MISTWOOD ACADEMY

AMY HART

For Ava,
For always believing in me.

1

SOMETHING DARK LURKED INSIDE ME. I knew it was there, forged in magic and shared in blood. It was an inescapable part of my destiny. The only thing was … I was having trouble finding it.

"Come on," I muttered, glaring at the blank piece of notepaper that lay in my hand. It wouldn't float. Or combust. Or melt. It wouldn't do anything.

Frustration prickled in my chest.

It had been three months since the night of the Sapphire Eclipse. Three months since I'd become the *putere*. I was still a vampire, but I was also something else. Something *more*. A creature who could absorb the powers of any supe I drained. A creature who was destined for darkness and destruction.

I was a secret.

A weapon.

A murderer.

I shook my head, my brown hair tumbling around my shoulders, and drew in a deep breath. *Focus. You can do this.* I pushed up to stand, leaving the comfort of my bed behind me, and tried again, staring at the small green square of paper that rested on my palm. It was thin and light—it should've been easy to manipulate.

But nothing happened.

Not even the slightest twitch.

I crumpled the notepaper into a ball, finally transforming it into another version of itself, a broken version of itself, but it wasn't the sort of change I was after. I was expecting something different. Something bigger. It wasn't like I wanted anything to happen, but I needed to know what I'd absorbed when I'd killed Mr. Olaru. Because I couldn't fight what I didn't understand, and I couldn't understand what I didn't even know.

With more force than necessary, I tossed the piece of paper at the bright pink trashcan that sat beside the door. It hit its mark, landing with an unsatisfactory plop, and I turned and reached out for the notepad, determined to try again. But there was nothing left. Not even the back cover. I'd used that already, hoping the heavier card would somehow offer a different outcome.

It hadn't worked, either.

I launched myself back onto my bed, covering my eyes with my hands. I'd attempted so many things already: clairvoyance, divination, teleportation, telepathy. I'd even gone to the nearest cemetery—a two-hour round trip on foot—to see if I could talk to the dead. It turned out, I couldn't. I also couldn't shape-shift, or control animals, or become incorporeal.

So I kept searching and searching.

And all I found was frustration and doubt.

No, that wasn't all. I *had* discovered two things I'd inherited: I could go in the sun without feeling like I was burning from the inside out, and I only needed to feed once or twice a month, instead of multiple times a week. They were abilities that made my life easier, but I wished I didn't have them; they were a reminder of what I carried inside me, a small piece of *him* that lived on in my blood forever.

I sighed and picked up my phone, scrolling absently through my unread messages, trying to distract myself from the underlying fear that never really went away. I'd been told so many times, by the handful of people who knew what had happened—my friends, my therapist, my housemistress at Worthington Hall—that prophecies were an art, not a science. That we'd changed the outcome, that we'd altered the prophecy, because of what we'd done that night. I mean, nothing's beyond the realm of possibility when your blood's been cleansed by magic and flame. But I couldn't shake the feeling that Mr. Olaru had left me something more than the ability to feed less and withstand the sun. The old ones spent their lives gathering powers and holding them close, hoarding them like treasure.

And Mr. Olaru had been older than most.

I took a deep breath and tried to find my center. Of all

the potential powers I'd tested, I always came back to telekinesis. I could still see the purple glow that had swirled around Mr. Olaru's hands and wrists when he'd moved me with his mind. According to the books I'd read, all it required—as long as you possessed the capacity— was intention, focus, and the ability to sense the connections between … well, between everything. But when I squeezed my eyes shut and lifted my hands, I felt nothing more than the mundane weight of my phone and my own disappointment.

What am I missing? Why can't I make this work?

A soft breeze blew through the open window above my desk, and I stared out at the cloudy night sky. The air was cool, but it smelled sweet, like spring. The fragrance of flowers, of jasmine and wisteria, drifted in from the gardens, and I wished I could be part of it. Everything out there was brimming with life. But I didn't know how I fit in with that. Not anymore. Not when I was destined for darkness and destruction.

No.

I lowered my hands, determination burning in my veins.

Destiny can be changed.

Familiar footsteps sounded in the hallway outside, and I plastered a smile on my face seconds before Haven Montgomery—my best friend, roommate, and one of the strongest witches I knew—walked into our dorm room. She had a pile of books in her arms, and a brown leather satchel bounced against her hip as she nudged the door shut with one heavy-soled boot.

"Were you asleep?" she said, crossing the room and dropping the books onto her desk. "It's still hours until sunrise."

"Of course not." I held up my phone. "I was just scrolling. And thinking." I couldn't let her know what I'd really been doing. Not when she finally seemed to be in a good mood.

"You were thinking?" She looked me up and down, her blue eyes sharp. There was something inscrutable in her gaze, an emotion I couldn't read even through her scent, but she straightened the cuffs of her lilac vintage dress and handed me one of the two brown paper bags that she drew out of her satchel. "Here—this is for you."

"Oh. Um, thanks." I took the bag, looking down to hide my confusion—Haven hadn't been in much of a gift-giving mood lately—then pulled out the chocolate chip cookie that was nestled inside and took a large bite. It was rich and buttery, more intensely flavored than anything I'd ever eaten when I was human, but even through the sweetness I could smell an undercurrent of something else in the room. Something dark. Something bitter. It drifted around Haven like smog, and while I didn't know what it was, it wasn't completely unfamiliar.

Late nights.

Pacing.

Nightmares.

It smelled like Haven when she dreamed.

"Where's Logan?" she asked, dragging me away from my fears. "I've hardly seen him all day."

I took another bite of cookie and shrugged. "I dunno. He had tons of homework to do, so we're not hanging out tonight."

She raised a disbelieving brow.

"What?" I wiped my mouth with the back of my hand. "We don't spend every waking moment together."

"Just most of them."

It wasn't exactly a lie. Logan Adams—my boyfriend—was everything I'd never expected to find when I'd started at Mistwood Academy. He was cute, with dark brown hair that was always messy, and chocolate-colored eyes that turned to amber when he shifted. He was a werewolf, warm and alive and vital, and even though I was perfectly capable of being alone, I missed him when we weren't together.

"You're good for him, you know," Haven said, her gaze softening. "I've never seen him so happy. So secure." She flopped down onto her bed and sighed, a deeply content sound that spoke of spring nights and unexpected magic. "This is nice, though. We haven't hung out like this—just the two of us—in ages."

I shoved the rest of the cookie in my mouth so I didn't have to answer. Haven was my best friend, and it wasn't like I'd been avoiding her, but I also hadn't *not* been avoiding her. It was just … something about her had changed since the night of the Sapphire Eclipse. I almost hadn't noticed it at first. It was subtle. Gradual.

Not much more than an occasional glare or a snappy remark.

But then the nightmares had started.

Now, she avoided sleep and spent her days pacing, working on spells that she couldn't—or *wouldn't*—explain. She was mercurial, a natural disaster in human form, and I never knew what sort of mood I'd find her in. Or how long it would last.

"I guess we've all been busy," I finally said, wiping my hands on my jeans. "I mean, I've got five assignments due this week. And another three next week." I toyed with the edge of the empty paper bag. "There's only so many hours in the day."

Haven swung her legs up onto her bed, her boots digging into the covers. "What do you need help with?"

"Nothing," I said quickly, my voice overly bright. "I'll be fine."

She considered me carefully, then tore open her own paper bag, revealing a huge blueberry Danish. "Well, I don't know about you, but I'm fascinated by the assignment Mrs. Miller set for English." She tore off a piece of pastry, then launched into an explanation of the topic, her hands waving in the air. The edge of a delicate floral tattoo peeked out from under one sleeve, and her hair—a platinum-blonde pixie cut—bounced around as she moved. She spoke quickly, barely breathing between words, between sentences, between concepts, but I didn't slow her down. Even when I could barely keep up.

Because I'd missed this.

I'd missed *her*.

"Here," she said, standing when the mostly one-sided conversation came to a lull. "Give me your paper bag."

I balled it up and tossed it toward her without thinking. For a while, I'd forgotten what I'd been doing before she came up to our room. I'd forgotten how much things had changed. But then she looked at me from beside the trashcan, her blue eyes darkening, and reality slammed back into place.

His blood flows through my veins.

"Again?" she said, her forehead wrinkling. "That's the third time this week."

"Nothing happened. I promise."

She pressed her lips together, her expression unreadable. "Did you want something to happen?"

"Of course not." I forced myself to smile. "I'm fine with failing at telekinesis, and pyrokinesis, and every other kind of kinesis. It's better than—"

"Stop." She held up a hand, but didn't say anything else. She just stared down at the evidence of my failed experiment. Everything about her had shifted—her tone, her posture, her scent. She was sea spray and soot, nightmares and storm clouds, and I swallowed past the sudden lump in my throat. I'd been so relieved to have the old Haven back, that I hadn't considered—hadn't *let* myself consider—that she might not be back for good.

When she finally looked up, her face was etched with worry. "You can't keep doing this," she said, the words unexpectedly gentle. "I know I helped you when you first started searching for what you'd absorbed, but you need to stop. We found everything. And it wasn't a lot."

"But what if—"

"No." She breathed out a weary sigh. "You can't keep looking for something that isn't there." She dropped the two takeout bags into the trash, then crossed the room, her boots scuffing against the floor. "We both know this isn't about his abilities." She thumped down next to me on the bed. "You're scared because you think you'll become him."

"No, I—"

She silenced me with a look. "You *are* scared you'll become him. But that whole power-hungry, homicidal, evil thing he had going on? It wasn't some sort of vampiric ability you were destined to inherit. He was just an asshole." She put a hand on my arm, and her gaze was steady as it met mine. "You won't do what he did."

No, I'll do something worse.

The prophecy was a tattoo in my chest, a beat I knew by heart: *The* putere *will come to power on the night of the Sapphire Eclipse. As the power ascends, a darkness will rise, and with it will come the destruction of our world.*

My breath caught in my throat at the memory of the words, and I reached across the bed and picked up Minikins, the stuffed toy cat I'd had since I was a baby. His patchy black fur was rough against my skin, but he was a memory of home. A memory of my humanity.

Haven squeezed my arm. She stood, her dress swinging out around her legs as she strode into the center of the room. "Maybe this'll help take your mind off things," she said softly. "I've been practicing, in case … Never mind. Just watch." She held her hands out in front of her, palms raised to the ceiling, and closed her eyes.

The scent of magic, dark and earthy and wild, drifted around her, mingling with the breeze that was still coming in through the window. There was a weight to it, a heaviness, like it had been pulled from a lineage that whispered in my mind like a long-lost memory. I leaned forward, goosebumps skimming over my skin.

There was a pause.

A breath.

Then a tiny orange flame, no larger than a grain of rice, flickered to life and hovered in the air above Haven's hands. Her eyelids fluttered open, the blue of her irises obscured by light and shadow, and the flame twisted, growing and changing.

It was beautiful.

Deadly.

Terrifying.

She won't let it hurt you.

The flame kept growing, safe and controlled, until—

—there was a knock at the door, and sparks leaped from Haven's fingers.

"Who is it?" she hissed, her gaze hitting mine. The scent of rotting leaves filled the air between us.

Shit.

"Well?" she demanded, stepping toward me.

Ice crept up my spine, stiffening my bones and

freezing my skin, but I pushed it away, breathing in the distinctive scent—peach pie and ice cream—that wafted in from beneath the door. "It's Ms. Emmerson. Put out the fire, and I'll go see what she wants."

"No." Haven's eyes glittered as the flame grew taller.

Ms. Emmerson knocked again.

"Please." I stood, my movements slow and careful. "You'll be suspended if she catches you."

Unsupervised magic was forbidden at Mistwood Academy. It had been that way for decades, ever since a student lost control of a spell and almost killed someone. There were wards around all of the buildings, including our dorm, Worthington Hall, that were supposed to prevent and report it, though I'd long since learned there were ways around everything if you knew what you were doing. And Haven was someone who knew what she was doing.

"The school won't touch me," she said. "No one else's parents donate even half as much as mine do." The flame in her hands rippled and changed. It was no longer a distraction; it was a weapon brought to life.

"Emily? Haven?" Ms. Emmerson knocked again. "Are you in there?"

I didn't move. Didn't speak. Didn't breathe.

"If you answer her," Haven said, turning slowly, "all of this will burn."

I didn't know what to do. The door was miles away—blocked off by fire and a pissed-off witch—and I couldn't get out the window. Not fast enough, anyway. My fangs tingled in my gums, but I lifted my hands placatingly and hoped I wasn't about to make a terrible mistake.

"This isn't you, Haven," I said, keeping my voice calm and steady. "Put the flame out. Please."

"Well, since you said *please* ..." The fire dimmed, just for a moment, then it burst up tall and bright, reaching for the ceiling. Haven stepped forward and brought her hands —and the flame—right up near my face, her expression twisting. "How much do you like your skin?"

My breath caught in my throat. "Please," I said again, trying to ignore the heat on my face. "Put out the flame before someone gets hurt."

"I can't."

"You can." I took a tentative step forward, remembering all the times I'd lost control. All the times I'd put Haven in danger. "I trust you."

We faced each other, frozen between heat and fear, until Haven moved and the flame shrunk down, crawling back into itself until it was nothing. It left no smoke, no lingering smell of burning or magic. It was like it had never existed.

I took one of Haven's hands in mine. Her skin was freezing, even against the clammy coldness of my own. "Are you okay?"

She pulled away, her shoulders slumping. Everything about her was wrong, like she'd been contained or muted, recast into a different version of herself. A version I barely recognized. "You should open the door," she said quietly.

I drew in a breath. "Ms. Emmerson's gone."

"Oh." Haven drifted over to the window, her gaze on the sky beyond. The soot-stained scent of fear was a swirl around her, and she scratched at her arm through the fabric of her sleeve. Her painted red nails were elegant and brutal; there was something desperate about the way they moved, as though she was trying to destroy something deep below the surface of her skin.

"Haven," I said. "Are you—"

"What?"

I'd tried giving her space, tried letting her deal with everything that had happened in her own way, and in her own time, but I couldn't leave things any longer. "What's going on with you?" I said. "You haven't been the same since the eclipse."

She kept scratching, the rose-gold rings on her fingers glittering in the lamplight. "I'm fine. Just … leave it alone, okay?"

"No."

Her eyes widened and her fingers stilled.

"Is it about what happened that night?" I asked, pushing for something, anything to get her talking. "With me? Or the spell? Or … Philip?"

"Philip?" Haven's gaze hit me like a punch to the head. "Is that how little you think of me? You think this is about some stupid boy?"

"I don't know what this is about! You won't talk to me!"

She stretched her hands out in front of her and the flame burst back to life. It was bigger this time, more vibrant and less controlled, and blue sparks flickered at its base. "Philip was a mistake. An error in judgement." She moved her hands apart, splitting the flame in two. "One I won't be making again."

"Wait," I said. "You don't—"

My words were lost as the door burst open and Cayley Rodriguez stepped into the room. "Holy shit!" she said as she slammed the door shut behind her, rattling the bowl of crystals that sat on the nearby shelf. The orb that stood beside them—a small, smoky-looking thing—shook dangerously on its stand. "What the hell are you doing?"

"I'm failing." Sparks flew wildly around Haven's hands.

"You're not failing," I said.

"I *am* failing." The flames disappeared and she sunk to her knees, her eyes bright with tears. "I'm not strong enough. I'll *never* be strong enough. I can't even do the spell. I tried to find everything, but ..." She covered her face with her hands.

"What spell?" I said, sitting down next to her on the floor.

Her shoulders shook, but she didn't reply.

"I can't keep doing this," Cayley muttered under her breath. She was leaning against the door, a storm dressed in black. "I'll come back later, when—"

"I found it in a book." Haven lifted her head, her face streaked with tears. "It's a spell to bind Emily's powers."

2

"A SPELL TO WHAT?" I said, my voice rising sharply.

"A spell to bind your powers. The new ones you got when you were turned into the *putere*." Haven rubbed her eyes with her hands, streaking her already-smudged mascara across her face. "I found it at the SCC facility in the city when I interned there over the break."

"And you didn't think to tell me?"

"I wanted it to be a surprise." She blew out an unsteady breath and bent forward, making herself smaller. "You've been so stressed out about the prophecy, and your inherited powers, and just … being the *putere*. I wanted to give you a choice. The option to make it all go away, if that's what you want."

I swallowed hard.

If that's what I want?

It's everything *I want.*

"But … it's impossible." Haven scratched her arm and

winced, her breath catching in her throat. "I can't find all the items the spell requires, and even if I could, I'm not an elf. Their magic works differently to ours, and I can't figure out how to replicate the effects."

Cayley pushed away from the door and crossed the room, her brown hair darkening to a deep, glossy black. "Where's the book? Do you still have it?"

"It's in there." Haven pointed at the wooden trunk that stood by the foot of her bed. It was large and beautifully decorated, with swirling symbols carved into the sides and the lid, and it housed all of her magical paraphernalia.

She'd told me never to open it.

"Go on," Cayley said, her lip gloss changing—from pink to red to burgundy—as she stopped beside the trunk. "Show us already." She was coiled beneath her perfect exterior, her fitted black sweater and jeans unable to hide the emotions she wore on her skin like perfume.

Haven gulped.

"It's okay," I said quickly. "I don't mind if she doesn't."

Cayley lifted her chin. "I do."

I closed my eyes, biting back the retort that burned on my tongue. We were all so on edge, exhausted from months of tip-toeing around emotions—both mine *and* Haven's—and fighting with each other wasn't going to help, no matter how much the predator in me wanted to.

Breathe.

Control it.

Don't mention the fire.

I opened my eyes and turned to Haven, keeping each

movement deliberate and slow. "What do you want to do?"

She bit down on her lower lip, her fingers rubbing at her arm. "I don't know. There's so much … I can't …"

"It's all right." I reached for her hand when she didn't say anything more. "We can wait until you're ready."

"No." She shook me off and stood, her legs trembling beneath her. "You need this. You *deserve* this. And if I can't do it, maybe somebody else can."

I didn't know what to think.

What to say.

How to feel.

Because as worried as I was about Haven, my chest filled with hope as she lifted the lid of the trunk and removed the book. The thin, gray volume was everything I'd been waiting for. If Haven was right, it could be my one chance to remove the echoes of Mr. Olaru from my blood forever. My one chance to be certain—completely and utterly certain—that the prophecy would never come true.

"It looks like that other one," Cayley said, picking up an apple from the fruit bowl on my nightstand and taking a bite. "*Putere: Prophecy and Destiny*, remember?"

How could I forget?

It was the book we'd taken from Dr. Norlgren's office on the night he'd been killed. The book that had told us about the prophecy, and warned us about my—and the world's—disastrous future. We'd held onto it for as long as we could, absorbing the history of the first *putere* and hoping to figure out how to stop what was coming, but now it belonged to the SCC. The Supernatural Citizens Council had seized every shred of evidence of the Sapphire Eclipse.

Except for me.

"It was written by the same elves," Haven said, sitting back down next to me on the floor. "I recognize some of the handwriting."

"What does it say?" Cayley asked.

Haven paused to cough, covering her mouth with the back of her hand. "It says that with the right ingredients and under the right conditions, Emily's powers, specifically those related to her existence as the *putere*, can be bound."

My heart stuttered in my chest as she slid on a pair of white cotton gloves and slowly opened the cover of the book. The scent of dust and vanilla drifted from the pages; they were yellowed with age, crumbling at the edges, but the script that filled them—the swirling, sinuous markings of a language I didn't understand—was dark, as if it had just been written.

"How do you bind it?" I said, my voice cracking uncomfortably. I hadn't forgotten what the other book had said about the original *putere*, how the elves had drawn the power out of him and sent it into his son. They'd thought it would be dormant forever.

They were wrong.

"Does it have to go into someone else?" Cayley asked.

"Because you know that would be impossible. Emily's the last of the bloodline."

My stomach twisted.

I didn't need the reminder that my parents had spent my entire life lying to me. That my dad wasn't really my dad. That—

No.

I won't think about them.

I can't.

"It doesn't need to go into a person," Haven said, carefully turning over another page as Cayley sat down next to her. "It can be placed into a vessel, like the one your blood was …" She trailed off, her face turning pale. "Like the one your blood was held in during the Sapphire Eclipse. But a person is better. Stronger. There's less chance of it accidentally being released."

My fingers found the scar that marked my wrist. It was a permanent reminder of what Mr. Olaru had done to me that night. And of what I'd done to him. "A vessel would be fine," I said quickly, pushing the memories away. "What else do we need?"

Haven opened her mouth to reply, but whatever she was going to say was cut off by the figure that came bursting in through the window above my desk.

"Hey," Logan said, pausing when he saw the three of us sitting on the floor. "I didn't expect a welcoming committee."

"I didn't expect *you*," I said, surprised.

"Yeah, well, homework got boring." He stretched out

beside me, then leaned forward, his brow wrinkling. "Why does that look like the book I stole last semester? The one about the prophecy."

I didn't say anything. I just rested my head against his shoulder and let Haven and Cayley explain. Worry still scratched at the corners of my mind—about Haven and her erratic moods; about the fire and how she'd threatened me; about the spell and everything that could go wrong. I didn't have a great track record when it came to magic and my powers. Before I'd come to Mistwood, I'd been tricked by a nightmare who'd promised me a potion that didn't exist. And then, three months after starting school, we'd tried—and failed—to stop the ritual on the night of the Sapphire Eclipse.

There's always a cost.

Always a price.

A shiver crawled up my spine.

"How does it work?" Logan asked when Haven and Cayley were finished. "What do you need?"

Haven cleared her throat and lifted the book closer to her face. "You need five items to complete the spell," she said, her voice crackly. "Something belonging to the *putere*. Something belonging to the one who was sacrificed. The Blade that was used during the ritual. An anchor. And the vessel—human or not."

I straightened, dropping my shoulders and trying to force the tension from my body. My head was spinning. Everything felt strange, like the air was stretched tight and thin, and I lifted a hand, pushing through the invisible layers of dust-gas-pollen-scent-sound that surrounded us.

Haven closed her eyes.

Logan tapped his fingers.

My vampire was close beneath my skin.

"Wait," Cayley said.

My heart gave an extra-loud thump, and the world slammed back into place. I ran my tongue over my teeth. "What?"

Human.

Stay human.

"Do you really want to get rid of your powers?" she said, shifting closer, her hazel eyes boring into mine. "We all do shitty things sometimes. It's part of being a supe. But it's not your fault you killed Mr. Olaru, and it's not your fault you ended up with his abilities. Why not make the most of them?"

"Because I don't want to." My predator rose up in my chest. "Don't you get it?"

"You should do what feels right," Logan said, putting a hand on my arm. He was calm, careful in that particular way he had, with his emotions held so far in check they were barely discernible at all. "Why don't you take some time? Think things through."

"I don't need time." I pulled away as my fangs sliced through my gums. "These powers aren't mine. I don't want them. I *never* wanted them." They were poison, destroying me from the inside out, and I was suffocating —forever linked to the man who'd tried to kill me.

Breathe.

Breathe.

Breathe.

"Em?" Logan said. "It's—"

"No, I—I can't do this." I squeezed my hands into fists, my nails cutting into my palms. My predator wanted me angry. It understood anger; it *coveted* anger. But … that wasn't me. Not all of me, anyway. *It was always part of him.* "I have to go." I stood, forcing my fangs to retract, and pressed the hunger down until it was no more than a simmer in my blood.

"Do you want me to come with you?" Logan said. "We could—"

"No." I stepped over his legs and made my way to the door. I needed to feed. And I needed my cello. "I'm going to go practice. Put the book somewhere safe for me. I'll take it to Mr. Green tomorrow."

He'll help us figure it out.

He has to.

"What do you mean you don't think I should do it?" I said, my eyes widening in disbelief.

"I didn't say that." Mr. Green's voice was steady, though his brow was furrowed. "I merely suggested taking some time to consider your options."

Ugh.

I didn't need time.

I needed someone to listen to me.

"I've made my decision," I said firmly. "I know what I want. And I want Mr. Olaru's powers gone."

I looked down as Fred, Mr. Green's miniature dragon, padded across the room toward me. Tendrils of smoke drifted from his nostrils, and he came to a stop at my feet, his spiny tail wagging.

"Here." Mr. Green took a dried apricot out of his pocket and threw it toward me. "You know the drill."

I caught it and held it out to Fred, who quickly snapped it out of my fingers. "Good boy," I said as I tapped my leg three times. "Come on. You can come up." When the dragon was settled, his body curled round and his head on my lap, I looked back up at Mr. Green, who was studying me carefully. "I know what you think." My voice was annoyingly defensive in the face of his scrutiny. "I got used to being a vampire"—*kind of, sort of, mostly*—"so I'll get used to this too. But … it's not the same. Mr. Olaru didn't just turn me. I absorbed some of his powers. It's like I still have this connection to him. Like he's living inside me."

Mr. Green crossed one leg over the other, leaning back on the old two-seater couch that sat by the window; the burgundy leather creaked lazily beneath him. When he spoke again, his voice was soft. "Do you understand you may never be able to get these powers back?"

I nodded.

I never wanted them in the first place.

"Well, then." He pressed his lips together, his dark eyes

shadowed as he picked up the laptop that was sitting beside him. His eyebrows drew down as he typed, but his expression was calm when he looked back up, his gaze catching mine. "I'll keep the book for now, and I'll make some enquiries, but you need to understand that this may not be an easy process. And it may not be a fast process. There will be forms to fill in, and decisions to be made by people higher up in the SCC hierarchy than I am. It may not be approved at all."

I nodded again.

Mr. Green rubbed a hand over his forehead, the deep brown skin wrinkling under the pressure. For a moment, he looked tired. He'd been working undercover at Mistwood Academy for years, managing a full-time workload as the school psychologist, while also keeping tabs on Mr. Olaru for the SCC. Miss Lassila, my housemistress at Worthington Hall, had worked undercover alongside him.

I'd expected them to leave after Mr. Olaru's death.

Instead, both had stayed.

Maybe they're keeping tabs on me.

"How many people know what I am?" I asked, my mouth suddenly dry.

Mr. Green blinked. "I don't know."

"Is that ... bad?"

Mr. Green clasped his hands in front of him. He was supposed to know everything; he was an adult, a therapist, a figure of authority in a pressed tweed jacket, but he couldn't hide the uncertainty that drifted around him in a wave of clouded mint and forest breeze. Truth. Worry. Practiced calm.

My throat tightened.

I knew I was dangerous. The prophecy had never specified *when* the world might end. Just that I was the one who would cause it. And I wasn't convinced that whatever we'd done on the night of the Sapphire Eclipse had been enough to change it. To stop it from ever coming true.

But that wasn't everything.

I was also a target. A prize for whoever could catch me.

I'd been warned more than once that I needed to lie low, that I couldn't tell anyone what I was. That there were creatures out there who'd exploit me for my power.

"Am I in danger?" I said, running a hand along the thick blue scales on Fred's back.

Mr. Green exhaled. "No more than on any other day." He offered me a reassuring smile, though it didn't quite meet his eyes. "Mistwood Academy is one of the most heavily warded institutions in the country. You're safer here than anywhere else."

"But what about Philip? And the person he was working for? The one who wanted my blood. The one who wanted my power."

Mr. Green's stiffened. "That's still under investigation."

"And?"

"And nothing. You just keep doing what you're doing. Keep your identity a secret, but you don't stop living your life." He glanced down at the stainless steel watch that encircled his wrist. "That's all we've got time for today. But you can message me anytime or stop by if you're worried."

I set Fred down on the ground and stood, slipping my messenger bag over my shoulder. "And you'll look into that spell for me?"

Mr. Green nodded. "I will. See you next week."

I gave Fred one last pat and left the room, not really feeling any better than I had when I got there. As soon as the door closed behind me, I pulled my phone from my pocket and unlocked the screen.

"Over here."

I looked up and saw Logan leaning against the wall further down the corridor. He wore dark jeans and a hoodie, and his hair was even messier than usual, a few errant strands hanging over his forehead. His face was lit up by the glow of his phone, but his eyes were hooded with tiredness.

I stopped directly in front of him. "Hey," I said softly.

"Hey." He reached for my hand, his fingers tentative. "I'm sorry about last night. I wasn't trying to tell you what to do about that spell. I was just … worried."

I pressed my lips together. "Do you trust me?"

He nodded.

"Then let me make my own decisions." I went up on my toes and kissed him. "Did you get breakfast?"

He blew out a breath and rested his forehead against mine. "No. I overslept. There was hardly anything left by the time I got to the dining hall."

"Well …" I drew back and opened my bag, then pulled out a cardboard takeout box. "It's a good thing you have the best girlfriend ever."

He took the box and opened it, his eyes widening when he saw what was inside. "You got me a muffin. And a Danish. And two scones."

"With cinnamon butter," I added.

His lips curved into a smile. "You *are* the best girlfriend ever."

I reached into the box and tore off a piece of cranberry muffin, then started walking down the corridor. "Did you get all your homework done?"

"Almost. I've still got a paper to finish for English, and a Werewolf Studies quiz to prepare for." He took a bite of cherry Danish and chewed. "You aren't mad anymore?"

I shook my head.

He smiled again, then leaned down and kissed me on the cheek.

We walked past the nurses' station and pushed open the heavy arched doors that led outside. The air was sweet and welcoming, unlike the large, eagle-faced chimera who stared down at us from the rooftop as we walked outside, his countenance strange and formidable. He moved forward on goat-shaped legs and followed us along the length of the building, only turning away when he couldn't go any farther.

"What did Mr. Green say about the spell?" Logan said, his voice pitched low.

I shook my head, unwilling to speak while I could still

see the chimera. "He said he'd look into it," I finally whispered when we were safely inside the science building. "But he also said it might take a while. And that the SCC might not approve it at all."

Logan touched my arm. "That's—"

"Logan Adams!" boomed a voice from down the corridor. "And Emily Sanderson! Just the sort of students I was looking for."

"Shit," Logan said, his jaw tightening.

3

LOGAN SQUEEZED MY ARM, then dropped his hand and turned toward the teacher who was coming down the corridor. "Mr. Davis," he said, a practiced smile spreading across his face. "What can we do for you?"

The rotund witch came to a stop in front of us, patting his thick dark hair into place. He taught Math, specializing in Mathemagical Formulas and Witchcraft, and though I hadn't been in any of his classes, I'd heard he was strict but fair. "I need volunteers for the upcoming parent-teacher conferences," he said, adjusting his jacket and beaming at us, his crooked teeth shiny and white beneath his black handlebar mustache. "I trust I can count on you?"

"Certainly," Logan said. "I'd be more than happy to help out."

"And you, Emily?" Mr. Davis asked, turning his attention to me.

"Oh," I said, faltering. "I—um, I don't know if I'll be there."

Mr. Davis' eyes widened. "My dear, but you must. It's one of the highlights of the semester. There's food, and music, and—"

"I don't know if my parents can make it," I said quickly, my tongue tripping over the words.

"Oh. I see." Mr. Davis' voice turned chilly. "I realize you haven't been here very long, so perhaps you aren't used to the concept, but supporting your community through service is expected at Mistwood Academy. Mandatory, even. The supe community is a tight-knit one, and we all must do our part." His blue eyes narrowed. "Do you understand?"

I nodded.

"Very well. I'll put you down for refreshments."

"Yes, sir," I said.

"As for you Logan ..." Mr. Davis tapped a finger on his chin as he thought. "You can be an official greeter. Your manners are impeccable and the parents all adore you."

"Thank you, sir," Logan said.

Mr. Davis inclined his head. "No, Logan, thank *you*. This is going to be our most successful event yet." A trio of senior students walked past and his dark eyebrows lifted. "Ethan!" he called as he waved a hand in their direction. "Ben! Sarah! Just the people I was looking for. I have jobs for you!"

I leaned against the wall and closed my eyes, willing Mr. Davis to disappear.

Logan nudged my elbow a few minutes later. "It's safe. He's gone."

"I know." I'd been listening to his voice, his heartbeat, his blood. He smelled like mustache wax and cologne, and though he'd gone into one of the classrooms, the scent still lingered in the hallway.

Logan leaned back against the wall beside me and sighed. "Refreshments and greetings. Should be better than last year, at least."

"What did you have to do last year?"

"Direct people around the parking lot."

I screwed up my nose. "Can we get out of it?"

"Nope. You already agreed. To Mr. Davis, that's an iron-clad contract." Logan looked up at the ceiling and blew out a breath. "It's easier just to go through with it."

Well ... shit. I didn't want to go through with it. I'd planned on spending the occasion hiding out in my room, where I could ignore the fact that parents were a thing.

"Have you talked to them yet?" Logan asked.

I stiffened. "I don't know what you mean."

"I'm not stupid, Em." His hand brushed against my wrist. "I know what you smell like when you think about your parents."

"You're wrong."

"I know what you smell like when you lie." He reached for my hand, his fingers tentative. "You don't have to talk about it, but you should be prepared for the fact that your parents might turn up on conference night. It wouldn't be the first time they've showed up here without warning."

Dammit.

Logan was right.

My parents had visited Mistwood once before. I'd been sitting near the front of the stage during our end of semester music concert, ready to play my solo, and suddenly … there they were. My mom. My dad. My brother, Sam. Sitting in the audience like they belonged. Like they hadn't been lying to me forever.

We wanted to keep you safe.

We did it for your own good.

We thought you'd never find out.

I'd run from them that night.

And I'd been running from them ever since.

"Maybe it's time you called them," Logan said, his voice soft. "They phone you every week."

"And every week I don't answer," I snapped, pushing away from the wall and turning toward the classroom. "Are you coming in?"

Logan didn't move. "It's been three months since they were here."

"So?" I spun back to face him, my hands clenching into fists. "Three months is nothing. They spent my whole life lying to me. *My whole life.* They're not human. And my dad isn't really my dad. I couldn't be the"—I glanced around, then lowered my voice to a whisper—"*putere* if he was."

"I know, but—"

"No, you *don't* know. You have no idea what it's like. Your parents have always been honest about what you are. About what you're meant to be."

Logan's shoulders tightened; everything about him became jagged and real. "Okay, yeah," he said, his tone suddenly harsh. "My parents *have* been honest. Honest about my lack of choices. Honest about the need to be the perfect alpha-in-training. Honest about what a fucking disappointment I am."

I lifted my chin, my eyes narrowing.

Logan glared, then looked away, pulling his emotions back until he was neutral, safe, blank. "Forget it," he said. "This isn't about me and my dysfunctional upbringing. It's about you and your relationship with *your* parents. And someday soon they'll end up back here, whether you like it or not."

"Fine." I pulled my phone out of my pocket, holding it tight as I stared at the screen. My pulse drummed in my ears. "Maybe I'll call them later."

Logan nodded once and reached for my hand. "Shall we go?"

I shoved my phone into my bag and let him lead me to class. My anger, the emotion my predator pushed forward —*test him, push him, fight him*—was dimming, and guilt roiled in my stomach. "I don't think you're a disappointment," I whispered, squeezing Logan's hand. "You know that, right?"

"Sure. But your opinion doesn't mean anything to my father." He dropped my hand and shoved his bag onto the desk in front of him.

"Does it mean anything to you?"

He looked at me as he lowered himself into his seat,

clearly taken aback. "Of course it does."

I exhaled slowly and sat down next to him. I knew he was telling the truth. He'd dropped his shields just enough for the honesty in his scent to shine through. He spent so much time hiding, molding himself to fit any situation, and being whatever—*whoever*—he needed to be. But when it mattered, when it really, truly *mattered*, he always let me in.

"You know you mean everything to me," he said, shifting so his leg was touching mine. "Don't you?"

"I—"

"Good evening, students." Miss Parker, our Chemistry teacher, strode into the room, and I immediately closed my mouth. She was a witch, tall and broad-shouldered, with curly brown hair and a low, resonant voice, and she had very little tolerance for extraneous noise in her classroom. "I hope you've all done the required reading," she continued briskly, slipping her arms into her lab coat. "We've got a lot to get through today."

The next forty-five minutes were a whirlwind of learning about chemical reactions and the transformative effects magic could have on them, and putting it all into practice. But I couldn't stop thinking about my parents. Would they turn up for the parent-teacher conferences? Was I going to have to *talk* to them?

I pulled my phone out of my bag.

"Could you pass me the acetone?" Logan said, his eyes narrowed in concentration. "We need to …"

"Sure," I mumbled, shoving the bottle across the table.

"Here." Then I tuned him out, staring down at the screen in my hands.

Should I?

Could I?

I bit my lip. My hands were sweating. I knew avoiding my parents was selfish, but they'd been lying to me for my entire life. And it hurt. It *hurt*. But no matter how much I hated them for it, and no matter how much I didn't want to admit it—either to them *or* to myself—I missed them.

The sweet smell of my mom's perfume when she gave me a hug.

The sound of my dad's laugh when he told a stupid joke.

The way my brother always crept into my room whenever there was a thunderstorm.

I missed them so much it was crushing me. And I hated them so much it was killing me. So, holding my breath, I swiped a finger across the screen. My mom's last message was still waiting, unread, and I skimmed it, my phone held beneath the lab counter, then typed: *Parent-teacher conferences are next week. Are you coming?*

Behind me, someone gasped.

My phone clattered to the floor, and I turned as a series of staccato *pops!* filled the air.

"Wilbur," said Kelly, a werewolf I'd never really spoken to. "What did you do? That's hemlock, not wild carrot!"

"Oh, for goodness' sake," Miss Parker muttered under her breath as thick green smoke began to drift from Kelly and Wilbur's beaker. "I've always said this class should be theoretical."

"It stinks!" someone yelled.

Miss Parker sighed and opened the door. "Everybody out. I have to get this cleaned up before next period." She straightened the cuffs on her lab coat and stood aside as everyone scrambled through the doorway. "Wilbur, go straight to the nurse. You're going to need some ointment on those hands."

I picked up my phone and followed everyone outside, slinging my bag over my shoulder. Wilbur took off toward the medical center, while the rest of us milled in the corridor, waiting for the bell. We weren't supposed to leave—the chimera would let the faculty know if we did—so I sat down on the floor and looked at my phone. *Nothing.* Logan dropped down beside me.

"Are we okay?" he asked quietly, his dark eyes catching mine.

"I guess so." I ran a hand through my hair and sighed. "Look, I shouldn't have mentioned your family before. It's just ... with Haven, and the prophecy, and my parents, and my powers ... Everything feels so messed up sometimes."

I feel so messed up sometimes.

Every time I got mad, every time I did something wrong, it felt like I was closer to losing my humanity. Like I was closer to becoming like *him*.

"I know it does," Logan said as he leaned his head back against the wall. "It's been a lot for all of us. For you, more than most." His fingers pulled at the hem of his hoodie, catching on a loose thread and drawing it free. "I shouldn't have snapped at you either."

I leaned over and kissed him on the cheek, moving closer as he turned his head toward me, his lips capturing mine. They were soft and sweet and tasted like cinnamon and cranberry, and I reached up and cupped his face with my hands, trying to hold onto my humanity as I held onto him.

"Get a room!" someone yelled.

"Best suggestion I've heard all day," Logan murmured.

***

By the time I got up to my room that night, ten minutes before curfew, I was exhausted. And worried. I'd had a full day of classes, then orchestra practice, and after that I'd gone straight to the library to work on my History assignment. Logan had come with me—though he'd been more of a hindrance than a help—and Cayley had stopped by to bring us dessert, but I hadn't seen Haven since before third period. She'd skipped out on Geography and English, and she hadn't turned up to orchestra. All I'd gotten from her was a text that said: *Cover for me.*

"Hey," I said softly as I opened the door and stepped into our room. "Are you here?"

"Yeah, I am." Haven was already in bed, propped up on a pile of pillows, a stack of loose papers resting on her lap. "Can you turn out the light?"

Relief flickered through me and I clicked off the main

light, leaving the room cloaked in shadow. My stomach churned as I remembered the night before.

Fire.

Magic.

How much do you like your skin?

Haven's lamp cast phantoms on the wall, but I set my bag down on my desk and forced myself to smile. "Where were you today?" I asked, keeping my tone deliberately light. "I told Mr. Townsend and Ms. Hanson you were finishing a project for English, but I don't think they believed me."

"I'll deal with them later." She waved a dismissive hand. "We have more important things to deal with. Like, where are we at with the spell?"

"What?"

"The spell to bind your powers. What did Mr. Green say? Is he going to do it?"

I kicked off my shoes and sat down on my bed, the mattress sagging beneath me. "I don't know."

Haven's eyebrows twitched.

"He said it might be a long process," I said, folding my legs beneath me. "And that the SCC might not approve it at all."

"Fine. We'll do it without him."

"But you said—"

"Never mind what I said." She sat straighter, her eyes wide and unfocused; the spiced scent of impatience ran through her veins. "Do you have any of the items yet? Did Mr. Green say he could get them?"

"Hold on, are you—"

"Did he say he could get them?" she repeated, rifling through the papers on her lap. "Because it'll be easier with his help, but it's not essential. Not anymore. I've been researching elven magic all day, and I think I can make it work."

"Why don't I—"

"We just need to find all the items," she said, ignoring me and holding up a piece of paper. "Here—take this. We can go through it together."

I got up and grabbed the crumpled sheet, my eyes skimming over the text. "You made a copy of the book?" I said, frowning at the full-color reproduction that took up most of the page.

"I didn't think Mr. Green would give it back." She looked at me, her expression hardening. "And clearly I was right."

I thumped back down on the bed.

"It's easy enough to find something of yours," she continued, glancing down at her own copy of the spell. "And there'll be something of Mr. Olaru's around here somewhere—the faculty wouldn't have thrown *everything* out. I'll keep searching for the Impure Blade. That just leaves the vessel and the—"

"Wait," I said, raising a hand. "You've been looking for the Impure Blade?"

"Yeah."

"But ... don't you remember what happened last time?"

She waved off my concern. "It's fine," she said,

scratching her arm, her rings clacking together. "That won't happen again. Anyway, look at your paper. I translated it for you down the side."

I did as I was told—mostly because I wasn't sure what she might do if I didn't. Haven had always been excitable; she was impatient and loud, and had a tendency toward exaggeration, but there'd always been a lightness to it, a joyful sort of engagement with the world and with her passions. But there was something different in her now. Something dark. The scent of fear and anger, of rotting leaves and soot, leeched from her blood, her bones, her skin.

"Have you figured out your anchor yet?" she asked, shoving her papers aside. A few floated down to the floor.

"I—I don't know what that means."

Her upper lip twisted. "It's an object that connects you to your family. Obviously."

Breathe.

Magic moved beneath Haven's skin, wild and undisciplined, and somewhere deep within me, my predator felt threatened. It wanted to fight. It wanted to feed. I pushed it down, swallowing past my fear, and picked up a pen from my nightstand.

Stay calm.

"Do you mean a literal connection?" I said, keeping my voice level. "Like a family tree? Or—"

"No." She tossed the rest of the papers on the floor and lay down, rolling over to face the wall. "You need an heirloom." She pulled the covers up to her head, her movements rough and jerky. "Why am I the only one taking this seriously?"

I didn't answer.

I knew whatever I said would only make things worse.

When it was clear she wasn't going to say anything else, I got ready for bed and slid beneath the covers. But I couldn't fall asleep. I thought about getting up, about going to take a shower or making a cup of tea, but curfew was strictly enforced at Worthington Hall by both Ms. Emmerson and Miss Lassila. So I lay there and stared at the ceiling until the sun came up, my mind whirling.

Heirlooms.

Prophecies.

Powers.

I couldn't fix any of it.

Reaching for my phone, I read over the message my mom had sent me half an hour earlier: *Your dad and I are so glad to hear from you. We'll be at the parent-teacher conferences next week, but we'd like to meet up before then. Text me back with a time and place. Sorry I didn't reply earlier. I was asleep and didn't hear the notification.*

I rolled over, pushing my hair out of my face. *A time and place.* Maybe they could bring me an heirloom. Maybe they could—

"No!" Haven screamed. "Don't!"

4

I CLUTCHED Minikins to my chest, adrenaline surging through me. Instinct made me push back my blankets, ready to fight, ready to flee, but when I sat and looked over at Haven's bed, I knew there was nothing I could do.

"Leave me alone!" she yelled. "Stop!"

The first time this had happened, the first time the nightmares had gripped her, I'd tried to wake her and she'd punched me in the face. The second, she'd tried to flatten me with a simple defense spell. I'd ended up with a hole in my pajamas and a broken nose. By the third time, I'd learned to stay quiet.

So I sat.

And watched.

And waited.

"Don't make me do it!" she screamed, her sheets twisting around her legs as she wrestled with the demons in her head. Sweat beaded on her brow. "Please, please don't."

Her eyes were still closed, but her fear was so real I could taste it. It coursed through her blood, acrid and sharp, and I pushed down the part of me that wanted to drink. *Take it. Take it. Take it.* She screamed again, something wordless and desperate, and her whole body trembled as she curled into a ball.

"Haven," I whispered, though I knew I shouldn't wake her. "Haven, you're having a nightmare."

She sat slowly, a puppet on a string.

"It's okay," I said softly, switching on my bedside lamp. "You're in our room. In Worthington Hall. You're safe here."

She turned to me, her eyes open, expression blank.

"Haven? Are you—"

Shit.

I barely had time to duck before the fireball hit the wall behind me. It exploded in a shower of heat and flame, and I scrambled out of bed, a scream burning in my throat.

"Don't," Haven commanded.

My knee twisted painfully beneath me, but I paused, half-sprawled on the floor.

Wake up, Haven. Wake up.

"Stop. I won't do it." Haven's eyes rolled back in her head, and a thin line of blood trickled from her nose. "I can't. Not again." She slumped over, her body going limp, and her head hit the mattress with a thud.

"Haven!" I pushed myself up and darted across the room. "Haven, can you hear me?" I grabbed her shoulder and shook it, but she didn't wake up. Her eyelids didn't even flutter.

Panic rose in my chest, but I drew in a breath and reached out with my senses. I could hear the blood in her veins, see the way her skin fell across muscle and bone. Her pulse was unsteady, skipping random beats, and she smelled of magic and fear, earth and soot.

No, not just soot.

Smoke.

And it was getting worse.

I turned and saw flames, yellow and orange, licking across my pillow and onto my blankets. Heat brushed against my skin.

My bed was on fire.

My bed was on fire.

"Haven, wake up!" I grabbed a bottle of water from my nightstand and tipped the contents out over the flames.

It wasn't enough.

"Fire!" I yelled, my voice cracking, and for the first time, I wished Haven hadn't soundproofed our room. It was a one-way spell—we could hear out, but no one else could hear in—and most of the time it was an assurance of privacy in a school full of supes with enhanced hearing. But now? Now it was a risk. A hazard we hadn't foreseen. "Haven, we need to get out of here! There's a fire! Haven!"

"What?" She sat slowly, her eyelids heavy with magic and sleep. "Oh, there's a fire? I can fix that." Reaching out with one hand, she murmured some faint words in Latin that I didn't understand.

The flames disappeared.

I sunk down slowly on the edge of her bed, my entire body shaking. "Is that it? Is it … over? It won't come back?"

Haven nodded. "It's gone."

I clasped my hands together and tried to remember how to breathe. "Are you all right?"

"I'm fine. The fire wasn't anywhere near me."

I leaned back and examined Haven's face, my gaze catching on the purple shadows beneath her eyes, the hollow cheeks, the ashen skin. I'd always thought she didn't like to talk about her nightmares, that she spent her days awake in order to avoid them. I didn't realize she didn't remember them at all.

"What's wrong?" Her forehead wrinkled in confusion. "Why are you looking at me like that?"

I bit my lip and tasted fear on my skin. *Hers? Or mine?* "You had a nightmare." I swallowed hard; my hands were still trembling. "You threw a fireball at me. You set my bed on fire."

"Oh."

"And your nose—it's bleeding."

She reached up tentatively to touch her face. "It'll stop in a minute."

I didn't know what to do. She smelled of aniseed and fog, shock and confusion, but beneath it there was something *wrong*. Something pungent, like decay.

"Come on," I said, tugging at her arm as I stood. "You need to go to the infirmary."

"No, I don't." She pulled away, her mouth twisting as blood dripped over her lip. She swiped a hand across it and lay back down, her body stiff as she faced the wall. "I'm not sick."

"But—"

"I don't need anyone's help."

I waited, my predator stirring inside me at the scent of Haven's anger, at the blood that still trickled from her nose, but she didn't say anything else.

Breathe.

I didn't know what to do. She'd become a hazard, a danger to herself and everyone around her, and I knew she wouldn't listen if I tried any more to convince her. I could *make* her go with me. It wouldn't be that difficult. I could restrain her, tape her mouth closed so she couldn't do any spells, and—

No.

The ghost of Mr. Olaru had risen in my veins, a memory of his words—*you do not have a choice; you are under my control*—and I placed a hand over my stomach as it churned. Was this how it was going to be? Every stressful decision marred by the influence of the monster that lived in my blood? He'd controlled me, and now I wanted to control Haven.

I shook my head, trying to dislodge the instincts that weren't mine. *He's part of you now.* I had to find something in me that was calm. Stable. Controlled. Something that was still *me*. I knew I shouldn't be frustrated by Haven; she was sick, haunted by nightmares and something I didn't understand. I didn't need to control her. I just needed to get her help.

But I wouldn't drag her to the infirmary against her will.

Instead, I paced the room, restless, and watched her until her breathing slowed. I listened to her heart, ensuring each beat was strong and steady as she fell back to sleep. I could've stayed there all day. *Just one more minute.* But half an hour later, Haven was sound asleep and the smell of charred polyester and cotton was burning the back of my throat, so I stripped the ruined covers from my bed, then stood back and surveyed the damage.

The wall was barely marked. My pillow was untouched. And my mattress looked fine, though it smelled vaguely of smoke. "At least you're okay," I whispered to Minikins as I set him down on my nightstand.

I opened the window a crack, then slid my feet into my sneakers and crept toward the door. The hallway outside was silent, and I slipped out as quietly as I could. If Haven wouldn't go to the infirmary, we had no proof that anything was wrong. Which meant I needed to get rid of the evidence—because setting your roommate's bed on fire would result in detention at best, or expulsion at worst.

All it took was a creaking floorboard.

A stumble on the stairs.

Three attempts to disable the alarm.

And then I was outside on the porch, the sun burning my eyes. I'd been outside during the day a few times since I'd inherited my new abilities, but never like this. Never alone. Someone had always been with me when I'd snuck out to test the limits of my powers. The first time, Haven had held my hand, an anchor for my fear when I didn't know if the sun would simmer in my blood, a painful reminder of the day I'd been kidnapped before the Sapphire Eclipse. She hadn't let me go. Not until she knew I was safe.

I wish she'd let me do the same for her.

I clutched my bedding closer to my chest and slunk around to the back of the dorm, to where they kept the trashcans. The sun was hot on my skin and I lifted my face, looking up at the sky. It was clear and blue, a perfect spring day, and I blinked back the tears that pricked behind my eyes. Frustration. Fear. Relief. There was so much within me that I didn't understand, so many emotions and needs and powers that I still had to work through, but at least I had this.

Daylight.

Warm and settled and free.

I tossed the remains of my bedding in the trash and held out my arms, soaking up the heat. Somewhere inside, I felt almost human. I wanted to stay longer, lost in the sun-washed paradise of cobblestone paths and Neo-Gothic buildings, but it wasn't worth the risk. I'd almost been spotted twice by the large, stone chimera that paced slowly around the roof of our dorm, constantly searching

for anyone or anything out of place. It wasn't dangerous—
actually, it probably was—but I knew it wouldn't hurt me.
I'd just be in *a lot* of trouble if it reported me for being out
after curfew.

After one last touch of spring-soaked air, I slipped
back into the dorm and reset the alarm before creeping
upstairs to my room. "It's just me," I whispered to Haven
as I closed the door behind me.

But I needn't have bothered.

Haven was gone.

"Still no answer," I said, my gaze catching Logan's as I
glanced up from my phone. "You?"

His jaw tightened. "Nothing."

I shifted uncomfortably in my chair, trying to ignore
the way its carved wooden edges cut into my thighs.
Everything at Mistwood Academy was beautiful, and the
auditorium where I sat, my hands clasped anxiously
around my phone, was no exception. Neat rows of chairs
filled the stately hall, and stained glass windows threw
light across the ceiling that arched high above us. Usually I
loved it, but for once I didn't care. I just needed to know
where Haven was.

I turned to Cayley. "How about you?"

She shook her head, wavy brown hair swinging
around her shoulders. "She hasn't answered any of my
messages. Or my calls."

Dammit.

Haven hadn't returned before sunset, and she hadn't turned up to breakfast. None of us knew where she was. For a while, I thought she'd just gone to take a shower, to get the smell of smoke out of her hair and off her skin, but when over an hour had passed and she still hadn't come back, I'd begun to get worried. We'd searched all the usual places—the library, the music rooms, the coffee shop—and asked everyone we could think of. But no one had seen her. We'd even checked the infirmary, but she hadn't been there either. Finally, we'd decided to try the auditorium, hoping she'd turn up for assembly.

So far, she hadn't.

"Where are you?" I muttered, looking down at my phone.

Thomas Callaghan—werewolf, Logan's adopted brother, and Cayley's boyfriend—leaned forward, his head thrust out over angular shoulders. "What if she's hurt? Or … or worse?" he said, his blue eyes worried. "We should be out there looking for her."

"She'll be back," Cayley said, squeezing his hand. "She has a physics quiz second period. Mr. Timmins will kill her if she misses it."

Logan's jaw twitched.

I moved my leg so my knee rested against his, then lifted my phone.

"Screw it, I'm going." Thomas stood, his brows drawing together.

"Sit down, Mr. Callaghan," a passing teacher intoned as

the stage lights came up and the main lights in the auditorium dimmed. "Assembly has started."

Thomas paused a beat too long. The scent of wolf, of fur and forest air, whirled around him. His eyes flashed amber, the predator ready to escape from beneath his skin, but Logan said his name and he sat back down in his chair with a thud.

"Haven will be fine," Cayley said firmly, her hair fluttering around her shoulders on a non-existent breeze. "She always is."

Logan's entire body tensed at her words, and I reached for his hand. He'd told me once that he didn't do well with absolutes; he'd said they made him nervous. Usually, he covered it up with a smile or a quip, anything to draw attention away from how he was really feeling, and usually it worked. No one at school—aside from our small group of friends and Mr. Green—knew that Logan had been diagnosed with anxiety and OCD. No one knew how much time he spent battling himself. The only thing he hadn't been able to keep secret were the self-inflicted scars that lined his arms.

Everyone knew about them.

And not everyone responded to them kindly.

"Good evening, students." Mr. Unsten, the deputy headmaster, strode into the middle of the stage. He was a dwarf, portly and dark-haired, with broad shoulders and a long curly beard, and I'd never heard him sound anything less than cheerful. "As you know," he continued, shifting closer to the microphone, "today is a very important day. We've got—"

"Oh, shit," Thomas said, turning in his chair.

I twisted around, but I already knew what he was looking at. I could smell her. *Haven.* She was magic and earth, sweetness and wild, tainted with something foul. Something broken and wrong. She stalked down the center aisle of the auditorium, her head held high and her eyes blazing with fire.

"Haven?" I whispered.

She thumped down into the empty seat beside Logan and leaned forward, her elbows on her knees. She wore a red flannel shirt, unbuttoned and unwashed, over a plain black T-shirt and paint-stained jeans. The laces on her boots were frayed and undone.

"What happened to you?" Logan asked.

She tilted her chin and stared straight ahead.

"Incoming," Cayley muttered as Mr. Longley—our music teacher and orchestra conductor—made his way toward us, his light green forehead wrinkled in a frown.

I dropped Logan's hand.

Mr. Longley stopped beside Haven and handed her a small yellow card. "Detention," he said briskly. "You're late."

Haven took the card and smiled; it was a slow, sinuous baring of teeth that transformed her face into something dangerous.

"Are you drunk, Miss Montgomery?" Mr. Longley asked, his green eyes narrowing.

"Of course not." Haven's smile deepened, but when she spoke her voice was sweet. "I'd never do something like that."

Thomas stiffened.

Mr. Longley tapped his pen against his fingers. "See that you don't."

I waited until he'd made it back to his spot by the wall before I turned to Haven. "Where have you been?" I whispered. "We've been looking for you. You haven't been answering your phone."

"Digital detox, bitch." She looked away, her gaze fixed on the stage where Mr. Unsten still stood. "You should try it sometime."

"And now," Mr. Unsten boomed into the microphone, "the moment you've all been waiting for. Please welcome your new headmistress, Ms. Siobhan Maguire."

There was a smattering of applause as a tall, blonde woman with pale skin and a wide, easy smile strode out onto the stage. She wore a business suit with black stiletto heels, and she moved with grace and confidence. "Good evening," she said, her voice bright and clear as she adjusted the microphone on its stand. "I'm Ms. Maguire and I'm—"

"Haven," Thomas hissed, drawing my gaze away from the new headmistress. "What are you doing?"

"Not you, asshole." She scratched furiously at her arm, her sleeve pushed up just enough to reveal a small patch of skin that was swollen and burning red. "And I never will. No matter how much you want me to."

Thomas' ears turned pink.

"What the hell, Haven?" Logan said.

Cayley's hazel eyes burned. "Have you completely lost your mind?"

Thomas' crush on Haven had been an open secret for years; she'd never felt the same way, but they'd always remained friends. As far as I knew he was over her—he and Cayley had been dating since just after the Sapphire Eclipse.

"Of course not," Haven said slowly. "I know what I am. The real question is: do you, *succubus*?"

Cayley opened her mouth to answer, but a sudden loud crackling filled the auditorium. Up on stage, Ms. Maguire was still speaking. "To sum up," she said, her words competing with the interference coming from the speakers, "I aim to … Mistwood Academy … a place … students and staff …" The stage lights flashed around her, a flickering strobe that made my head ache. "Excuse me … technical …"

She ducked as an explosive boom shook the auditorium.

A stained glass window shattered.

And everything went dark.

5

I WAVED a hand in front of my face. Someone was screaming, but I could barely hear it over the pounding of my pulse. I couldn't see anything. I couldn't see *anything*. I reached out slowly, my fingers splayed through the darkness. My breath caught in my throat.

The putere *will come to power on the night of the Sapphire Eclipse. As the power ascends, a darkness will rise, and with it will come the destruction of our world.*

Was this it?

Was this how the end began?

"Em."

Something warm and solid touched my wrist, and I screamed. "What—"

"It's me," Logan said. His scent was clouded and uncertain as his fingers threaded through mine. "I guess the electrical system overloaded."

"This isn't electrical." I swallowed hard, my mouth burning with the taste of magic. "It's worse. It's—"

Wait.

I blew out a breath, trying to slow my panic. The scent of vanilla and spice, familiar and fragrant, drifted around us, but it was laced with something bitter. Something burned. Something *wrong*.

This wasn't my darkness; it belonged to someone else.

"What's going on?" someone yelled. "Why can't I see anything?"

"I know why," Cayley murmured under her breath. She nudged me with her elbow, her hair brushing against my cheek as she leaned closer. "And so do you."

It had nothing to do with the prophecy.

"Haven," I said, straightening, all of my senses searching for the sound of her heartbeat in the dark. I hadn't forgotten what had happened the last time this darkness had fallen. The weakness. The blood. The strange silver marking that still snaked up her arm. "Haven, are you there?"

The last time, her heart had stopped.

Logan shifted beside me. "She's not in her seat."

I reached across him, my arm outstretched, pushing through the inky blackness. "Are you sure?"

"Yeah, I'm sure."

My hand met the empty wooden surface of her seat and I swore under my breath. I straightened, pushing up to stand—*find her, help her, save her*—but an elbow smashed into the side of my face.

"Watch it," snapped an abrasive voice.

I didn't know who it belonged to, but she smelled like strawberries and entitlement, and I fell back into my chair, its legs squealing painfully against the floor as I tried to arrange myself correctly in space.

"Something's wrong," Logan said quietly. His breath was hot on my neck as he grabbed my arm. "This isn't a regular outage."

"No shit," Cayley said.

"You said you know what it is." The air shifted around Thomas as he moved; his wolf was close beneath the surface of his skin. "Tell us."

Cayley sighed and I could almost imagine her glancing up at the ceiling in frustration. "It's because Haven's an idiot, okay? She's been looking for it again."

"Looking for what?" Thomas said.

I closed my eyes against the darkness and tried to shut them out. I needed to find Haven before it was too late, before the spell overtook her and her heart stopped working, but—

"My phone's dead!"

"Miss Taylor, Josh hit me!"

"I can't see anything!"

"Students, stay in your seats. I repeat—stay in your seats."

"I have to get out of here."

"Miss, where's the door?"

It was fear and panic and blood rushing through veins, and my predator rose up in my chest like a challenge I couldn't refuse. My fangs tingled in my gums. There was so much to taste, so much to—

"She's looking for the Impure Blade?" Thomas said suddenly, his chair clattering to the floor. "After what happened last time? What the hell is she thinking?"

"She's not thinking," Cayley muttered.

I squeezed my hands into fists, my nails digging into the skin—*breathe, breathe, breathe*—and then I finally heard it. Haven's pulse. It was thin and fast, a hummingbird in her chest, but it was close, and it was real.

She was alive.

I stood, my head spinning with relief. Pushing my predator down, I stumbled past bodies and chairs, holding onto that sound, willing myself to move faster.

"Did you find her?" Cayley said from somewhere behind me.

I didn't answer.

I was close.

So close.

Then the overhead lights flashed back on, followed quickly by the lamps that lined each wall, and my retinas burned. I closed my eyes, clapping my hands over my ears as the speakers roared to life, sending feedback screeching across the auditorium. It was too much, too fast, and my fangs shot through my gums as I bent double, trying to find equilibrium.

Breathe.

You can do this.

I took one step, then another. Haven's blood still called me forward.

"You're standing on my foot."

I flinched as something prodded me on the arm. "What?"

"You're standing on my foot."

I blinked, slow and painful, and the world came into focus around me, still too bright, too loud, too much.

"Haven's over there." Mia, a statuesque dryad with smooth brown skin and masses of untamed hair, was standing beside me. She raised her eyebrows expectantly. "And you're still standing on my foot."

"Sorry," I said, already moving away.

There were people everywhere. Some were still sitting where they'd been when the lights went out, while others were standing in the aisles or winding their way back to their seats. Everything was colored by chaos—the brush of skin against my hand, a laugh that was too long and too loud, the blood that buzzed and hummed and beckoned.

It slid over me and through me, wild and unfettered.

I wanted to hold onto it.

I wanted it to take me under.

I was made for darkness and destruction.

But that wasn't an option.

Not now. Not ever.

"Haven?" I said, forcing my fangs to retract as I stopped right in front of her.

She was sitting on the floor, her body hunched over,

and fresh blood trickled from her nostrils. "Don't touch me," she snapped, her voice low and raspy.

I stepped back. *Breathe. Stay human.* Everyone around us was distracted. Only Mia looked our way, her dark eyes curious.

How much had she seen?

"Can you stand?" I said carefully, crouching down in front of Haven.

She didn't move.

"It's okay." I extended a hand. "I can help you up."

"No." She pushed me away and stood, her legs trembling beneath her. "I can do it myself."

I followed her back to our seats, ready to catch her if she fell, but she didn't even falter. She just moved through the crowd, glaring at anyone who got in her way.

"What happened?" Thomas demanded before we'd even sat down. His eyes flashed amber, his wolf still wild and waiting.

"I told you what happened," Cayley said as she leaned forward, her hand resting lightly on Thomas' knee. Her fingernails darkened from red to black, and her voice dropped to a whisper. "She was looking for the Blade. I just don't know why this didn't happen *during* the spell like last time."

Logan turned to Haven, his dark eyes troubled. "Why were you even looking for it? I thought you couldn't do the spell to"—he lowered his voice—"bind Emily's powers."

"Screw you. Screw all of you." She crossed her ankles

in front of her and stared up at the stage, a stranger in my best friend's body. "I can do the binding spell if I want to. You have no idea what I'm capable of."

It smelled like the truth. And I wanted to believe it. But there was something else behind her words, something I couldn't quite name. It was a faint twist of acid, bitter and corrupt, like truth and a lie combined. "Did you find it?" I said, not sure if I wanted to know the answer.

"I told you, I—"

"Shit," Cayley said, suddenly straightening. "Haven, what's wrong with your arm?"

I followed her gaze, my stomach clenching when I saw what she was looking at. After everything that had happened, I'd forgotten about the patch of red, swollen skin I'd seen earlier on Haven's wrist. But now her sleeve was pushed up to her elbow as she scratched. And her skin? It was scorching, the flesh stretched cruelly around the silver marking that twisted up the inside of her forearm.

It wasn't a normal tattoo.

It was a mark she'd received the very first time she'd searched for the Blade. Someone else had been on the other side of her spell, protecting the Blade with dark magic, and the silver mark was the result of the collision of their opposing forces. Haven had said she was dangerous.

And we still didn't know who she was.

"I'm taking you to the infirmary," I said, standing. "Now."

But Ms. Maguire had already stepped back up to the microphone. "Everyone, settle down." She waited a few moments, then moved on with her speech, and one of the teachers at the side of the room motioned for me to sit. "As I was saying, the study of witchcraft was the high point of my education."

Haven coughed, thick and loud, and a dark-haired vampire in the row in front of us turned around, his mouth pulled back to show his teeth. "You've got a little something above your lip," he said to her, leaning closer as hunger and desire weaved their way across his features.

My own appetite rekindled, deep in my belly.

"Get it under control, Sylvester," Cayley snapped.

Haven wiped her mouth with the back of her hand, smearing blood in a crooked line up the side of her cheek. She stared at Sylvester and raised a middle finger.

Inhale.

Exhale.

Control it.

Ms. Maguire kept talking, unaware of what was going on in the seats halfway across the room. "A lot has changed since my days at Mistwood Academy," she said, "but I can also see that much has remained the same."

I stopped listening again when I heard the familiar click of a camera in the row ahead. The top of Sylvester's phone—a sleek, shiny thing that probably cost more than my cello—was sitting above his shoulder. He cleared his throat, moving the phone a little higher, and there was another click.

Haven snatched the phone from his hands. "Screw you, Sylvester." She jabbed sharply at the glass-covered screen, deleting the last five photos. "I won't be part of your blood-fixation spank bank."

The vampire's ears turned pink. "Give it back."

"Make me." A smile stretched across Haven's face, and she placed the phone in her palm, holding it out in front of her.

"Haven …" I said in warning.

The phone exploded into flames.

"You're insane!" Sylvester said as he leaped to his feet. "Do you have any idea how much that cost? Put it out. Put it out!"

Haven laughed, her head tipping back as the flames grew higher.

"That's enough." Mr. Longley appeared beside us. He held himself up to his full height and pointed first at Haven, then at Sylvester. "You two are coming with me. Now." He raised a hand, extinguishing the flames with a few muttered words, and plucked the device from Haven's palm.

"It's all his fault." Thomas's skin rippled as he stood, and he pointed at Sylvester. "He was—"

"Silence, Mr. Callaghan. Unless you want to spend the rest of the week in detention, you will sit back down in your seat and stay there until the assembly is finished."

"But—"

"Thomas," Logan said quietly. The scent of wolf, of

forest air and power, swirled around him, reaching toward his brother.

"Stop it," Thomas snapped, his fingernails turning to claws.

Mr. Longley sighed. "Very well, Mr. Callaghan, you may join us. Retain your human form please, and hurry up." He began walking up the center aisle of the auditorium, motioning for Thomas, Haven, and Sylvester to follow.

Sylvester made his way past the rest of his row, his face flaming red as everyone whispered. Thomas growled. Haven stood, stretching her hands out in front of her. Dark shadows played across her face, her hollow cheeks sinking in as she murmured something in Latin under her breath. *"Ignis—"*

But that was all she said before her eyes rolled back in her head and she crumpled to the floor.

"Haven!" I yelled, launching myself forward. "Haven, wake up."

Logan's gaze skimmed over the staring crowd, and he gestured at the people in the rows around us as he stood. "Everyone move. She needs space. Quickly!" The air around him rippled with power, and chair legs scraped loudly against the tile floor.

"Has this ever happened before?" Mr. Longley said as he bobbed down beside me.

"I—" I swallowed hard as I took Haven's hand in mine. It was cold and clammy, but her chest moved up and down with each shallow breath. *She's breathing. She's alive.*

"I don't know. I don't think so."

I gazed down at Haven's face, her skin so pale the veins were visible at her temples, and I wished there was something I could do. Some power I could use that would wake her up. That would make her okay again.

"What about my phone?" Sylvester said, his face contorting as he stood over us. "She's just doing this for attention. She—"

"Shut up, Sylvester." Cayley stepped past me and pushed him back into the aisle. "You were photographing her without her consent. Total dick move."

"Everyone stay calm," Mr. Longley said. "This isn't helping Haven."

Thomas snatched up Sylvester's phone from where it lay beside Mr. Longley on the floor. It was blackened and warped, the screen marked with scattered cracks, and it smelled toxic, like burning plastic. And magic. *Dark* magic. "How are we supposed to stay calm?" he demanded, his eyes glowing amber. "This asshole was taking photos of Haven. And now she's unconscious."

"That's enough," Mr. Longley said sharply as he lifted his own phone to his ear. "I will handle this."

Ms. Maguire surveyed us from up on the stage, her expression sober as she whispered in Mr. Unsten's ear. She might've seemed young for a headmistress, but she spoke with absolute authority when she stepped back up to the microphone and said, "You are all dismissed. Go straight to your classes. Do not dawdle. And do not stop and stare." She clapped her hands, the amplified sound ringing out across the auditorium as everyone started talking at once. "Quietly, please."

To her credit, almost everyone listened, and the noise lowered as people began to stand and make their way toward the exits. Logan, Cayley, and Thomas all stayed where they were, and I turned back to Haven as her hand stiffened in mine.

"What happened?" she said, her eyelids fluttering.

I smoothed her hair back from her forehead. "You fainted. But you're going to be fine."

Mr. Longley lowered his phone. "The nurse will be here soon."

Haven's skin was cold, her face still impossibly pale, but she tried to smile even as her eyes filled with tears. "What will they do?" she said. "Will I—will I have to go to the infirmary?" She tried to sit and she coughed, showering tiny specks of blood over her lips and her chin.

"What's happening?" Thomas said. "Why is she bleeding?"

"I don't know." I swallowed hard.

Haven coughed again.

"Coming through," snapped a familiar voice. "Get out of my way. Everybody move."

I looked up at Mr. Lopez, one of the school nurses, who stood over me, scowling, his dark eyebrows furrowed over hard brown eyes. "Hi," I said weakly.

His lips thinned. "That includes you, Miss Sanderson."

I gave Haven's hand one last squeeze and scrambled out of the way.

"What happened?" he asked as he knelt down beside Haven, his steady fingers reaching for her wrist.

"She fainted," I said. "She wasn't herself and—"

"She set my phone on fire," Sylvester interrupted, leaning over the chairs in the row in front of us. "With magic."

"You don't even deserve a phone." Thomas threw the offending object at Sylvester's face, hitting him on his already-crooked nose. "You were—"

"Out!" Mr. Lopez thundered, placing Haven's hand back in her lap. He stood, eyes blazing. "All of you. Now."

Shit.

"Can I st—" I started, but Mr. Lopez turned his glare on me.

"You will leave with the others."

Cayley was already dragging Thomas down the center aisle, her hand tight on his wrist, avoiding the claws that had once again sprouted from his fingertips. Logan touched my shoulder. I put my hand over his and he looked down at me, his jaw set, eyes dark and troubled.

"I'll be back," he said, before taking off after Cayley and Thomas.

"Emily," Mr. Lopez said, his voice rising in warning. "Go."

No.

Haven's breath fluttered in her throat. "Can't she stay? Please?" She put her hand over her mouth and coughed again, her narrow shoulders shuddering.

Mr. Lopez shook his head, his face set in stone.

I wanted to stay, to fight him, to fight *anyone* who said I had to leave, but every second he spent trying to get rid of me was another second he could've been helping Haven.

"I'm sorry," I said, leaning down to hug her. "I'll come and see you in the infirmary, okay?"

She bit her lip, and tears slipped down her cheeks. "I can't keep doing this," she whispered. "It's too much. I can't remember—"

"You can't remember what?" I said when she looked away, her pulse unsteady.

"I need to help my patient." Mr. Lopez towered over me, a giant in tennis shoes and scrubs. "And you are in my way."

"Okay, okay." I blinked back tears of my own and kissed Haven on the cheek. "I'll come and see you soon. I promise."

6

My HASTY WORDS had turned me into a liar. It was almost curfew and I'd had to sit through an entire night of classes, orchestra practice, dinner, and homework, and I *still* hadn't seen Haven. I had no idea how she was doing. Or even what was wrong with her.

"We could just go back," Thomas said, his leg jiggling under the table. "Wait outside her room until someone tells us she's okay."

I clasped my hands in front of me. The scent of coffee and sugar filled the air, and I breathed it in, hoping it would help me think. We usually came to Coffee and Cake, the little café on campus, to chill out and relax, but now Logan, Cayley, Thomas, and I were there because we didn't know what else to do.

"You know we can't go back," Cayley said. "They *just* sent us away."

Between the four of us, we'd visited the infirmary at

least twelve times already. Probably more. We'd mostly gone between classes, slipping in during those brief moments of chaos when no one really knows or cares where anyone else is supposed to be. Thomas had also gone during class, claiming headaches and nausea to get out of both History and Math, though neither the teachers nor the nursing staff believed him. Then there were the visits before and after orchestra. And before and after dinner.

No one would let us see her.

I picked up a sugar packet and ran my finger across it. "We could—"

"Chocolate cake?" said the shaggy-haired waitress who appeared at our table.

"That's mine." Logan lifted his phone out of the way and put it in his pocket. "Thanks."

She set the rest of the orders down on the table with a smile, then headed back to the counter, humming along with the music playing over the café's speakers as she walked.

"Why are we even here?" Thomas said, glaring at his apple pie before pushing it away. "We're wasting time."

"We're here because Mr. Lopez said he'd give us a month of detention if he caught us in the infirmary one more time," Cayley said. "And we have to eat, so ..." She shrugged, putting a forkful of Neapolitan Cheesecake in her mouth.

Thomas just glared harder.

I knew how he felt. Haven hadn't answered her phone

all night. And despite our repeated visits to the infirmary, no one would tell us anything—not even Mr. Green or Miss Lassila. They all said it was because they had to abide by federal privacy laws and we weren't family.

It was bullshit.

Because after everything we'd been through, Haven *was* family.

Picking up my red velvet cupcake, I wished there was something more I could do. I had all this power—abilities I knew about, and maybe ones I didn't—but I couldn't *do* anything with it. There were rules and regulations that had to be followed; there were consequences for breaking the law. It was no different than when I was human.

I put the cupcake back down on my plate.

"You know you should have something," Logan said, nudging my arm with his elbow. "You've barely eaten since breakfast."

He was right.

I'd managed half an apple at lunch, and a bread roll at dinner. But I also knew that no matter what influence my feelings had on my appetite, eating regularly was something I *had* to do. It was a rule that had been drilled into me from the time I woke up at the Paranormal Program. Food, exercise, meditation, sleep—they were all integral for retaining control.

I took a small sip of tea, hoping it would settle my stomach.

It didn't work.

Anxiety tightened my throat and I pushed the cup

away. So much had happened in the last two days—the fire, Haven's collapse, finding out about the spell. Maybe I should've visited one of the Nutriments at dinner. I mean, the extra control I'd stolen from Mr. Olaru's blood only went so far. It wasn't like he'd been a paragon of moderation. He'd been short-tempered. Power-hungry. Homicidal.

His blood runs through my veins.

How long could I resist it? How long until I snapped?

"What if we called the medical center?" Thomas said, drawing me away from my fear-induced spiral. "Or what if you went there?" He turned to Cayley, his blue eyes widening. "You can make yourself look like anyone. If the staff thought you were Haven's mom …" He trailed off, leaving the idea hanging between them.

Cayley shook her head. "It's not gonna happen."

"What?"

"I said, it's not going to happen."

I choked down another sip of tea as they argued, and Logan moved closer, his leg coming to rest against mine. "It's not a bad idea," he whispered, his voice so low I could barely hear it.

"I'm going." Thomas suddenly stood, his phone clenched tight in his fist. "Stay here, come with—I don't care. But I'm not coming back till I have some answers."

Cayley raised an unimpressed brow. "Seriously? That's—"

Beep. Beep. Beep.

Our phones buzzed in unison.

"It's Haven," Thomas said quickly, almost dropping his phone. "She's … got an infection?" His forehead wrinkled in confusion.

"She says it made her magic go haywire," Cayley continued, her face tilted down. "But she's being treated, and she's feeling okay."

I skimmed the message twice, my phone trembling in my hands, then lay my forehead down on the table. The wood, fragrant with the scent of sugar and spray cleaner, was cold against my skin, but it didn't matter. None of it mattered. Because Haven was awake. She was awake and coherent and alive.

And she's going to be fine.

The table shook as Thomas sat back down. "We can't go and see her," he said, disappointment clouding his words. "Not until tomorrow."

"So?" Cayley put her phone down on the table. "It's not like she can entertain you right now."

I lifted my head, surprised by the sharp undercurrent beneath her words. "That's not—" I started, but she huffed and turned away. Her jaw was set, her shoulders rigid, and her hair had darkened to a black so deep it barely reflected light.

Thomas flushed. "I don't want to see Haven for *entertainment.*"

"Whatever," Cayley muttered. "She's still not going to want us there."

I quickly sent Haven a message, then slid my phone into my pocket. "She will," I said. "Soon."

Cayley rolled her eyes.

"I know supes don't usually get sick," I continued, resisting the urge to glare at her, "but you used to be human, Thomas. Don't you remember what it's like?"

He frowned, then wiped the back of his hand across his lips, nodding slowly. There was something behind his eyes that I couldn't quite read, but now wasn't the time to deal with it.

I turned to Logan.

"I've never been human," he said quickly.

"Yeah, but you must remember how you felt when we were attacked by Derek in the quad last semester."

"Ah." He paused. "I do."

"And you," I said, shifting my attention to Cayley. "I … um, I actually don't know if you've ever been injured."

She lifted a shoulder, her expression stony. "A couple of times. But I'm a succubus. I have a high pain tolerance."

I tilted my head, breathing in slowly. My predator was close, pressing against my skin like a guardian. It didn't matter that Haven was okay. It wanted to claw its way out; it wanted to protect me. But I didn't need protecting from Cayley. Because while she was a mess of emotions, over-flowing with relief and drowning in fear, I knew why she reeked of anger. It sat on her skin beneath sea spray and cookies, carnations and apples. Beneath aniseed. Daisies. Tobacco. It was the scent of rotting leaves, acrid and sharp, and sometimes it was easier to hold onto than anything else.

"What I'm trying to say," I said, "is that we need to give

Haven some time. It doesn't mean she doesn't want to see us. And it doesn't mean …" My gaze drifted to Thomas. "It doesn't mean that we didn't protect her."

His throat moved painfully as he swallowed.

Everyone was silent.

"We should finish up here," Logan eventually said, his dark eyes on his brother. "It's not long until curfew."

The tables around us had emptied as we'd talked, leaving the café almost deserted. A couple of people still sat near the front of the room, but the waitress had already started clearing the food from the display cabinets at the counter, so I finished my tea and ate most of my cupcake, trying to ignore the tension in the air.

The old-fashioned bell above the door chimed.

"Shit," Logan muttered under his breath.

I looked up as three of my least favorite people walked in: Courtney Beckett, Vanessa Green, and Danielle Hunter. They were tall and pretty, with shiny hair and vicious mouths, and it felt like a cliché to hate them.

"Looks like someone forgot to take out the trash," Danielle said, her green eyes narrowing as she saw us.

The scent of rotting leaves intensified, twisting around Cayley like a second skin, and Thomas growled low in his chest.

"Be cool," Logan murmured. "Don't let her get to you."

I watched silently as the three of them ordered—two iced coffees and a large cappuccino—and bit my tongue as they turned, drinks in hand, and stalked toward our table. They smelled of perfume and spite, an odd juxtaposition of chemicals and sulfur, and I wished they were anywhere else.

"So," Courtney said, stopping beside Logan, hand on her hip. "We've got Logan, Thomas, Cayley, Emma"—her blue eyes hardened as they cut to me—"and, oh. What's this? No Haven?"

My fingernails dug into my palms.

Don't do it.

Don't give her what she wants.

"Don't be such an asshole," Cayley snapped, unwilling —or unable—to hold herself back. "You know what happened at assembly. You were there."

Beside me, Logan straightened his shoulders. His skin was warm with the power of his wolf, but his expression was neutral. Polite. "We were just leaving," he said firmly.

"What about Haven?" Courtney's blue eyes were wide. "Supes don't pass out. And we don't get sick. What's the matter with her?"

"I heard she was drunk," Danielle offered.

"I heard she was pregnant." Vanessa smiled, showing perfect white teeth, yet something about her seemed off. Her makeup was layered on thicker than usual, and her carefully-lined eyes were tired. Still, her voice was as sharp as ever when she turned to Thomas and raised one perfectly-shaped brow. "Is it yours?"

Thomas stood, his hands braced on the table. "Fuck you." His wolf was so close it was moving beneath his skin.

"Control it," Logan whispered, putting a hand on Thomas' arm.

Thomas snarled.

My fangs prickled beneath my gums and I breathed in slowly, adrenaline coursing through my veins. I unclenched my fists, but the room was too bright and my heart was too fast. The room shifted around me.

Breathe.

I blinked, exhaling as the floor tilted up.

Control it.

My hands found the edges of my seat, holding me in place as my focus sharpened.

Don't let yourself change.

Beneath my skin, my blood ran hot.

As the power ascends, a darkness will rise, and with it will come the destruction of our world.

I was strength. I was power. I was connected to everything.

The neatly-folded napkin on the table in front of me began to shake.

I lifted my hands, the faintest wisps of purple dancing in the corners of my eyes—

—then the front door slammed and I flinched.

The spell was broken.

"Come on," Courtney said, flicking her honey-blonde waves over her shoulder as she turned to go. She took three steps forward, the heels of her ankle boots moving smoothly on the tile floor, then she spun back around. "Logan, I'm sure you're aware, but your father will be hearing about this. You cannot keep associating with these people—especially with your history. You're going to destabilize the Adams' pack and your family's hold on it."

Logan pushed his chair back and rose. "Get out."

"We've all seen your arms, Logan. And the scar on her" —she tilted her chin at me—"wrist. Cayley's going nowhere in life. Haven's a screw up. And the only reason Thomas is tolerated in the pack is because he was a stray and he's obviously still learning."

"He's been learning long enough to know better," Danielle muttered. She tucked her copper-colored bob behind her ears and took a step toward Thomas.

He bared his teeth and lunged.

"Stop," Logan said, his muscles straining as he held Thomas back. "Let them go."

The waitress from earlier walked toward us, drying her hands on a dish cloth. "We're closing," she said mildly. "You all need to leave."

Danielle's eyes narrowed, but the waitress cocked an eyebrow, her body elongating and changing as she let us see the monster beneath her skin. Her skin shimmered iridescent blue, and though her face remained human, the faint outline of wings spread out behind her.

"Half dragon," she said when she saw my mouth drop open. "Now, leave. Don't make me complete this change."

Courtney, Danielle, and Vanessa were already halfway to the door, and the rest of us quickly followed. Thomas took off as soon as we got outside, not even slowing to say goodbye, while Cayley stormed away in the opposite direction. Her hair flew out around her shoulders and she nearly walked straight into Mia, who was carrying her violin case over her shoulder. I could almost hear what they were saying, but Logan touched my arm, drawing my attention closer.

"I need to run," he said.

"It's nearly curfew."

"I know." He reached out and squeezed my hand, then pressed a kiss to my lips. His skin was burning. "But I have to go. I have to change now."

I kissed him again, but when he left I didn't follow. I was restless, filled with a longing I didn't understand. It was a prickle in my chest. A memory of depth, of brightness, of *knowing*. But no matter how many times I tried to draw it out, I couldn't make it real.

Did I imagine it?

"Em!" Cayley called, beckoning me over to the side of the path where she and Mia were still talking.

"What's up?" I nodded a greeting at Mia, who adjusted her violin case and frowned.

"Have you seen Jenny tonight?" she asked.

"Jenny Williams?" I rocked back on my heels, waiting for confirmation. Mistwood Academy was small, at least compared to my school back in Michigan, but I still didn't know everyone who went there. Especially the supes who weren't in any of my classes.

"She didn't turn up to practice after dinner," Mia said, her voice pitched somewhere between irritation and

concern. "She's never missed a rehearsal before. Like …
ever."

"Oh." I paused, trying to think, but I'd been so worried
about Haven that I hadn't really been paying attention to
anything—or anyone—else. "Was she at orchestra?"

Mia's frown deepened. "She was sitting two seats away
from you."

"Yeah, but …" I rubbed a hand across my forehead. "I
didn't notice."

Mia watched me carefully, her dark eyes assessing
every movement I made. She was a dryad, a sort of nymph
who sometimes took the form of a tree, and like the oak
that she intermittently became, she was strong and steady.
Dependable. She took her time getting to know people;
she was unwavering in her loyalty.

And somehow I felt like I'd let her down.

"I'm sorry I can't help," I said.

"Let me know if you see her." Mia touched Cayley's arm,
her long fingers moving with a familiarity that surprised me.
"Come on. I haven't checked the library yet. And if she's not
there"—she stopped as the warning bells chimed—"we can
swing by Hollyfield Hall on the way back to Worthington."

"Is there anything I can do?" I said.

"Yeah." Cayley lifted her chin, her gaze focused on
something behind me. "Go and see what Mr. Green wants.
I think he's waiting for you."

I turned as Mia dragged her away, and my eyes came
to rest on the therapist, who was standing beneath a lamp

post farther down the path. Fred sat at his feet, his long tail thumping on the ground, smoke drifting lazily from his nostrils.

"Emily," Mr. Green said, gently tugging on Fred's lead before walking toward me. "I have something for you."

I waited until they'd stopped. "What is it?"

Mr. Green smiled, then pulled a large white envelope out of his bag and handed it to me. "Your papers."

My stomach tightened. "For the spell? Already?"

"Yes," he said, "but take your time. Read them slowly. This is only the beginning of the process. It will take months, possibly even longer, before the spell can be completed."

"I know, but …" I clutched the envelope to my chest. "Thank you."

I ran up to my room, my mind spinning. By the time I'd sat down, my legs crossed beneath me on my bed, I'd forgotten everything else. All that mattered right now was this. The envelope sitting in front of me. My name was printed on the front in elegant writing, the packet sent care of Mister James Edward Green, Head of Psychology, Mistwood Academy, Washington State. The address never got more specific than that, but it had been delivered anyway. I wondered if—

No.

Focus.

I drew in a breath and tore open the seal. I could do this. I *would* do this. With shaking hands, I pulled out the stack of papers and set them down in front of me. There were forms to read, and forms to fill out, and—

No. Oh, no, no, no.

"Parental permission?" I said aloud, my shoulders slumping.

7

I READ THE SHEET AGAIN, focusing carefully on every single word, but I couldn't see any way around it. *Signature of parent or guardian.* It was there at the bottom of each page, in glaring black text.

What the hell am I supposed to do?

I'd be eighteen soon—this was my second time doing junior year because I'd missed so much school after the attack that had turned me into a vampire—but I didn't want to wait. I could feel Mr. Olaru's hold on me, subtle yet threatening, a noose being tightened inch by burning inch.

I lifted my hands.

His blood runs through my veins.

I pushed out with my powers, trying to sense, to see, to *feel*, but the world was static and stable. There was no purple glow on my skin, no otherworldly wisps catching the edges of my vision. The papers sat immobile on my bed.

Maybe it didn't actually happen.

I'd spent so long searching—all that time measured in notepaper and hours and fears—that maybe I'd seen what I wanted to see. A figment of my imagination. Or a panic attack that had altered my vision.

Or maybe Thomas had bumped the table when he stood.

The truth was, though, that it didn't really matter. Because Mr. Olaru lived within me. He was there every time I was thoughtless. Or mad. Or a liar. He was in my blood, and there was nothing to stop me becoming just like him. Nothing to stop me destroying the world.

Nothing except the spell.

"Dammit," I muttered, reaching for my phone.

I was going to have to text my mom. *Again.* I pressed my lips together and wondered how much I could get away with not telling her. *It's not like she ever told* me *the truth.* But when I unlocked the screen, the words wouldn't come, so I lay back on the bed and stared at the ceiling, my phone lying heavy on my chest. I could text her tomorrow, when—

Shit.

Someone was knocking on the door.

I sat, ignoring my phone as it fell, and gathered up the papers, stuffing them under my pillow. *You're a target. A prize. No one can know what you are.* I'd just set Minikins down on top of it all, pulling the covers up as high as I could, when the scent of rye bread and cheese drifted under the door. Sighing with relief, I pulled everything back out.

Miss Lassila already knew what I was.

"Emily," she called. "May I come in?"

"What is it?" I asked before the door was even open. "Did something happen to Haven?"

The housemistress stepped inside and closed the door behind her. "Haven's fine." She clasped her hands in front of her body and looked up at me, her blue eyes appraising. She was tiny, a haltija who barely came up to my waist, and though she seemed harmless, with simple clothes and white-blonde hair that hung in a braid down her back, I'd learned never to underestimate her. Her magic was stronger than I was.

"Can you tell me anything?" I asked, trying to swallow the desperate note that crept into my voice. *Stay calm. Be rational.* I wasn't scared of Miss Lassila—she wouldn't do anything to hurt me—but I also didn't want to piss her off. "Do you know what caused the infection?"

Her lips pursed in disapproval.

Oops.

"You know I can't comment on Haven's medical situation," she said.

I sighed and sat down on the bed. "Do you know if she found the Blade?"

"The what?"

"The Impure Blade. She was—" I stopped abruptly. "Oh. With everything that's been going on, I guess I forgot to mention it earlier."

Miss Lassila's gaze flicked to the papers that were scattered all over the bed. "Mr. Green informed me about the binding spell. I was not, however, aware that you'd started looking for the items yourselves." Her shoulders stiffened. "You need to stop—*all* of you—and leave it to the professionals."

"But Haven was just—"

"No." Miss Lassila lifted a finger, her eyes dark with warning. "There is no *just* about it. This is a dangerous spell and a dangerous situation. Do you understand?"

I didn't—not really—but I nodded anyway.

"I mean it," she said as she walked slowly around the room, scrutinizing the desks, the beds, the bookshelves. She stopped beside Haven's trunk; it was almost as tall as her, and she ran a hand over the intricately-carved wood before pulling it back, her expression thoughtful.

My stomach fluttered. "Do you think it's in there?"

"The Blade is in storage at a facility owned and maintained by the SCC."

I touched the scar on my wrist, my fingers lingering on the memory that would never quite heal. "Have you checked?"

Her teeth snapped together. "Are you questioning my ability to do my job?"

"No, ma'am," I said quickly. "Of course not."

My phone beeped, the screen lighting up with a message, and Miss Lassila sighed. "I only came up here because I wanted to check on you before curfew," she said. "You've been through a lot, and I know you're not used to sleeping alone." She swept across the room in her kitten-heeled boots, her braid hanging primly down her back. "Ms. Emmerson and I will be outside if you need us."

I waited until the lock clunked back into place, then straightened the mess of papers on the bed. A sigh escaped my lips. *Why does everything have to be so hard?* All I wanted was to be free of the influence of a homicidal vampire and to ensure that an apocalyptic prophecy never came to pass. Was that too much to ask?

I was pouring through the first few pages, wondering why the SCC needed to know my blood type and what they'd say if I told them I didn't know, when another knock interrupted me, this time from the window. I set the papers aside and frowned.

"It's me," Logan called. He waited a beat. Then another. "Can I come in?"

The curfew bell had already rung, but I made my way over to the window and threw open the shutters. "What are you doing?" I said as I unlatched the window. "We're supposed to be asleep."

He slipped into the room silently and kissed the top of my head. "You didn't answer my message. I was worried."

I leaned in as he wrapped his arms around me. He was warm, the lines of his body fitting perfectly against mine, and I let myself get lost in his lips before reluctantly pulling away. "You could get both of us expelled."

"I come up here all the time."

"Not after curfew. What if your housemaster notices you're not in your room?"

Logan reached out and took my hand. "He's already done the room check, but I can go if you're uncomfortable."

"It's not that, it's just … I dunno." I blew out a breath, not even sure what I wanted to say. "I'm just worried about Haven. And the conferences. And that stupid spell. The forms already arrived—Mr. Green gave them to me tonight."

"That's good though … right?"

"If good means needing to get parental permission."

Logan's fingers tightened around mine, his skin hot and his scent uncertain. A dark curl slipped over his forehead as he lowered his chin, trying to catch my gaze. "So … are you gonna call your mom?"

Not if I don't have to.

I let go of his hand and backed away, only stopping when my legs hit the side of the bed. "I texted her yesterday. She's coming to the parent-teacher conferences next week."

"I—oh, she is?" Logan blinked. "That's great."

I sat down on the mattress and reached for my phone, trying to ignore the irritation that tightened my chest. "She can sign them then."

"Don't you want to give her a heads up?"

I swallowed hard and stared down at the screen in my hands. It was blank, empty, but the phone itself was filled with her messages:

We wanted to keep you safe.

We did it for your own good.

We thought you'd never find out.

Bitterness rose in my throat, coating the back of my tongue, and Logan put his hand on my knee as he sat down beside me. "Do you think your mom will sign it?" he said.

"I don't know. Maybe."

"You could—"

"Stop," I said, moving away from him until we were no longer touching. "Just … stop."

Logan clasped his hands in front of him, his emotions folding back inside of himself until every part of him was neutral and bland. Usually I found it strange, how he could compartmentalize this way, but for once I just felt relief. I didn't think I could handle his fears. Not when I already had more than enough of my own.

"You could've told me," he said quietly. "You didn't have to deal with it alone. I know you've been—"

"I said *stop*." My fangs prickled, the tips sliding through my gums, and I whirled around to face him. "It's not like you tell me everything."

"I … what?" Logan's brow furrowed. "What are you talking about?"

"Why do you hide so much of yourself?" I demanded. "You're doing it now. Why won't you let me in?"

His eyes widened in disbelief. "I *do* let you in. I let you in more than anyone I've ever known."

I tossed my phone down on the bed and snatched up the unsigned forms. "Tell me the truth—do you want my mom to sign these? Because *I* want her to. Every day I feel what he tried to take from me. He tried to kill me. He tried to kill *you*. And he almost succeeded. It was—" I broke off, the words sticking in my throat.

"It's okay," Logan said softly.

It's not okay.

It'll never be okay.

"You're not like Mr. Olaru," he said. "You're not a bad person."

"Not a bad person?" I echoed, my voice rising as I cast the papers aside and stood. "Look at me. *Look at me.*" Adrenaline surged through my veins, crawling over my skin, and my hands curled into fists.

I hated this.

Every day I was getting worse—angrier, sharper, colder. No matter what I did, no matter how much I tried to control it, I could feel him like poison in my veins. It seemed almost inevitable, this slow decline into something monstrous, but there was still enough of me left to know that it wasn't what I wanted.

I have to bind my powers.

No matter what it takes.

"I'm sorry," I said, scrubbing my hands over my face and trying to find a spark of humanity. "You've been so amazing through all of this and I've ..." My gaze dropped to the floor. "I've been a total disaster. You don't deserve that."

"I know."

My head jerked up. "Wh—"

"I know I'm amazing," Logan said, his lips lifting at the corners. "I mean, look at me."

A laugh burst from my throat, loud and unexpected. "I thought—"

"What? You thought I'd disagree?" Logan stood, lifting his t-shirt; the lean lines of his body were highlighted in the warm, yellow glow of my bedside lamp. "See? Amazing."

He grinned down at me, a smile so genuine it made my chest hurt, and I reached out and took his hand. So many times, I'd seen him use humor as a distraction, as a way to ensure people couldn't get too close, or see too much of the truth. But this wasn't like that. He'd done this for me. For no other reason than to make me smile.

He pulled me closer. "I should probably go."

I bit my lip. My hands were clammy. "You don't … you don't have to."

Logan stepped back, his eyes searching mine, then he cupped my face in his hands and kissed me softly, slowly. When he finally pulled away, his face was flushed. "Are you sure?"

I nodded. "It doesn't mean we'll … um …" I trailed off, suddenly uncomfortable. We'd done a lot of things—making out behind the library; doing more than making out in my bedroom when Haven wasn't there—but we'd never actually slept together. In any sense of the word.

"Of course," Logan said. "We don't have to do anything." He reached up, his fingers gentle as he brushed my hair back from my forehead. "I mean, it's not that I don't want to. I pretty much always want to. But right now, I think we both need to get some sleep."

I looked at the bed.

"Come on, I'll help you tidy up."

Logan gathered up the bundle of forms I'd thrown down on the blankets and put them on my desk while I changed into my pajamas. When I was done, I closed the window and the shutters, locking us in for the day.

"Should I take Haven's bed?" he asked.

I paused, then swallowed hard. "I don't know. Do you want to?"

He inhaled slowly, his dark eyes rising to meet mine. "No."

I climbed into bed first. The sheets were wrinkled and cold, but I burrowed down into them, shoving Minikins aside to make room for Logan.

"You can move closer. I won't bite." He shot me a crooked grin. "Unless that's something you want."

"I—um—"

"I'm teasing," he whispered, his breath warm against my neck. For a moment, I forgot about spells and fears and powers. I forgot about everything. All I could feel was him. His lips against mine. His hands lifting my shirt. The heat of his skin beneath my fingers. "I thought you didn't want to do anything," he whispered, his mouth still against mine.

"Sometimes you're hard to resist."

The sun was approaching by the time we rolled over, both of us facing the wall. I didn't think I'd be able to sleep

—not with Logan's arm around my waist and his legs curled behind me—but I closed my eyes and drifted off.

I was safe.

I was happy.

I was home.

I sat, sweat dripping down my back.

Thump.

Thump.

Thump.

My pulse was off-the-charts fast.

"Logan?" I said, confused as the dusky scent of boy and wolf invaded my senses. I tried to push the blankets from my legs, but they wouldn't budge. "Is that you?"

"It's too early," he mumbled. "Go back to sleep."

I pressed my hands against my eyes, starbursts of color exploding in the dark, and tried to slow my pulse. A warm hand touched my leg and I almost slumped back down, but I was hot—unbearably hot—so I wiggled myself free and padded toward the door.

"Where are you going?" Logan asked, his words slurring.

"Bathroom," I whispered.

He closed his eyes, sleep pulling him back under, and I slipped on some shoes before making my way out into the hallway. I never liked getting up by myself during the day, not since I'd been kidnapped on my way back from the bathroom, a few weeks before the Sapphire Eclipse. But it wasn't like Logan could go with me. I hesitated, glancing back at the door, then straightened my spine and kept walking.

I'm seventeen years old.

I can go to the bathroom by myself.

I shivered as I swung open the door, but the bathroom was empty, the luxury fittings illuminated softly by the chandelier that hung from the ceiling. The carved wooden benches by the walls smelled faintly of furniture polish, and the doors to each cubicle hung open, revealing gleaming white porcelain. I kept searching, looking for anything out of place, but by the time I washed my hands, my reflection staring back at me from the mirror above the sink, I was able to let myself believe that everything was fine. My hair was tangled and my face was flushed, but—

My face.

My face in the mirror.

I'd seen it, just before I'd woken up, but … I hadn't been at Mistwood. I'd been back home in Michigan, surrounded by my memories, by echoes of the past. My bedroom had been exactly the same as it had been when I'd lived there, from the bedspread to the dresser to the half-used pencils on my desk. But it wasn't my bedroom that was important. It was something else.

I leaned closer to the mirror, my vision blurring.

Why can't I remember?

I thought of Kitty, the mara I'd met at the Paranormal

Program, who'd invaded my dreams and preyed on my fears. She'd promised me a different life, and she'd destroyed the lives of others. But I knew this couldn't be her. She was locked up. Incarcerated indefinitely and separated from her powers.

This was just a dream.

Nothing more. Nothing less.

I tucked my hair behind my ears and walked back to my room, nodding to a girl down the corridor who was creeping away from the kitchenette, a steaming cup of tea in her hands. The dream kept playing in my mind, slipping and shifting like gossamer in the wind, but when I reached for the door handle, a single image became crystal clear.

My old living room, and my hand—reaching for a vase.

"That's it!" I said as I shut the door behind me, kicking off my shoes. "I know what it means."

Logan blinked. "What?"

"I figured out the anchor." I climbed back into bed, accidentally elbowing him in the side. "You know, the heirloom."

"What?"

"Argh, nothing," I whispered, leaning over and kissing him on the cheek. "Go back to sleep."

I lay back down and Logan shifted closer, his body molding against my own. His breath came slow and steady, and he flung an arm across my waist. The scars that marked his skin were visible, even in the dark; each thin silver line was a reminder of the pain he'd felt, of the relief he'd sought. He'd been clean for over a year, but it still hurt my heart to know what he'd been through.

I slid my hand beneath his and he mumbled something under his breath. I closed my eyes, and the next thing I knew my phone was beeping, its alarm accusing in the otherwise silent room. Rolling over, I bashed Logan's thigh with my knee, and reached for my phone.

"Logan," I said, my eyes widening when I realized what day it was. "You have to get up."

He groaned and pulled the blankets up over his face. "Later."

"No, you have to get up now." I scrambled out of bed and rushed around the room, picking up random items off the floor and putting them away. "Ms. Emmerson will be here any minute. It's room inspection day."

The blanket shifted and Logan's head popped out. "Inspections are on Fridays."

"They might be at Emberfield, but at Worthington Hall they're on Tuesdays."

He pushed his hair back from his forehead, looking puzzled.

"That's today," I said, tossing an empty chip packet in the trash. "You have to leave. Now."

Logan swung his legs over the side of the bed, then stood up and stretched, covering a yawn with his hand. He'd slept in his clothes—a black t-shirt and a loose pair of sweatpants—and he looked rumpled and delicious and—

Focus.

"Quick," I said, opening the shutters and unlatching the window. "You can go out—"

"Wait." He slipped his arms around my waist, his sleepy gaze searching my face. "Did you wake me during the day?"

"Yes, but you have to go. I'll explain everything later." I went up on my tiptoes and kissed him, melting against the heat of his lips as the scent of boy and wolf invaded my senses.

The scent of boy and wolf.

"She'll smell you," I said, fear widening my eyes. "We'll get kicked out. I can't—"

My words were cut off by a sharp knock at the door.

"I guess that's my cue." Logan slid his feet into his shoes, not even bothering to tie the laces, and planted another quick kiss on my lips. "She won't know I've been here. See you at breakfast?"

"Room inspection!" Ms. Emmerson called before knocking again.

I grabbed a small bottle of perfume from the top of Haven's dresser and sprayed. It was a mild scent, like wildflowers and honey—and very *unlike* Haven—but it would probably be enough to cover the smell. *I hope.*

"Emily." Ms. Emmerson's key sounded in the lock. "Emily, are you in there? I'm coming in."

8

LOGAN DISAPPEARED out the window and I slid the latch back into place, shivering as the gigantic stone talons of Worthington Hall's resident chimera scraped loudly against the glass. Its shadow flashed across my room as it turned and silently watched Logan's descent. It should've used its magic to inform the senior staff of our transgression. It should've stopped him before he got away. But no matter how many times Logan came up to my room, no matter how many times he sneaked in before class, before practice, before dinner, the chimera never reported us.

And I didn't know why.

"Emily," Ms. Emmerson said as she eased the door open. "Are you awake?"

I forced myself not to glance back at the window and held up my phone, a sheepish smile on my face. "Sorry, I forgot to set my alarm."

Ms. Emmerson tutted. "That's not like you." She swept around the room, her long brown skirt swirling around her ankles as she went. She was tall and thin, a witch with pale white skin and long silvery hair caught up in a bun, and her blue eyes were sharp and assessing.

I nudged a missed sock beneath the bed and quickly straightened the covers before she wondered why my bed was so mussed up. "Have you heard anything from the infirmary today?" I asked.

She shook her head. "You'll have to be patient."

"But—"

"No buts. Go and have breakfast. Something nourishing, like oats or scrambled eggs on toast—not one of those sugary, artificially-colored cereals. Then, and *only* then, can you go to the infirmary and ask how Haven is doing."

I nodded.

She gave the room one last appraising glance and stopped beside the door. "You're doing a decent job of keeping things tidy, but you do need to clean more often. Look at the dust on these crystals, and all over this beautiful orb." Her nose wrinkled, the lines on her creased skin deepening. "And that smell … What is it?'

"Oh, I knocked over Haven's perfume bottle when I was looking for a hair tie."

Her mouth tightened with disapproval. "Leave the windows open for the night. And be more careful next time."

I waited until she was gone, then flopped down on the

bed, covering my eyes with my hands. *So exhausted.* Turning my head to the side, I breathed in the lingering scent of Logan and artificial fragrance, and my thoughts slipped back to the spell.

I had something belonging to the *putere* (otherwise known as me).

I'd figured out the anchor.

Now all I needed was something of Mr. Olaru's, the Impure Blade, and—

"Hey!" My door swung open and Cayley bounced in. "You ready for breakfast?"

—the vessel.

"Earth to Emily," she called. "I said, are you ready for breakfast?"

I looked down at my pajamas.

"Obviously not." She draped herself over my desk chair and spun it around, her dark hair swirling. As always, she looked perfect, from her classic winged eyeliner to her denim cutoffs, and she lifted a hand to shoo me away. "Go. Get ready. I'll wait."

Ten minutes later, I was showered and dressed, and I hurried back to my room, hoping Cayley was still there. When I opened the door, I found her rifling through Haven's bookshelf.

"Have you seen Petrov's *Introduction to the Arcane?*" she asked, pulling out a leather-bound book with a cracked, red spine. "Haven said I could borrow it, but it's not here. Or on her desk." I shook my head and she tucked the book back in its spot. "What about Alexander's *Dictionary of Obscure Magical Terms and Phrases?*"

"Sorry." I reached past her and grabbed a couple of Haven's favorite novels. "Why don't you ask her after breakfast?"

She rocked back on her heels. "Because I want them now. Mia and I were planning to use them in our Photography assignment, and I should've picked them up last week. Normally I wouldn't care but …" A small frown creased her forehead. "It's not just about me."

I slipped Haven's novels into a tote that was hanging by the door. "You and Mia seem to be getting on well."

Cayley lifted a shoulder. "She's okay."

"And Thomas?"

"He doesn't really know her." Her hazel eyes narrowed. "Unless you meant …?"

"I was asking how he is."

She picked up Haven's hairbrush and tossed it in the bag, her gray sweater shimmering like she wanted to change it but couldn't settle on a color. "He said he was fine."

"But?"

She arched an irritated brow. "I couldn't really hear what he was saying. It was after curfew, and there was a lot of noise in the background. I guess some of the guys were hanging out in the common area." She folded her arms across her chest. "They don't let us do that here."

"And you guys?" I asked quietly. "Are the two of you okay?"

Her gray sweater darkened, the sleeves loosening around her arms. "We'll be fine. And if we're not, at least it's been interesting." I wanted to ask exactly what she meant, but she opened the door and strode out into the corridor. "Come on. Breakfast's almost over."

I stuffed Haven's cell phone charger and laptop into my bag and followed her out, locking the door behind me. By the time we got to the dining hall, there wasn't much food left, so I filled a bowl with cereal—the sugary, artificially-colored kind—while Cayley tried to sweet-talk the supervising teacher into letting her into the kitchens.

It didn't work.

"Stupid rules," she muttered under her breath.

I waited as she grabbed a cup of black coffee, then we made our way across the room to our usual table. It was positioned beneath an expansive window, the stained glass throwing shadows on the battered oak surface. There was something strangely comforting about it—the dash of red that lit up the water rings on the right; the streaks of blue that shimmered across multiple carved initials. It was life and light. History and stability.

I wanted that.

I *needed* that.

Logan looked up from his seat at the end of the table and smiled. "Pastry?" he said, pushing a plate toward me.

I sat down beside him, slinging my bag over the back of the chair.

"Where's mine?" Cayley nudged Thomas with her shoe.

"I—uh, I—" He smiled sheepishly as she lowered herself down next to him. "I meant to save you some French toast, but I got hungry." Pushing a hand through his dark hair, he leaned over and kissed her. When he pulled back, his eyes were bright, but his skin looked paler than usual, his cheekbones razor-sharp. "I'll get you something from Coffee and Cake on the way to class. Something better."

"I'll allow it." She ran her fingers through the steam that wafted from the top of her coffee cup and looked up at him, her hazel eyes serious. "Are you okay?"

"I'm fine."

His voice was pitched low, barely even a whisper, and I looked away, ignoring the obvious lie. Thomas was taking Haven's illness harder than the rest of us. A few years before I'd come to Mistwood, Haven's ex-boyfriend, Marcus, had posted private messages and photos she'd sent him online. She'd been devastated, and Thomas had promised he'd never let her get hurt again.

It was an impossible vow, but he'd meant every word.

"So why did you wake me up during the day?" Logan asked, breaking into my thoughts. "Did you say something about ... a ship?"

I snorted. "I said I found the anchor."

"The what?"

I lowered my voice. "The anchor for the spell. And I didn't actually *find* it, as such, but I know where it is." I finished the pastry he'd saved me and told him about the house I'd grown up in—a pretty, one-storey bungalow with a sloping roof and covered veranda. Everything in it had been new, from the dining table to the sofa to the ornaments that lined the mantlepiece.

Everything except the vase.

It was long and gray, made of unpolished ceramic—and it looked more than a little boring—but my mom had always loved it. She'd said it had been in our family for generations, passed down from her—

Huh.

I couldn't actually remember.

"Are your parents gonna bring it?" Logan asked carefully.

"I don't know." I slid my phone onto the table in front of me. "I guess I should ask them."

I unlocked the screen and started a new message, but before I'd finished the first word, a notification popped up from the group chat.

"It's Haven," Thomas said, his fork clattering to the table. His angular shoulders hunched forward as he picked up his phone and started reading.

Haven's message was short: *This place is a nightmare. So bored. Send help.* But I couldn't help the smile that slid over my face. "See?" I said. "She just needed some time. She's sounding better already."

Logan pushed back his chair. "We've got twenty minutes till first period."

"We should go and see her," Thomas suggested, cutting off whatever Logan was about to say next. "Great idea."

Cayley reached for his arm. "We still need—"

"Shit." He pulled away, his eyes flashing yellow, and he covered his mouth with his hand. "I think I'm gonna—" He didn't say anything else. He just ran for the door, his chest heaving.

"What the hell?" Logan said.

"Was he just about to … throw up?" Cayley's head tipped to the side. "Werewolves don't get sick. Unless I missed something basic in Biology?"

Logan's face was pinched with worry. "It can happen sometimes. Usually if a wolf's changed too often and hasn't left time for recovery. Or maybe it's just stress. You know, about Haven." He pulled the sleeves of his hoodie down over his wrists and stood, his features morphing into something calm. Authoritative. "I'll go talk to him. See what's going on."

I looked down at the table, almost as worried about Logan as I was about Thomas. He tried so hard to keep everything under control—his body, his mind, his life—but he spent so much time hiding, suppressing everything that scared him. *What's he gonna do when he realizes it's not working? When he can't control the world on his own?*

"We should go," Cayley said, touching my arm. "We can get food at Coffee and Cake and be back before Logan and Thomas are done."

"You sure?"

"Absolutely."

We made it to the café and back in less than ten minutes. Cayley had bought enough food for three people

—and another cup of black coffee—while Haven texted us relentlessly.

I'm in room three.

Save me.

I'm dying.

There's nothing to do.

Hurry up.

Hurry up.

Hurry up.

"Drama queen," Cayley muttered, taking a sip of her drink.

I'd just finished my own cup of coffee when Logan came back, his dark eyes troubled. "I couldn't find him," he said. "I checked the bathrooms in every building between here and Emberfield, but it's like he disappeared."

"Maybe he didn't go into the bathrooms," I said.

Cayley's fingers tightened around her cup, her painted nails darkening. "Did you track him?"

"Of course I tracked him. His scent went as far as the bushes outside the science building. Then it just … stopped."

I chewed the inside of my cheek, trying to figure out what to do. "We could tell someone. Your housemaster? Or Mr. Green?" I paused, knowing he'd hate my final suggestion. "Your father?"

Logan's response was immediate. "No. Thomas won't want him getting involved. And *I* don't want him getting involved. Whatever this is, we can deal with it here." He looked down at his phone as another text came through.

"Let's go see Haven before she combusts. I'll look for Thomas later."

We made our way to the medical center, each of us quiet and worried. Logan and I texted Thomas as we walked, and Cayley tried calling, but by the time we got to the large stone building, its imposing façade washed out in the moonlight, we still hadn't heard from him.

"I guess we're going in," Cayley said, stuffing her phone into her bag.

There was no one at the nurses' station, or in their main office—a large room filled with first aid supplies, a bed, and a couple of desks and chairs—so we headed down the corridor, straight to room three.

"Haven?" I called, knocking quietly on the door.

There was no reply.

I knocked again, harder this time. "Haven, it's us. Can we come in?"

Still no reply.

"Maybe she can't hear us," Logan said from somewhere behind me.

"They might've discharged her." Cayley leaned against the wall, her arms folded over her chest. Everything about her had been arranged to say *I-don't-care*, from her bored expression to the way her oversized sweater draped loosely over her body. But she smelled so much like Logan —like smoke and anger and fear—that she wasn't fooling anyone.

"Hey! You three!" called a voice from down the corridor. I turned and saw Mr. Lopez striding toward us, his face pinched and angry. "Didn't I say you'd get a month of detention if I saw you here again?"

Cayley rolled her eyes, but Logan straightened, pulling his hands from his pockets. "Haven requested our company," he said. "And we were under the impression she was allowed visitors today."

Mr. Lopez glowered. "You have five minutes." He knocked on Haven's door, then eased it open, watching as we all trooped inside. "I'll be timing your visit," he snapped, then he marched back down the corridor, muttering under his breath.

My predator stirred at the hostility in his tone, but I pushed it down and concentrated on Haven. Her room was dimly lit, illuminated by two small lamps, and she lay propped up in a hospital-style bed near the window. An IV dripped liquid slowly into her arm, and a heartrate monitor, complete with moving graphics and numbers, beeped softly in the background.

"Haven?" I said quietly.

Her eyes were closed, and her phone lay on her lap. She looked washed out and sickly in the yellowish light, the skin beneath her eyes marked by purple bruises.

"Haven?" Logan said, taking a tentative step forward. "Are you awake?"

Her eyes flew open. "Mom?" she said, her voice scratchy.

I walked toward her, holding out my bag. "No, it's us. We brought you some things. Are you … are you feeling okay?"

She pulled out her earbuds—a shiny black noise-canceling pair—and frowned. "Sorry, what?" Her frown deepened. "Why do you smell like my mom? Is she here?"

"No, it's your perfume. I needed something to cover up the scent of Logan in our room." I smiled uncomfortably. "I know I shouldn't have used it, but—"

"It's not mine. It's my mom's." Haven licked her lips—they were swollen and chapped—then reached for the glass of water on the tray table beside her bed. "I thought someone might have told her."

"Do you want us to?" Logan asked.

"God, no." She grimaced, and the largest gash on her lips, a line that ran right through the center of the lower one, opened up further. Blood oozed out, dribbling toward her chin, and she wiped it away with a tissue. It smelled strange, tainted with chemicals and magic. "You know what she's like."

I'd never met Haven's parents, but I knew her mom was an SCC ambassador who worked somewhere in Western Europe, and her dad was a high-powered executive, working with supe-run businesses in both the US and France. Neither was complimentary in their assessment of Haven. *Excitable. Peculiar. A liability who'll ruin the family name.* Haven brushed it off, but I knew it still hurt, so I sat down and quickly emptied my bag on her bed to distract her.

"We brought you some stuff," I said brightly, pulling out her books, her laptop, and—

"My phone charger! Thank god!" She grabbed it out of

my hand and held it to her chest. "My battery's almost dead. I thought I'd be cut off from the world forever."

Cayley rolled her eyes. "Here," she said, handing Haven the bag of food from Coffee and Cake. "Eat."

They started bickering over the best bagel toppings and I turned my attention to Logan, who was standing in the middle of the room. His hands were in his pockets. One leg jiggled back and forth like his body wasn't big enough to contain everything inside him. He hated the infirmary. Not just because we'd both been patients there; and not just because we'd both seen Dr. Norlgren die there.

His hated the infirmary because of OCD.

It wasn't something he usually talked about, but I knew that it affected him in different ways, from the intrusive thoughts that flooded his mind to the compulsions he felt like he *had* to do. He hid the worst of it—the counting, the tapping, the desperate desire to change all his clothes and throw out his shoes.

What I didn't understand though, was what it actually felt like.

Sometimes I thought I could smell it on him, a subtle shift in scent that reminded me of fear and darkness. An increase in his pulse. A flicker of anxiety behind his eyes.

But mostly, I think I couldn't tell at all.

"Knock, knock," came a voice from the door. It swung open slowly and a tall, thin elf walked in. "How's the patient today?"

"Feeling better," Haven said, holding up a half-eaten bagel.

"I'm pleased to hear it." The elf smiled, showing straight, white teeth. "I need to run a few checks, but first—who are all these lovely visitors?"

"I'm Logan Montgomery," Logan said, his voice smooth and polite, though his throat bobbed painfully when the doctor shook his hand.

Cayley stood. "Cayley Rodriguez."

"And you?" The doctor turned to me, hand extended.

"I'm, uh—" I rose, memories of blood and magic flooding the space behind my eyes. *Dr. Norlgren.* I'd known he was different from the first time I'd seen him. He'd been an elf, a doctor, and he was supposed to have saved me. *I wish I could've saved him.*

The elf kept smiling. "I'm Doctor Owens," he said, his voice deep and lilting.

I reached for his hand. It was cool and dry. Ordinary. "Emily Sanderson."

"I'm pleased to meet you all," he said, his gaze sweeping across us before settling on Haven. "Will your friends be staying while I examine you? Or would you like one of the nurses to come and act as a chaperone?"

Haven wiped her mouth with the back of her hand. "They can stay if they want." She looked at us, her eyebrows raised.

"Of course," I said. "I'll stay as long as you want."

Cayley nodded in agreement.

We all looked at Logan. "Sure," he said. "I can stay."

"Very well." Dr. Owens snapped on a pair of white latex gloves and strode over to the bed. He tilted his head as he peered at Haven's arm. It was still red and swollen; the skin around the silver swirl was stretched unnervingly tight. "How's the pain today?"

"All right." Haven shrugged.

The doctor fell quiet, his expression focused as he checked Haven's vitals. He was tall, fine-boned beneath his long, white coat, and his skin was pale green and dotted with light brown freckles. In some ways he reminded me of Dr. Norlgren, but he moved with a different sort of grace and his accent was broader, the consonants noticeably flat.

"I'll have one of the nurses give you another dose of antibiotics," he said to Haven, "and I'll make arrangements for a few more tests. There should be no problem with the efficacy of the medication because you're technically human beneath your magical abilities, but there are some anomalies in your last test results I want to investigate further."

"Is she going to be all right?" Cayley asked, folding her arms across her chest.

"Absolutely." Dr. Owens peeled off his gloves and threw them in the trashcan in the corner. After washing his hands, he typed a few notes on the tablet he'd brought in with him, then considered us all with sharp green eyes. "Haven has infections in both her skin and her chest, but we're treating them with a combination of medicine and magic, and I have no reason to think she won't be on top of this within the next few days. I'm just wanting to cover all our bases."

The crisp scent of disinfectant cast a layer over everything in the room, but I could still smell that Haven was sick, and Cayley was angry, and Logan was hiding. And Dr. Owens? He was sandalwood and mint leaves. Sincerity and truth.

Haven was going to be fine.

"When can I get out of here?" she said.

"Hopefully by breakfast tomorrow," Dr. Owens replied. "We just need to run those tests and see how you manage today."

"And my magic?"

"Will be back to normal soon enough. But you need to refrain from performing any spells for the next three days, no matter how simple. Magic uses a large amount of energy, and you need to let yourself heal."

Dr. Owens turned to leave, and the warning bell for first period rang out. Haven scratched her arms absently, her fingernails digging into the skin around the silver marking.

"No scratching," the doctor ordered as he looked back from the doorway. "That's probably how the infection got in." He strode into the hallway, the door banging shut behind him.

"We'd better go," I said. "But we'll—"

"Wait!" Haven leaned forward, her eyes widening. "Have you got any of the items yet? The anchor? The vessel? Something of Mr. Olaru's?"

"No," I said, "but you shouldn't be worrying about the spell right now. You need to rest and get better. Mr. Green gave me the forms and we'll look at them when—"

"You don't understand." Her shoulders sagged. "I'm the only one who can help. Mr. Green's been lying to you."

9

"Wʜᴀᴛ?" I said, a disbelieving laugh escaping my lips. "Mr. Green wouldn't lie to me. He's trying to *help*. He gave me all the papers and—"

"Stop." Haven's voice was filled with regret. "I'm telling you the truth."

I shook my head. "You're wrong. He has no reason to lie to me about the spell."

She looked down at the sheets, smoothing the wrinkles away with her fingers. Her face was shadowed, and her frame was thin beneath her hospital-issued nightgown. There was something uncharacteristically uncertain about the way she moved, almost like she was nervous.

"This *is* about the spell to bind Emily's powers, right?" Cayley said, her eyes narrowing. "Mr. Green didn't lie about something else?"

Haven's head snapped up. "What are you implying?"

"That you're—"

"Hold on," Logan said, cutting Cayley off before she could say anything more. His power pulsed out around us, warm and compelling, but Haven wasn't a werewolf. Logan couldn't use his abilities to influence her.

"You think I'm a liar," she hissed, her features contorting. Her eyes—normally pale blue—faded to silver, and she thrust out an arm, pointing at Cayley, then Logan, then me. She didn't seem to notice the needle pulling at her vein, or the way the machines beside her beeped in warning. "Why would I lie about this? What would I have to gain?"

"Nothing," I said, raising my hands slowly. "You have no reason to lie."

"I know what I heard. I'm not stupid, no matter what you guys think." She covered her face with her hands, and when she lowered them her eyes were blue again, like nothing had ever changed. "He was talking to Miss Lassila. And he *has* been lying to you about the spell."

I drew in a breath and reached out with my senses, checking her scent on the air. It was earthy and bitter, both elements I'd expected, but somewhere beneath the magic and decay lay the mint-fresh aroma of truth.

Shit.

"What did he say?" Cayley asked.

Haven scratched her arm and grimaced, then pushed the needle back into place. "He said the spell would never be approved. That he'd given Emily the forms so she wouldn't keep asking. And Miss Lassila said the *putere* was too valuable for them to lose."

I didn't know what to think. I wasn't a *thing* that needed protecting. I was a girl, a vampire, a creature with agency who deserved to make her own decisions. "I need to talk to them," I said. "Once they understand how I feel, I'm sure they'll change their minds. If I tell them—"

"They won't," Haven cut in. "Em, you'll just … disappear. Mr. Green has it all planned out. He'll tell everyone you've been having issues with your powers and need extra tuition at the Paranormal Program." She blinked, and a single tear rolled down her cheek. "But it'll all be a lie. If you try and do the spell, he's going to have you locked up in the cells."

I froze. "What?"

Still mint.

Still truth.

"He'll have you incarcerated." She wiped her face with the back of her hand. "He told Miss Lassila you'd be left there till they need you."

"Why would they need you?" Logan said. "It's not like you have a whole bunch of extra powers. You only absorbed a couple from Mr. Olaru and you wouldn't kill anyone …" He stopped, his face suddenly pale.

"They want you to drain supes," Cayley said flatly. "Drain them, absorb their powers, and then do god knows what with them. You could be the most powerful creature on the planet. And they want you under their control."

I closed my eyes.

My heart was a hammer and each beat shattered my chest.

"Breathe," Logan whispered in my ear.

I inhaled slowly, drawing in the scent of succubus and wolf, mint leaves and witch, and something inside me died. I'd trusted Mr. Green and Miss Lassila—they'd saved my life. And all because the SCC wanted to control me? I couldn't—I *wouldn't*—let my abilities as the *putere* be used again. I wouldn't drain another living being.

But what if they make me?

"One thing doesn't make sense," Cayley said, moving over to the window and staring out into the night. "Why give her the forms at all? Why not just tell her the SCC said no?"

Haven's lips thinned. "I told you already. He gave Emily the papers so she'd stop asking about it. They're stalling. Don't you understand? It'll give them time to find all of the items. To gather up everything left of Mr. Olaru's. To steal the anchor. To reinforce the security around the Impure Blade." Her fingers drifted to her arm, nails digging in as she scratched. "Then Mr. Green will tell her the spell wasn't approved, and we won't be able to do anything about it."

Cayley tilted her head. "It's a good theory, but I still find it hard to believe."

"It feels ... wrong," Logan said. "They've done so much to help us. They saved Emily's life. And when—"

"Whatever." Haven's mouth twisted, her eyes turning silver again as she glared up at the ceiling, anger bubbling in her veins. "Get locked up. I don't fucking care." She swiped a hand across the bed and the books stacked on the tray table toppled to the floor.

I took a step back.

"We should go," Logan said.

"No, wait." Haven sagged against the pillows, her chin quivering. Her pulse was thready, and her eyes slowly changed back to blue. "I didn't mean to get mad. It's—it's the infections. They've messed everything up—my body, my magic, my emotions. There's … there are things I don't remember, snatches of time where I've … lost myself. I think I've been sick for a while—haven't you noticed how difficult I've been?"

"You've always been difficult," Cayley retorted. "These last few months have been something else."

"It's just—"

The bell signaling the start of first period rang out.

"We really need to go," I said, picking up the books and stacking them back on the tray table. "Get some rest and we'll finish this later."

When you're in a better mood.

"But we don't have much time," Haven said. "Are you sure you haven't got—"

The door swung open and Thomas walked in.

"—the anchor?" she finished. "Or anything at all? Because I can find the Impure Blade if you guys get everything else, and I can—"

"No," Thomas snarled. "Why would you even consider that? Look at where you are!"

"It's our only chance." Haven clenched her fists and

turned to me, imploring. "Find everything you can. Check the headmaster's—no, the headmistress's—office. Look in the supply closet in the administration block. Call your parents and ask about heirlooms. Promise me. *Please.*" She sucked in a breath, her shoulders shaking. "Emily, promise me."

"I—" I paused, looking around the room at Logan and Cayley and Thomas. They were dangerous. Supes. Predators. I could feel their power, surging through their blood, carrying their fear and their anger. Their confusion. None of them knew what to do any more than I did. But I had to be careful—there was so much emotion suppressed beneath their skin. One wrong move, one wrong word …

Someone will explode.

"We need to go," Logan said. "First period already started."

Thomas sat down in one of the chairs and crossed his arms over his chest. "Tell Mrs. Barker I'll be late," he said to Logan, his blue eyes sparking a challenge.

Logan's jaw clenched.

Thomas had cleaned himself up—he was wearing different clothes and reeked of mouthwash and soap—but his complexion was still pale and dark circles stained the skin beneath his eyes.

"Where were you?" Logan said. "I followed you earlier, but it was like you'd disappeared."

Thomas scowled. "It's none of your business."

Haven watched them carefully. There was something dispassionate in the way her gaze tracked their movements; it was like she was studying them, memorizing their strengths, their tactics, their weaknesses.

But Logan didn't notice—he just crossed the room, his hair falling over his eyes as he shook his head. "Fine," he said, anger singing in his blood as he reached for the door handle. "But you can talk to Mrs. Barker yourself."

I glanced at Cayley, then followed him into the corridor. "Wait," I said, tugging on the back of his hoodie. "Slow down. Are you okay?"

He shoved his hands in his pockets and backed away. "Am I okay?" he repeated, incredulous. "Am I okay? You're being set up for a life as a god-knows-what by the SCC, Haven's in the infirmary, Thomas is being an asshole, Cayley's constantly angry, and you're asking me if I'm okay?"

I swallowed down the predator that burned in my chest. "I care about you, Logan. I know this is hard. It's hard for all of us."

He made a weird noise in the back of his throat.

"We could skip class," I offered. "Go somewhere and talk. Or not. Whatever you want."

He didn't say anything for a few moments, then shook his head. "I can't. I just … can't." The door to Haven's room banged shut and he flinched as Cayley stepped into the corridor.

"Where are you guys going?" she asked.

"Algebra," I said.

"English," Logan added.

Cayley smoothed out her hair, the brown strands lightening around her face, and moved past us, looking back at me as she walked. "What are you going to do about the spell?"

I glanced down at the floor. My black sneakers were dull against the polished tiles and I wished I could change them. I wished I could change everything. All I knew was that I couldn't risk being locked back up. I'd spent months in a cell at the Paranormal Program, and I'd vowed never to go back. Sure, they'd helped me deal with being a vampire, taught me how to feed, how to maintain control. But they were brutal and strict, and the penitentiary cells were even worse—they'd been filled with creatures who'd failed the Program, who were caught between animal and human, who couldn't control their powers.

They were locked up forever.

That could be you.

"I don't know what I'm going to do," I said as I shoved open the big arched doors at the end of the corridor and stepped out into the night. "Haven's too sick to help me. And the SCC *won't* help me."

Cayley followed me to the bottom of the stairs. "There's no harm in being prepared. Or so I've been told." She lifted a brow. "I have a free period after Photography. You know, if you feel like raiding the supply closet."

She took off toward the Arts Center without waiting for an answer, and Logan slid his hands from his pockets, his fingers worrying at a thread on his sleeve. It unraveled, pulling a small hole in the fabric. "Shit," he said under his breath.

"Logan, I—"

"It's okay," he said. "I didn't mean to … you know. You're the one being manipulated by the SCC. I should be asking you how *you* are."

"Yeah, you should. But I get it." I offered him a small smile. "There's a lot going on right now."

He nodded. "I have to go, but text me if you need anything, okay? Maybe not about raiding the supply closet, but …" He backed away, his dark eyes searching mine. "Actually, I'd raid the supply closet with you any day."

Something loosened in my chest as I watched him go. Because as horrible as all of this was—and as much as I couldn't do anything to fix it—at least I wasn't alone.

For the rest of the night, everything was deceptively normal. I went to my classes, I practiced my cello, I *didn't* raid the supply closet, and I pretended that my life hadn't been turned upside down. *Again.* I stared at the people in front of me in Mr. Dufort's History class, wondering what their secrets were. It was easy to hide behind a well-timed smile, a polite nod, a carefully-prepared excuse for whatever emotion they'd failed to mask. Even now, I could smell happiness and hope, lust and sadness, fear and impatience.

I dipped my head and looked down at my laptop.

"When will this be over?" Cayley groaned as she lay her head down on the desk. "We've been here for hours."

I shushed her and tried to concentrate on the article we were supposed to be reading—*An Examination of the Role of the Nutriment in Renaissance Italy*. It was fascinating, an anecdote-filled account written by a vampire who'd actually been there, and any other day I would've devoured it quickly, absorbing everything I could about the history and culture of our world. But my thoughts kept slipping—back to the infirmary, back to Haven and her anomalous test results, and back to the spell.

You could be the most powerful creature on the planet.

And they want you under their control.

I shivered. Who was I supposed to trust? Even if I could find all the items needed for the spell, who would I get to perform it?

"Finish your work and close your laptops," Mr. Dufort said, clapping his hands. He cast his washed-out gray eyes over the class. "I know some of you are eager to get out of here"—his gaze landed on Cayley—"but before you leave, I have something you've all been waiting for. Your last assignments."

My heart sank. *More bad news.*

Cayley sighed.

Beside her, Thomas stiffened.

"Do you think he'd notice if I slipped out the back door?" Logan whispered, shooting me a grin.

Mr. Dufort raised his eyebrows, his lips twitching, then began moving around the room, passing out papers and occasional remarks. When he got to me, he stopped. "Well done," he said, setting the assignment down on my desk. "Top of the class."

"Really?" I snatched up the paper and stared at the big red A that was circled on the top corner. "Are you sure?"

He bent down to face me, his eyes twinkling. He was ancient—a vampire with steel-gray hair that hung halfway down his back and an air of old-world elegance—but sometimes he didn't seem very old at all. "I can lower it if you like, but it wouldn't be fair to the essay. Or to you."

"Oh."

He tapped the paper with his long fingers, the once brown skin now tinged with gray. "Have a little confidence in yourself. You've earned it."

He kept moving down the row, the musty odor of age following in his wake. "Decent attempt, Logan," he said as he handed him his paper, "though it could've been longer. Next time think about how you can flesh out some of those ideas." He stopped in front of Cayley, his voice quieting. "Not your best effort, Miss Rodriguez. You could do with a bit more focus."

"In life? Or in this?" she said, holding up the assignment.

Mr. Dufort pursed his lips as he considered her question. His entire body went still. It was something only the oldest supes could do, a complete absence of movement that often seemed predatory, though it was never like that with him. He only seemed to pause when he concentrated, like all of his energy was being used by his brain. It was one of the few things that reminded me how ancient he really was.

"I think perhaps both," he said softly before moving on.

Cayley lay her head back down on the desk, her hair falling over her face.

"It can't be that bad," Thomas said.

She thrust her paper toward him, not bothering to hide the glaring red D that was written at the top.

"Oh." He stuffed his own paper in his bag. "It'll be okay. Just do better on the next one." He seemed so different than he had earlier, at breakfast and in Haven's room. I still didn't know why he'd been unwell, and I didn't know what he and Haven had talked about after we'd left, but the tension in him had gone. Well, mostly. His shoulders hung loose and his eyes were clear, but the faint scent of worry still clung to his skin.

"Just do better on the next one," Cayley muttered, crumpling her failed assignment into a ball. "Like it's that easy." She took Thomas' hand and followed him out into the hallway, her expression serious until he leaned down and whispered something in her ear.

"Do you think they'll stay together?" I said to Logan as I stood.

He lifted his shoulders. "It doesn't matter what I think. They'll do what's best for them." When he spoke again, his voice was almost inaudible. "I hope."

We caught up with the two of them outside the dining hall and were about to go inside when someone called my name. "Emily! Hey, Em! Wait up!"

I turned, curious.

Devon Williams—a vampire and the most incredible pianist I'd ever heard—was striding toward me. "I've been looking for you all night," he said, slowing to a stop. The vowels of his upper-class English accent were round, each consonant crisp and clear. "I need a favor."

"Oh?" I'd spoken to Devon a couple of times in music class, but we weren't exactly what I'd call friends. "What is it?"

He ran a hand through his shaggy brown hair, his gray eyes hopeful. "How would you like to play in a quartet at the parent-teacher conferences?"

"At the conferences?" I repeated. "But … they're next week. And Mr. Davis already roped me into organizing the refreshments. I mean, I'm flattered you asked, but I don't think I have the time."

"Please," he said, clasping his hands in front of him. "We're desperate."

"What happened to Jenny Williams?" Logan asked. "Wasn't she supposed to do it?"

"Yeah, but …" Devon lowered his voice and leaned closer, his gaze darting from side to side. "She got suspended. Apparently she snuck out the other night and went to a party somewhere off campus. When she came back she was wasted. Threw up in the garden outside the admin block and called Ms. Maguire a fascist."

Logan's mouth dropped open. "Are we talking about the same Jenny Williams? The one who's always on time?

Who's never had a single detention? Who won't even walk on the grass?"

"That's the one," Devon said, shrugging a shoulder. "I know everyone gets curious sometimes, but I wish she'd waited until after the conferences. She's messed everything up."

"It's always the sheltered ones," Cayley said. "They never know when to stop."

Thomas coughed, his hand flying up to his chest.

"Thomas?" Logan's eyes were wide as he thumped his brother on the back. "What happened? Are you all right?"

"Fine," Thomas said, dragging in a breath. "Swallowed wrong." He bent low, his hands on his knees, his hair a dark halo around his head. His jeans were creased beneath his fingers, the fabric worn, and his shoulders swayed as he coughed again.

I reached into my bag for a bottle of water. "Here. Take this."

He held out his hand, but before he could grab the bottle, our phones all buzzed with an incoming text.

All except Devon's.

I pulled out my phone, my muscles tense as I looked down at the screen and saw a picture of something against Haven's infirmary pillow. Something I wanted. Something I needed. *Something that's caused me nothing but problems.*

The Impure Blade.

10

"I have to go," I said to Devon, dragging my gaze away from my phone. "I'll play in your quartet—just let me know when rehearsal is, and I'll figure out how to make the performance work around the refreshments issue. I— I'm sorry, but I need to be somewhere else right now."

"Is everything all right?" Devon said, his eyes flickering with uncertainty as he handed me my water bottle.

When did I drop that?

"Everything's fine," Cayley said smoothly. "We just have to go and see someone."

Everything's not *fine.*

My mouth was so dry I could barely swallow, and panic was flooding my system.

"What's going on?" Devon said. "I can smell your fear. All of you. What aren't you telling me?"

"Lots of things." Logan smiled, a practiced expression that looked more genuine than it was. "I haven't told you what I had for lunch. Or that I got a B on my History assignment. Or that I haven't done any practice this week for orchestra."

"That's one's a given," Devon said. "You never practice."

Thomas coughed, his eyes flickering between blue and amber, and I silently handed him the bottle. I chewed on my lower lip, trying to slow my pulse, trying to *think*. Haven had the Impure Blade. Which meant I was one step closer to removing Mr. Olaru from my blood forever. One step closer to ensuring the prophecy—the darkness, the destruction—could *never* come true.

"I'm going," Thomas said, tossing my now empty bottle back before taking Cayley's hand. "We'll meet you guys there."

Logan nodded. "Tell Haven we're on our way."

Devon waited until they'd left, then dipped his head and stared into my eyes. "Are you sure you're okay? Is this situation—whatever it is—going to interfere with your ability to play?"

I shook my head. "I'll be fine."

Logan tensed, his hands balling into fists, knuckles white; I shot him an apologetic look.

"Mia will give you the music tomorrow," Devon said as he turned to go. "And please—no drinking. I can't lose another cellist. There's a lot riding on this performance."

I didn't know exactly what he meant, but I knew I wouldn't be drinking. Supes weren't allowed to—at least, not while underage. It wasn't even a legality thing. It was about safety. Control. It was about what might happen when young, volatile, potentially dangerous creatures lowered their inhibitions.

Even adult supes didn't drink a lot. As far as I knew, anyway.

"Logan," I said when we got closer to the infirmary. "Why would Jenny have been drinking?"

He shrugged, his dark eyes catching mine. "I dunno. Sometimes people just want to try it, but the penalties are pretty harsh. The school has to report every incident to the SCC." He glanced up at the chimera prowling the roof of the nearest building and lowered his voice. "The first time, they let you off with a suspension and a warning. The next time, it's suspension, curfew, and a daily check-in with the SCC."

"And after that?"

"If you're a minor," he said, pulling his phone out of his pocket as it buzzed with an incoming text, "you're put through the Paranormal Program, with a specific focus on control and rehabilitation. If you're an adult, it's not dealt with as forcefully unless you've got a history of being drunk and disorderly. And then it's the Paranormal Program for them, too."

I shivered.

I won't be drinking anytime soon.

"It's Haven," Logan said, looking down at his phone. "She says we need to hurry up."

We increased our speed, rushing over the cobblestone paths toward the medical center, while I tried to keep things in perspective. "This is a good thing, right? I know what Haven said about Mr. Green and the SCC, but we can find someone else to do the spell. Someone who can—"

"Haven shouldn't even have the Blade," Logan interrupted. "She's not supposed to be doing magic." He tugged at his sleeves with restless fingers. "There's something weird about this whole situation. I know Mr. Green—he's a good man. And he and Miss Lassila helped save you. I can't believe they'd set you up for an eternity of being manipulated by the SCC."

I didn't know what to think.

So I just hurried up the stairs to the medical center and ran directly to Haven's room. Pushing open the door, I stumbled at the expression on Thomas' face. He stood next to Haven's bed, Cayley at his side.

"What is it?" Logan said, reaching out to steady me.

Haven looked up. Blood streaked over her chin and her skin was gray, but she smiled, her bloodstained tongue flicking out to lick her lips. "I did it," she said, her eyes shining as she watched me. "I found it."

"I know," I whispered.

"You shouldn't have been looking for it," Thomas said.

"Why not?" Haven pulled back the blanket that covered her legs and raised the long, slender dagger, her fingers curled tight around the dark wooden hilt. "Does it scare you?"

Yes.

But I still reached for it without thinking.

"Not yet," Haven said, jerking it away. "It's mine."

I lowered my hand and my fingers subconsciously slid beneath my sleeve. Found the scar on my wrist. Pressed down on the skin that would never fully heal.

His blood runs through my veins.

Haven laughed at my expression, and more blood spilled out of her mouth, dribbling down her chin. It dripped onto her chest, staining the thin gray nightgown that swamped her skeletal frame.

"Holy shit," Cayley said. "What the hell were you thinking, Haven? Why didn't you listen when they said you shouldn't do magic?"

"Because I'm stronger now." Her lips twisted in a brutal smile, teeth streaked with red. "Didn't you notice the lights? They didn't even flicker."

"I'm getting the doctor." Thomas turned to go. "And I'm telling him about the Blade."

"No." Logan stepped in front of his brother. "I mean, yes, get the doctor—I won't stop you doing that—but you can't tell him about the Blade."

Thomas' eyes flashed yellow. He straightened, his angular shoulders thrust back, and the bones shifted under his skin, his muscles lengthening and growing.

"I'm serious," Logan said. "You'd be putting Emily in danger. You'd be putting *all* of us in danger."

"You're not my alpha. You can't tell me what to do."

"You're right," Logan snapped. "I'm not your alpha. I'll never be *anyone's* alpha. But that doesn't mean I don't know how to work the system. And if you tell Dr. Owens —or anyone else—about the Impure Blade, I'll have my father send you away so fast you'll have motion sickness for a week." He leaned in close, his voice harder than I'd ever heard it. "You know what banishment does to a wolf."

Thomas lunged.

Logan's power—burning hot and fragrant—slammed into his brother, forcing him back. It filled the room, growing and swirling around us until Cayley walked toward him, her footsteps steady. "You wouldn't actually do that," she said slowly. "Would you?"

Logan's expression tightened. "No." He blew out a breath, his hands shaking at his sides. "But that doesn't mean you can tell anyone about the Blade. It's too dangerous. For all of us."

Thomas glowered, caught on a knife-edge between chaos and control, but he lowered his shoulders, his head dipping as he managed to steady his shape into something almost human. "I won't tell anyone," he said. "But I'm doing it for her"—he pointed at me—"not you."

Logan nodded once. "Fine."

"Are you two done with the pissing contest?" Cayley said. "Because Haven needs the doctor. *Now.*"

I turned, swallowing a gasp. Haven's arms were thrown out to the sides and her back was arched sharply, lifting her torso off the bed. She laughed and her eyes rolled back in her head; blood bubbled slowly from the corners of her mouth. The machines to the side of her bed —the ones that measured her heart beat, her blood pressure, her *life*—beeped dangerously.

Logan and Thomas ran for the door.

"What should we do?" I asked Cayley, hoping she had more of an idea that I did. "Should we … move her??"

She reached for Haven's hand. "I don't know, but I'm taking the Blade." Her fingers closed around the hilt and she gently extricated it from Haven's grip.

"Stop," Haven said. "You can't have it. It's mine. *She's* mine."

"You can have it back soon," Cayley started. "After—"

"No!" Haven's back straightened and her eyes flew open. The irises were silver. Volatile. Intense. "Give it back. Give it back now!"

The door swung open.

Cayley stepped away from the bed, the Impure Blade already hidden behind her as Dr. Owens rushed in, followed closely by Ms. Maguire and Mr. Lopez.

"Get out of the way," the doctor said as he pushed past me, his white coat flying around his legs. He barked instructions at Mr. Lopez, and Cayley and I hugged the walls, silently watching them work.

"Hold still," Mr. Lopez said to Haven, murmuring a spell beneath his breath as he slid a needle into her thigh.

She screamed, her back arching again, and her fingers curled, scrabbling for purchase on the sheets.

Ms. Maguire walked toward us. "I think you ought to leave," she said quietly. Her voice was kind, and her scent spoke of nothing more than witch and authority, but the skin around her mouth was pinched.

I wished I could do something.

I wished I could help.

"Come on," Cayley whispered, sliding the Impure Blade into her bag. It smelled like magic. It was silver and wood and the memory of blood, but no one else noticed it as we turned to go. They were gathered around Haven's bed, applying medicines and spells, trying to ease her pain.

A scream tore from her throat.

"Get me a stronger sedative," Dr. Owens said, and Mr. Lopez nodded.

"What the hell?" Cayley muttered as she dragged me out into the corridor. "Is that what it's like when humans get sick?"

I pressed a finger to my lips and leaned against the wall, listening at the door that hadn't quite closed behind us.

"There," Dr. Owens said, his words followed by a metallic clang and the sound of footsteps. "That should settle her for now. The antibiotics are working, but—"

"The antibiotics are the least of our concerns," Ms. Maguire said briskly. "This isn't physical. Not anymore." The earthy scent of magic, sweetened with something I didn't recognize, drifted through the gap in the door. "See that? Right there, in her aura. I've never—"

But I didn't hear anything else.

The door burst open and Mr. Lopez strode out. "Go," he snapped, his eyes flashing with anger. "Get out of here before I throw you both out."

We hurried away, though every part of me wanted to stay. Cayley lifted her tote, the Blade still tucked safely inside, while her other hand skimmed the wall, bouncing off door handles and nameplates, knocking lamp glass and paintings. Her hair swung angrily down her back.

My stomach churned.

Breathe.

Breathe.

Breathe.

We followed the low hum of Logan's voice to the end of the corridor, where he and Thomas stood talking to Mr. Green. Fred sat quietly in Thomas' arms, smoke rising lazily from his nostrils.

"Haven's gotten worse," Logan was saying. "She was bleeding from the mouth, and maybe her nose, and she looked—"

"Like she did after that spell," Thomas cut in. "The one she did yesterday when she was looking for the ..." He cleared his throat, glancing away from the heat of Logan's gaze. "When the lights went out."

"It was worse this time," Logan said. "I've never seen her like that. I've never seen *anyone* like that."

Cayley and I came to a stop behind them. Logan tugged at his sleeves, his fingers winding around a loose thread, and Thomas just stared with worried blue eyes. They were scared—I could smell it on their skin and in their blood, that dark tang of smoke that overpowered everything else—and I pressed my hands against my stomach. *This is all my fault. If she'd never tried to find the Impure Blade, back before the eclipse had even happened, she never would've connected with that witch and been marked. She never would've got the infection. She wouldn't be sick at all.*

"Hello, Emily," Mr. Green said, nodding his head. "Cayley."

"They're sedating her," I said shakily, my mind sifting through everything I'd heard at the door. "They don't … they don't really seem to understand what's wrong."

"It's her own fault," Cayley said. "They told her not to do magic."

Thomas ran his fingers over Fred's spiny back and the small dragon purred, settling his head down on Thomas' shoulder. "It's not like you're such a paragon of virtue," he said.

Logan closed his eyes.

There was a moment of silence, our emotions laid bare by the scents that swirled around us: Anger. Fear. Jealousy. Love. It was a moment of truth. A flash of vulnerability.

My fangs pressed against my gums.

"Would you like to come into my office?" Mr. Green said, his voice calm as always.

"No." Something cracked inside my chest. My predator reared up, drinking in the hurt that surrounded us, and I clung to it as the edges of my vision burned red.

He'll have you incarcerated.

They're stalling.

My hands balled into fists. "Why are you here?"

"I'm not sure what you mean." Mr. Green took a step toward his office. "Let's—"

"Mr. Olaru's dead," I snapped, my fangs sliding free.

"You don't have to monitor him anymore. So why haven't you left?"

"I—"

"Is it so you can watch me? So you can lock me up if I don't do what you want?"

Mr. Green's lips thinned. "My office. Now."

I moved forward slowly, the red closing in. "What if I just tell everyone what I am?"

"Stop fighting your predator, Emily." Mr. Green's eyes never left mine. "Let it flow over you and through you. You're still in control."

"I'm not fighting it," I said, blood blooming on my palms as my fingernails cut into the skin. "I'm embracing it. You want me to be like Mr. Olaru? You want me to kill supes and take all their powers?" I raised a hand to my mouth and licked it; the blood was coppery-sweet on my tongue. "Maybe I should start with—"

"Wait," Logan said.

"You," I finished, running my hand down his cheek. Dark streaks of crimson stained the white of his skin, but my predator burned for something deeper. Something more than hunger. I blinked slowly, my breath hitching as my skin flickered with purple, and Logan pulled me into Mr. Green's office.

"Sit," the psychologist said, motioning toward the couches.

I can't.

Because I could see everything. Smell everything. *Feel* everything. The ceiling light set the room aflame; the books on the desk reeked of dust and vanilla; the plant in the corner was sweet, like perfume.

The floor tilted beneath my feet.

I spun slowly as tendrils of light, vibrant and purple, sprung to life all around me. Lifting my arms, I whispered, "Can't you see them?"

Logan's heart thumped.

"They're so beautiful." I flicked my fingers and the curtains fluttered, moving with a breeze that only I could see. The hunger stirred in my veins, pulling at the anxiety in the room, but my predator pushed it away. *It's not important right now.* "They're around you," I whispered. "Around all of you." My gaze drifted to Cayley's bag, settling on the thick violet cord that snaked around it.

The Impure Blade.

It was made for this. Made for me. Because while I could lift each tendril of light, each violet thread, push them until the world around me shifted, I'd never be able to break them. Not by myself.

My hands itched with need. I wanted to feel the heft of wooden hilt, the silver blade passing through each strand …

The Blade can sever.

The Blade can unmake.

It was a truth that existed within me, a shivering moment of déjà vu, but the knowledge … that had never been mine. Somehow I knew it belonged to *him*, to Mr. Olaru; it had been passed down to me through blood and violence. Through death.

I froze, goosebumps skimming over my skin.

What did he do to me?

"Em." A deep voice, familiar and worried. "Breathe. I don't know what's going on, but we'll fix it, okay?"

I turned, squinting at the violet glow. It stretched between us, brighter than anything else in the room, a series of threads that tethered us together. "Logan?" I whispered.

"I'm here." He reached toward me.

The threads flickered and merged, and I plucked at them without thinking, sending a wave of movement through his hair. *Magic.* Turning, I pulled at the strands that led to a stack of books. They were perched precariously on the edge of Mr. Green's desk, and all it took was one last—

No.

This isn't my power.

The books crashed to the floor.

It's his.

"Shit," I whispered, my hands shaking as I lowered myself onto the nearest couch. "That was … that was …"

"Telekinesis," Cayley said.

Proof that Mr. Olaru will always control me.

"Eat this," Mr. Green said, his voice businesslike as he handed me a cookie. "Thomas, go and get a glass of water from the kitchen down the hallway. Quickly please."

Thomas nodded and left the room, Fred still nestled in his arms.

Logan sunk down beside me.

"I was right," I said softly. "I knew there was something else. Another ability I couldn't find." My predator prickled beneath my skin—it wanted more, more, *more*—but I shoved it away and looked up at Mr. Green. "Are the forms you gave me real? Or did you just give them to me so I'd stop asking about the spell?"

"I'm sorry, what?" Mr. Green's forehead wrinkled. "Those papers are very real. Why would you think they're not?"

"Because of Haven." I finished the cookie and let Cayley explain. My eyelids fluttered closed.

"Well," Mr. Green said when Cayley was done, and I straightened, trying to focus. "That's certainly a lot to process. However, I can assure you right now, Emily, that you will not be taken into the cells."

"But—"

He silenced me with a frown. "Your powers make you valuable—that's why Miss Lassila and I remain at Mistwood—but we're not watching you for the benefit of the SCC. The organization will not be forcing you to kill people to absorb their powers."

"Then why did Haven smell like the truth?" Logan asked.

Mr. Green lifted his shoulders. "I suspect she heard part of a private conversation and either misunderstood it or didn't hear enough to get the full story." He smiled sadly, his dark eyes meeting mine. "There was one manager at the SCC who did suggest locking you up for your own safety. And another who was interested in how your powers might benefit the council. Both were informed that you would be completing your education at Mistwood Academy as a free and equal citizen, and both were demoted when they argued the point."

I blinked. "I don't even know what to say about that." Thomas slipped back into the room and handed me a glass of water, but I barely even noticed. "What about the spell?" I continued. "Did you really tell Miss Lassila it would never be approved?"

"I told her I was *concerned* it would not be approved. Not that it would never happen."

I breathed in slowly, searching for the telltale scent of citrus, but it was conspicuously absent. There was only mint leaves and truth.

The SCC aren't going to lock me up.

They're not stalling.

And they're not going to make me kill anyone.

"Okay," I said, ignoring all the feelings that still swirled in my chest. "This is good. I can fill in the forms and—"

"Emily," Mr. Green broke in gently. "You're not going to like this, and it's not going to do my credibility any favors, but I have to tell you—I got a call from the head of the SCC earlier this evening. He's declined to approve the spell, even if you get parental approval."

11

"Wʜᴀᴛ?" My stomach dropped. "Are you sure?"

Mr. Green nodded. "He's had a number of elves—in addition to the council's three most experienced witches—look over the requirements and it's just too risky."

Cayley's eyes narrowed.

Then Mr. Green will tell her the spell wasn't approved, and we won't be able to do anything about it.

I set the glass of water down by my feet. "But Haven said—"

"I know what Haven said." Mr. Green held up his hands. "And all I can tell you is that she was wrong. Use your senses—it's clear I'm not trying to deceive you."

"How can I be sure?" I demanded. "You might be manipulating your scent."

"I might be ... but I'm not. Breathe, listen, look." He folded his arms across his chest. "I'll wait."

I glared at him while I checked everything I could

think of. His scent, his respiration, even the way his head tilted slightly to the side. Each blink was slow and steady, each heartbeat solid and sure. I didn't know him well—I mean, he was my therapist and an adult—but I'd dealt with him enough times that I was pretty sure he *was* telling me the truth.

"Fine," I said. "So why can't we do the spell?"

Logan swallowed. "What makes it so risky?"

"Well," Mr. Green said, rubbing a hand over his close-cropped hair, his expression caught somewhere between concern and professional neutrality, "there are a number of potential difficulties, including injury to both your physical body and your mind. Many of those scenarios could be considered minor. However, some of them are not."

"Okay," I said slowly. "And what does that mean, exactly?"

His dark gaze settled on mine. "At the most extreme end of the scale, it could result in you losing *all* of your abilities—not just those relating to your status as the *putere.* You would be left neither wholly vampire, nor entirely human, unable to feed and unable to survive."

Logan's leg started shaking.

Up and down.

Up and down.

The couch cushions shifted.

I put a hand on his knee and pressed on, the memory of the purple threads still fresh in my mind. "Give me the numbers," I said, resisting the urge to push my palms forward, to see if I could still feel the light. "How much of a risk are we talking about?"

"I don't know the exact figures"—Mr. Green paused, his brow wrinkled in thought—"but you're looking at around a fifty percent chance of injury or death."

The words hung there, like an echo between us. Thomas' eyes widened; Cayley stiffened, her ponytail tightening and her lips turning black; Logan's fingers gripped my thigh.

"It's not worth it," he said, his voice constricted.

But what if it is?

I looked Mr. Green square in the eyes. "Can you get the exact figures for me? Like, is it a fifty percent chance of serious injury? Or forty percent minor and ten percent serious? And what about—?"

"Slow down." Mr. Green lifted a hand. "I can try and get more specific figures if it'll give you peace of mind, but they're only going to be estimates, based on the outcome of other binding spells that have been performed in the past and the elves' assessment of the features particular to this one."

I don't want to slow down.

I stared down at my hands, at my wrists, searching for the power that wouldn't quite come. There was a mole by my thumb, and a scar on my finger from when I got it caught in the garden gate when I was six, but no purple threads. Nothing but a vague sensation of connection, and the echo of words that weren't mine.

The Blade can sever.

The Blade can unmake.

The hunger stirred in my chest, and I curled my hands into fists. "I don't care about the SCC," I said. "I have to do this spell."

"Emily." Mr. Green's voice was serious. Quiet. "From the day you were turned, you've wanted to be someone —*something*—else. And I get it, I really do. You've undergone a series of huge transformations in an incredibly short space of time. It makes sense that you want to go back to something familiar."

"But—"

He raised his brows at my interruption. "Change is difficult. And scary. Yet that doesn't mean it's bad. For the next few days, I want you to try and just *be*. Sit with your changes, with your powers, with your species. You don't need to embrace it, and you don't need to alter it. Aim for neutrality—nothing more."

I bit down on the words I wanted to say, and stared at the rug on the floor. *I don't need neutrality. I need these powers gone.* But he wouldn't understand, so I just shifted my foot against the faded woolen fabric and nodded. "I'll try," I said.

It almost sounded like I meant it.

Mr. Green scratched his forehead, his mouth turned down, and glanced at the clock at the back of the room. "Send me an email or text tomorrow and let me know how it's going. Remember—you're aiming for neutrality."

Logan's hand was heavy on my thigh.

"Can I go now?" I said.

Mr. Green nodded. "You're all free to go. Unless anyone else has anything they need to talk to me about?"

Cayley was already moving toward the door. "Nope," she said quickly. "I'm good."

"Same," Thomas said, scratching Fred on the head one last time before following Cayley into the corridor.

I wanted to go with them—I needed to be somewhere, *anywhere* else—but I glanced up at Logan, my vampire still close beneath my skin. "I'm going to the dining hall. I have to … um, feed." After everything that had happened, I needed blood to quell the predator in my veins. "Are you coming?"

"I—" He looked at Mr. Green and hesitated, his throat bobbing awkwardly as he swallowed. "There's something I need to—uh—talk to Mr. Green about first."

"Oh." I blinked. "Okay. I'll see you later then." I picked up my glass of water from the floor, then slipped out into the corridor and shut the door behind me. Cayley and Thomas had already gone, so I took the glass back to the kitchen and stood for a while with my hands under the faucet, letting the cold water wash the emotions from my skin.

It didn't really work.

But at least it slowed me down.

By the time I walked out, my footsteps dull against the tiled floor, my pulse had eased and my thoughts had steadied. I still needed to feed but—

Wait.

That scent—magic, hostility, decay. I sped up, making

my way toward it, and found a hospital-style bed, its rails pulled up at the sides, tucked next to the wall near Haven's room.

No one else was around.

"Haven?" I said. "Are you—"

"Help me." The bed shook as she pulled at the rails, blue sparks flaring around the restraints that encircled her wrists. "You have to get me out of here. She's—I can't —I can feel her …" Her gaze slammed into me. "I remember."

I came to a stop beside her. "What are you talking about? And why are you in handcuffs?"

"Because no one believed me when I said I was feeling better." Her voice cracked, her eyes wet with unshed tears. "I want my bed. My clothes. My room."

"And you'll have them," I said softly. "Soon. The doctor's just being thorough. I'm sure you have nothing to worry about."

She strained at the handcuffs, hissing as more sparks lit up her skin. "You don't understand. I have to get out of here so I can help *you.*"

"But—"

"The prophecy isn't over." Her blue eyes lightened to silver. "She showed me."

"Who showed you?" I reached out, grabbing hold of the rail on Haven's bed. Her fingers closed over mine.

"I know how you do it. Do you want to see?" She lifted her chin. "Let me touch your face."

I wasn't sure why, but I did as she said. I leaned my

head closer, and she twisted her wrist, running an index finger over my forehead. Her skin was ice cold. *"Vide. Impertio. Scire."*

A burst of pain took my vision, and I tightened my grip on the bedrail as the world disappeared. For a moment, there was only darkness. And then I found myself standing outside the entrance to Mistwood Academy, the woods burning in the background.

Pain.

So much pain.

At first, I didn't know where it was coming from. Only that it was everywhere, invading my mind, twisting itself into my body, destroying everything in me that was mine.

"Stop it," I whispered, my stomach lurching.

There were bodies, lining the path to the parking lot.

Each one broken.

Each one lifeless.

I recognized them all.

"Look behind you," Haven whispered, her words cutting through the agony that was ripping me apart.

I turned. "No. No no no no no." Bending double, I closed my eyes and clamped my hands over my ears. But I could still feel everything. Every breath, every thought, every moment of love and hate and indifference. My body glowed purple.

It's too much.

I can't—

"Open your eyes," Haven ordered. "Look at them. Look at what you've done."

I shook my head.

"Do it." Haven's voice was a whisper in my ear. "You need to understand."

Body trembling, my hands slid down my cheeks as I stood, and I looked out at the driveway behind me. At Logan. At Cayley. At Thomas. Their throats were ripped out, their bodies gray and cold. I covered my mouth, my stomach heaving. The taste of blood was sour on my tongue.

"Make it stop," I whispered. "Please, make it stop."

"I can't." Haven's voice was inside my head. "*Vide. Scire. Aufero.*"

I opened my mouth, but nothing came out as I was torn in two, my body moving forward while my mind soared free. I couldn't speak. Couldn't scream. I just floated, high above everything, and tried to get back to my body.

"It's time," Haven said.

I watched my body move toward the school gates, purple threads encasing me that reached out toward … everything. Somewhere beneath the glow, the Impure Blade glinted. I—no, *she*—stopped beside the broken chimera that lay behind the fence, one hand dipping down to touch the crumbling stone.

"Haven," I shouted in my mind, "I don't want to—"

"Wait," she commanded, and a burst of darkness erupted from my other self's body, tearing it apart and spreading across the school grounds. Across everything I could see.

Thirty seconds later, there was nothing left.

Nothing but razed buildings and dry, scorched earth.

"It engulfs the entire world," Haven whispered. "And it's all because of you."

My thoughts were a scream and I slammed back into my body, my hands still clutching the bedrail. I fell to my knees, gasping, and Haven tugged at the handcuffs that still bound her in place.

"You'll be powerful beyond measure," she said, "and you won't even want it. But time's running out." Her eyelids fluttered, and when she looked at me again her irises were blue. "Something bad is coming. Soon. You have to …" Her body stiffened and her legs began to shake. "Get what you need for the spell. And as soon as they let me out we'll do it. I'll fix everything. Okay?"

"I—I don't—" I stood as Mr. Lopez opened the nearest door and stepped into the corridor.

"Let's get you upstairs for testing," he said to Haven, shooting me a glare as he started wheeling the bed down the corridor. "Dr. Owens is waiting."

I stayed until they were out of sight. And then I ran. First to the dining hall, where I fed as quickly as I could, and then to my room. My fingers itched for my cello, for the cut of the strings beneath my fingers, but I knew I might run into someone I knew. Like Devon or Mia. Someone who'd want to talk.

And I didn't want to talk.

So I threw on some running gear and bolted across campus, increasing my speed when I got to the woods. Usually, I kept to the path, but tonight I didn't care. I pushed myself forward, faster and harder, ignoring the branches that scratched at my skin. My chest burned with the effort, and I stumbled over a log, falling to my knees, my hands scraping across the ground.

It engulfs the entire world.

And it's all because of you.

I sat back on my heels, my breath coming in loud pants. I didn't know how Haven had shown me what she had, but I couldn't let it happen. My predator surged. Violet light swirled around me and I plucked at the leaves on the nearest tree, sending a shower of debris fluttering down to the ground.

Something bad is coming. Soon.

I slid my phone from the pocket of my tights. I knew what I had to do.

"Hello?" a voice said after three short rings. "Emily? Is that you?"

I nodded, even though she couldn't see me. "Yes, Mom," I said, ignoring the tears that burned behind my eyes. "It's me."

She drew in a shaky breath. "Are you okay? What's happened? What's wrong?"

"Nothing's happened. I'm fine." I wiped my eyes and stared up at the sky, searching for a sign. A star to lead the way. "Could you do me a favor?"

"A favor?" My mother sounded surprised. "What do you need?"

"It's the vase from the living room at … your house. I—"

"Wait," my mom said. "This will always be your house. Your *home*. I hope you know that."

I swallowed past the lump in my throat. "Things have changed, Mom. Maybe we can meet up before the parent-teacher conferences next week and talk about it then." *Or maybe I'll just take the vase and run.* "But I need you to bring it. I know it's old, and I know it's an heirloom, but I'll look after it, I promise."

"What do you mean?" The speaker crackled for a second, and something scraped in the background, like chair legs grazing the floor. "Are you talking about the gray vase on the mantlepiece? That not old, Emily. I bought it at Pottery Barn when you were four."

"You what?"

"I remember it distinctly. We'd just moved to Michigan and I wanted to get something nice, something to liven up the house a bit."

"But … you told me it had been in our family for generations."

"You must be mistaken. I wouldn't—" She stopped suddenly. "Oh, I think I know what happened. Do you remember being in Miss Riley's class at school? You must've been six or seven."

"I was eight. And what's that got to do with anything?"

"You made family trees that year and you were desperate for something historical. An item that would connect you with your ancestors. I didn't have anything in the house that we hadn't bought new, so I showed you the vase and told you it was an heirloom to make you feel better."

"You lied to me?" My hand tightened around my phone. "Is that your answer to everything? Deception?"

"No, I—"

"And what about Dad?" I hadn't meant to say it, but the words kept coming, brittle and uncontrolled. "He's just as bad as you are. Were you really going to let me believe he was my father for the rest of my life?"

My mother sighed. "We wanted to keep you safe."

We did it for your own good.

We thought you'd never find out.

The cold of the earth seeped through my clothes, mixing with the ice in my heart. "Goodbye, Mom."

"Wait," she said, a pleading note creeping into her voice. "I'll explain everything. I just … I want to do it in person. Your dad and I will be at Mistwood on the night of the conferences. Can we meet up before they start? Just name the place and we'll be there."

"Fine." I glared up at the sky. So much for guidance. This conversation was an unmitigated disaster. "I'll text you details on the day. And Mom?"

"Yes?"

"You'd better have a damned good explanation for all of this."

I hung up and stood, sliding my phone back into my pocket. My bones were still restless, my thoughts still scattered, so I walked a while longer, roaming the woods until my legs ached more than my heart. I kept off the path, avoiding supes of all forms, slowing only when I came to a small group of witches in one of the clearings. Standing behind a tree, I watched as they practiced a spell with a dark-haired teaching assistant. Not for the first time, I wondered what it would be like to be one of them. To create something out of nothing. To change the things we couldn't otherwise see.

"Do it now, Audrey. Lift your hands," the assistant said. "Pull the water out of the air and spin it into this crystal."

"You're doing it," said one of the girls in the circle. "Keep going. Look!"

A small cloud appeared over Audrey's hands, soft and fluffy like gray cotton candy, and she chanted in Latin as it started turning, her words rising in volume until it vanished into the crystal that lay at her feet.

"Excellent," the assistant said, smiling with obvious pride. "We'll use that later when we scry for—"

"Wait," someone said, and I turned as two well-dressed seniors walked by, their heads bent together. "We need to go that way." They laughed, and I almost wondered where they were going so close to curfew, but another scent filled the air.

Someone familiar.

Someone who smelled like anticipation and fear.

"Thomas?" I said, frowning at the darkened form who sloped between the trees, phone held to his ear. "Thomas, is that you?"

"I've gotta go," Thomas muttered into his phone. He jabbed at the screen, ending the call, then came to a stop in front of me. "What's up?"

"Nothing much." I shrugged, inhaling as I tried to get a better read on his emotions, exhaling as I tried to stabilize my own. "What are you doing?"

"Walking."

My gaze swept over him. He smelled like the truth, but he wasn't dressed for a casual stroll. He wore stylish black jeans, shiny blue sneakers, and a fitted gray sweater that clung to his arms.

"New look?" I asked.

"Something like that." He cleared his throat and glanced down at his phone. "I'd better go."

"Where?"

He lifted his brows. "What?"

"Where are you going?"

Sniffing, he pulled at the collar of his sweater. "Nowhere interesting."

The lemon-sour scent of his words washed over me and my predator reared up, close beneath my skin. I pushed it away, my hands balling into fists. *Breathe. Keep it together.* "Can I come with you?" I asked.

"No. It's not somewhere you should—I mean, I can't—I'm not going—"

"What do you think I am, Thomas? I'm a vampire. The *putere*." I moved toward him, closing the gap between us. "I killed Mr. Olaru. Wherever you're going, and whatever you're doing, it can't be as bad as that."

He paled, his razor-sharp cheekbones white in the moonlight.

"Oh my god." I took a step back. "You're not going to …"

"Of course I'm fucking not!" Thomas looked around, like he was checking to see if anyone else had heard us. "How could you even think that?"

"I don't know. It looked like … I didn't mean it, okay?" I leaned against the trunk of the nearest oak and blew out a breath. "I'm sorry. It's just … everything keeps going wrong."

Thomas shoved his hands in his pockets, and his features crinkled in a very human expression of concern, though his wolf stalked close beneath his skin. "You wanna talk about it?"

No.

Maybe it would've been sensible—to talk about the

spell, about Haven. About my parents and their lies. Maybe Thomas could've helped. *But talking's not enough. I need to do something. I need to fix this.* I pushed away from the tree, my mind made up. "I need you to help me break into the supply closet in the admin block."

Thomas immediately shook his head. "No. Not if it's for that spell."

"But—"

"You can't ask Haven to do it."

"I don't have any other choice." Lifting my head, I glanced around and scented the breeze, then stepped closer, lowering my voice. "I saw Haven in the hallway when I left Mr. Green's office. She did something—some sort of magic, like a prediction or something—and she showed me what happens when I …" I swallowed hard. "When I destroy the world."

Thomas' forehead wrinkled. "That doesn't make sense. Haven's not an oracle. She can't see the future." His eyes gleamed yellow. "Anyway, there is no prophecy. You guys stopped it with everything you did during the Sapphire Eclipse."

"We don't know that," I whispered. "I'm still the *putere.*"

He watched me for a moment, then grabbed my arm and started walking. "I'm taking you back to your dorm. If you try and involve Haven in any of this, I'll go straight to Mr. Green and Miss Lassila."

I wrenched my arm away and stopped, glaring. "You're not *taking* me anywhere, dumbass. And you're not telling anyone." I inched toward him, my head tipping to the side as I studied the veins that showed blue on his neck. "And if you ever threaten me again, it'll be the last thing you do. Understand?"

His phone beeped and he glanced down at it, his mouth tightening. "Go back to Worthington Hall. I have somewhere else to be. Somewhere important."

He stalked off in the opposite direction, moving with none of the grace that werewolves often had, his human skin fitting him like a poorly-made suit. His arms were too long, his legs too thin and awkward, but there was still power in his muscles. Power I could use. Power I could *take*.

"Hey, asshole!" I yelled out, my fangs sliding free as he slowed. "Wait up!"

"Emily." His voice was a growl. "Don't."

"Don't what?"

"Don't do this." He turned, his eyes glowing amber, fingernails stretching into claws. "I don't want to fight you."

But I *want to fight* you.

"What would Logan think?" he said, breathing heavily as his arms shifted and changed. Wolf to boy; wolf to boy.

"He'd think I was—"

No.

Inhale.

Control it.

I forced my fangs to retract. "I don't want to fight you either," I said, the lie tasting sour on my tongue. "But you're not usually such a dick."

"And you're not usually so reactive."

My jaw twitched. "I know."

I hated this. I was losing it; I was losing me. *You'll be powerful beyond measure and you won't even want it.* How long until I was nothing at all?

"Look, I didn't mean for this to happen," Thomas said, his voice low. "Do you want me to call Logan for you? He could walk you back. Make sure you're safe."

My lips twisted in a strange sort of smile. "It's okay," I said softly. "I'll be fine."

I watched him as he left, his angular body moving clumsily through the trees, then I made my way back to my dorm, feeling lower than ever. I had no heirloom, no SCC approval, and I was going to blow up the world with a single burst of darkness.

How is this even my life?

My thoughts were a whirl as I showered and got ready for bed. The spell. The prophecy. Darkness engulfing the world. It had all felt so real. So *painful*. But Thomas' words were a warning that wouldn't let up in the back of my mind. *Haven's not an oracle. She can't see the future.* What if he was right? Haven had never predicted anything before. What if it was just a side effect of her illness? Another misinterpretation of something she'd seen or heard?

I went back to my room, my damp hair loose over my shoulders, and slid my feet into my softest slippers. Curling up on the bed, I picked up Minikins and hugged him, breathing in the memory of my humanity, remembering the person I still wanted to be, the one who wouldn't destroy the world.

Then I reached for my phone.

"Hi, you've reached Haven Montgomery. Please leave a message after the—"

Click.

I tossed my phone down on the bed. This wasn't a conversation I wanted to have via voicemail. Turning to face the wall, I wondered what I was supposed to do. Sleep? Eat? Break into the supply closet? Then a sharp knock sounded on my window.

Logan.

"What are you doing here?" I asked, unclipping the latch to let him in. "It's ten minutes till curfew."

"I wanted to say good night." He perched on the windowsill, his legs tucked beneath him. "You didn't come to dinner. And you haven't answered any of my texts."

I looked down at my hands, reaching for the violet glow that had connected us back in Mr. Green's office, but it was nothing more than a phantom, a shimmer beneath my skin. "I was busy. In the woods."

"Running?"

I nodded, my throat uncomfortably dry. "I saw Thomas. But he wouldn't tell me where he was going. We fought, and I ..."

"You what?" Logan said, sliding over the desk, his feet hitting the floor with a muffled thump.

"I challenged him." I stared at Logan's shoes, too afraid —too *ashamed*—to meet his eyes. My voice dropped to a whisper. "It's like … every day I'm a little less me, and a little more *him*."

Logan pulled me close, arms wrapped around me so tight I could barely breathe, and the world around us paused. We were suspended in time, caught in a single moment, until he pressed his lips to my head and drew back, staring down at me carefully, like I was something that might break. "It's okay. You're safe now, and Thomas is safe." He swallowed awkwardly. "He is safe, right?"

I nodded. "That's not everything, though." Resting my head against his chest, I let my hair slide over my face and told him what Haven had shown me. The bodies. The destruction. The all-encompassing darkness. "We didn't stop the prophecy."

"But—" The warning bell chimed, stealing the words from his mouth. "I don't know what Haven showed you," he said when it was finished, "but we'll figure something out. I have to get back to my dorm—I need to sign in or Mr. Wright will come looking for me—but I'll be back as soon as I can."

I reached for his hand as he moved toward the window. "I need you to break into the supply closet with me."

"What?"

"The supply closet in the admin block. I asked Thomas earlier, but he won't do anything to help me with the spell." I went up on my tiptoes and kissed him, needing to feel something more than fear. Something gentle. Something *real*. "Everything keeps changing and I'm just supposed to accept it. But I can't."

"I know what you're saying," Logan said gently. "And I get it. But maybe we should wait. Mr. Green said there's a fifty percent chance of injury or death. That's—"

"No." I backed away, my hands shaking. "You don't get it. This is my choice, and I'm going to do it whether you help me or not."

The warning bell chimed again, and Logan glanced back at the chimera who stalked past my window. "Eat something," he said, climbing outside. "I'll meet you round back of the admin block in thirty minutes. Bring Cayley."

He sloped away, and I closed the window then sat back down on my bed. Reaching for an apple from the fruit bowl on my nightstand, my face flushed with embarrassment. *How could I be so stupid?* Aside from my brief visit to the Nutriment earlier, I hadn't eaten anything since the cookie in Mr. Green's office. *No wonder I've been flipping out.* After finishing the apple, I grabbed a protein bar and my phone and messaged Cayley: *Wanna raid the supply closet? I need a vessel. And something of Mr. Olaru's.*

Her response was immediate: *When do we go?*

Twenty-five minutes—and two more protein bars— later, I knocked on her door. "Hurry up," I whispered, looking over my shoulder. "We need to get out of here before Ms. Emmerson comes back."

Creeping down the stairs, we narrowly avoided the house matron, who was comforting a crying student in her office, and Miss Lassila, who was pacing the first floor corridor. After disabling the alarm—and swiping a handful of chocolates from the bowl on the front desk—we slipped outside, closing the door quietly behind us.

Cayley stuffed a pecan caramel cluster in her mouth. "I'm gonna change. That way, if the chimera—or anybody else—notices us, they won't think anything's wrong." Within seconds, her hazel eyes turned blue and her dark hair lightened, her body shrinking until she barely came up to my waist. She marched down the stairs with the formidable confidence of the *actual* Miss Lassila. "Let's go."

I quickly followed. "How are we supposed to get into the admin building?"

"Did you grab Miss Lassila's keys when you disabled the alarm?" When I shook my head, Cayley's borrowed face pinched in a look of disapproval. "What kind of thief are you?"

I threw a chocolate at her forehead. "A bad one."

The school was almost deserted, the sun still well below the horizon, so we hurried along the cobblestone paths, avoiding the lamplight wherever we could. Cayley nodded politely at the groundskeeper, a weathered old dryad, who was pruning dead branches off a tree and tossing them into a wheelbarrow.

"Not another drunk one, I hope," he muttered.

"She's nothing of the sort," Cayley retorted. "This young woman is in need of pain relief. For *cramps*."

The groundskeeper's cheeks turned pink. "I see."

Cayley was still smirking when we came to a stop behind the admin block. "Still need those drugs?"

Logan slipped out of the shadows. "I thought this was a simple B&E," he said.

I ignored them both and stepped up to the arched wooden door that sunk into the side of the building. Like everything else at Mistwood, it was carved and beautiful, and I placed a hand against its surface, feeling the ridges that had been shaped so many years before. "How do we get in?"

"Universal key." Logan's voice was suddenly close behind me. "Opens every door on campus. *And* keeps the chimera off my case."

Uhhh ... what?

I didn't know what I'd been expecting. Maybe a spell. Or a potion. Or the use of sheer brute force. But a universal key? That had never been on my radar.

"Where did you get that?" I asked, watching as Logan slid the scratched brass key into the lock. The metal lit up with a faint gold shimmer, and there was a loud *clunk* as the lock disengaged.

"I ..." He cleared his throat, then threw a glance over his shoulder at Cayley. "I swiped it from my father's office years ago, when things were ... you know, bad. He'd been given it when he taught a special studies class on werewolves and pack hierarchy, a few years before I was born, and he never returned it." Logan opened the door and ran his thumb over the key. "It gave me options, when all I wanted was to get away from everything."

"He mostly used it to sneak into the dining hall after hours," Cayley said.

"I did not." He ushered us inside and pulled the door closed. "That was only twice a week. And I always took you with me."

We crept silently down the corridor, past locked rooms and offices, until Logan stopped in front of a door labeled "Supply Closet."

"The building's not alarmed, is it?" I asked, my gaze lifting as I searched for electronic sensors.

Logan shook his head. "Not by physical means, if that's what you're getting at. There are wards, obviously, but they don't count"—he slid the key into the lock and twisted—"when you've got one of these." Turning to Cayley, he said, "We'll go in. You keep watch in case someone comes."

"I know the drill," she said, leaning back against the wall.

Logan opened the door and we stepped inside. I'd never had any reason to visit the supply closet before, and I'd been expecting to find a small, dusty room filled with overflowing cartons and unevenly stacked paper. But when I crossed the threshold, I realized that—as with almost everything else at Mistwood Academy—my expectations didn't match the reality. The supply closet was large, technically more of a room than a closet, and it was filled with rows of tall, wooden-framed shelves housing neatly-labeled boxes.

"I'll look for something of Mr. Olaru's," Logan said,

already moving off to the side of the room. "You search for the vessel. Unless you wanna swap?"

"No, it's fine." I turned around, trying to figure out where to start. "How's this place organized? Is it alphabetical? Color-coded? Random?"

Logan snorted. "It's arranged by type. Crystals to the left, candles in the middle—somewhere between a selection of incense and resins, I think—and herbs, roots, and powders are in the next row along." He tilted his head, his eyes narrowing in thought. "Magical vessels should be somewhere near the back. Unless they've shifted things since the last time I was in here."

He sounded upbeat, like this was nothing more than a game, but I knew he didn't want me to do the spell. His eyes flickered with worry when he didn't think I was watching, and a tiny muscle kept twitching in his jaw.

"Why are you here?" I said.

He hesitated, his expression turning serious. "Because I believed you when you said you'd do the spell whether I helped you or not. It doesn't mean I like it. And it doesn't mean I agree. But I don't want you to go through this alone."

"Oh." I didn't know what to say, but an unexpected warmth filled my chest. "Thank you."

There was an awkward pause, then we both moved off in opposite directions. My gaze drifted over the tidy stacks of wooden storage boxes as I walked along the central aisle. Each box had a small barcode on the front, just beneath the label that denoted its contents.

"Won't someone notice what we've taken?" I asked as I lifted the lid on a box labeled "Anointing Oils." It was filled with tiny glass bottles, some prosaic, others beautifully decorated. They were fascinating, but not what I needed.

"Eventually," Logan answered from across the room. "They do stock take once or twice a year, but minor discrepancies are usually put down to scanner malfunction or user error."

"Scanner malfunction?"

Logan appeared at the end of the aisle, holding up a small, black object with a glowing screen and an assortment of buttons.

"A barcode scanner? For a school supply closet?" I frowned, taking the high-tech device from Logan's hands. It was sleek and modern, and it seemed completely out of place in the decorative wood-paneled room.

"Some people think the best way for supes to survive is to move with the times." Logan plucked the scanner out of my hands and turned it off, his lips pressing together. "Other people—my father, for instance—are a little less progressive."

"I'm sorry." I touched his arm, wishing I could stop the pain that crept into his voice whenever he spoke of his family. "Change takes time."

"They've had more than enough."

"Hey," Cayley hissed from her spot by the door. "Hurry up. We don't have all day."

Logan went back to whatever aisle he'd come from,

and I moved to the end of the room, searching through boxes of urns and jugs and jars. The specifications for the vessel had been noted in the spell book Haven had taken from the SCC—*old, preferably between eight and twelve inches in height, with a tight-sealing lid and a sturdy base.* But I couldn't find anything that fit the description.

Too big.

Too small.

Too new.

Too fragile.

"There's nothing here," I called to Logan as I examined a shiny glass jug. "How are you going?"

"I think I have … there." A few seconds later, he came up behind me, a fountain pen in his hand. He held it up, examining its faded black exterior beneath the overhead light. "Mr. Olaru had a whole bunch of these. He used to keep them in a drawer in his desk." Lifting it to his nose, he inhaled deeply and grimaced. "It smells kinda musty. Which is how I remember him, I guess."

"Quick!" Cayley barreled into the room, pulling the door shut behind her, her form caught somewhere between Miss Lassila's and her own. "We have to hide. Now!"

13

"WHAT'S GOING ON?" I whispered, stumbling as Logan dragged me to the end of the aisle, the glass jug still in my hands.

"Miss Lassila's coming." Cayley ducked down low behind me, peeking between the shelves.

"Why didn't you distract her?" Logan said.

"Because I couldn't change all of this"—Cayley gesticulated wildly at her face—"in time."

"Be quiet," I whispered as the housemistress entered the room, her boots clicking loudly against the tile floor.

Cayley's features shifted and changed as we huddled in a pocket of shadow by the back wall; her clothes stretched out with her body. I shuffled over to give her more room, and the jug slipped through my sweating hands.

No.

I raised my arms. Purple strands materialized in front of me, curling around my hands and wrists, and I pulled at the one that reached toward the jug. It was shiny, laced with the faint buzz of static. And it worked. *It worked.* The jug paused, just above the floor, then flew back toward me, pushing me into the wall as I caught it.

Logan grabbed my arm.

"Nice catch," Cayley whispered.

I held the jug to my chest, the purple threads fading away. *That was close. So, so close.* I had no idea what Miss Lassila would've done if she'd caught us. Detention? Suspension? Expulsion? A tiny sigh escaped my lips.

Maybe this power could be useful.

It was a traitorous thought. And even though I hated it, it still wove itself under my skin, burrowing deeper and deeper until I wasn't sure how I felt about anything anymore.

Do I actually want this?

"No. We can't let her go through with it," Miss Lassila said, stopping my questioning in its tracks. An electronic beep punctuated her words and a wooden lid closed, her footsteps coming closer. "She can't be cut off from her powers again."

Goosebumps lifted on my skin.

"Her body will remember, Jessica. And not just these powers—it will remember the others. She's been living with loss for most of her life."

Jessica.

My mother.

My fangs tingled in my gums.

"I think she's talking about you," Cayley whispered, poking me in the arm.

I shook my head, trying to listen to what Miss Lassila was saying. But she was quiet now, and the buzz of that familiar maternal voice was nothing more than an incomprehensible hum through the tiny speaker of Miss Lassila's phone.

I moved forward.

Careful.

Quiet.

Slow.

"I know she doesn't know," Miss Lassila said, her voice suddenly loud, "but her powers are a part of her being. They can adapt and change—you know that as well as I do —but there are always, *always* consequences." The electronic scanner beeped again and Miss Lassila sighed. "I wish I'd never agreed to participate in that ill-considered spell when she was a child. It was dangerous. And illegal. If the SCC knew…"

I could feel Logan's and Cayley's eyes on me, but I stared straight ahead, unflinching.

"You need to talk to Emily," the housemistress said as she crossed the room, heading toward the exit. "Help her come to terms with what she is. This was always supposed to be her life, whether you like it or not."

The lights flicked off.

The door snapped shut.

And I stepped forward.

I have to know. I have to know. I have to—

"Stop," Logan said. "You can't go after her."

I whirled around. "Why not?"

"Because we'll be expelled. And my dad will kill me. I'm not supposed to have this key. He thought he lost it when—"

"I don't care about the key," I said, my voice hitching. "She was talking to my mother. *My mother*, Logan. How do they even know each other?" I clutched at the jug in my arms, clinging to it like a lifeline. "What did she mean about a spell? And living with loss? And remembering other powers?"

"I don't know," he said quietly. "But it's not worth getting expelled over. Not when you could just talk to your parents."

I don't want *to talk to my parents.*

I stalked down the aisle and shoved the jug back in its box. It rattled against a jar—sturdy and floral and ten inches tall—and I snatched it up angrily, inexplicably annoyed by how perfect it was.

"Why did I think I knew them?" I muttered under my breath. "Why did I think I knew *me*?"

Logan came up beside me and took the jar from my hands. "You *do* know you," he said as he gently tucked a stray strand of hair behind my ear. "You're loyal and kind. Talented and brave." His lips curled up in a lopsided smile. "And you're an excellent kisser."

I tried to keep glaring, but there was something so earnest beneath his words that I snorted instead. Then, sagging down into his arms, I lay my head against his chest as exhaustion surged through me. "Do you think I can trust Miss Lassila?"

"I don't know," he said softly. "But we'll have to figure it out later. The longer we stay here, the higher our chances of getting caught."

We made our way out into the corridor, Logan and I creeping out behind Cayley, who was now tall and gray-haired, a disconcertingly exact replica of Ms. Emmerson. "It's clear," she whispered. "Let's go."

Five minutes later we were standing outside Worthington Hall. "Can I come up?" Logan said, handing me the vessel and the fountain pen, his fingers warm where they brushed my own.

I nodded, barely able to hold myself up.

"Great B&E, Logan," Cayley said as she grabbed my hand and pulled me toward the steps, her long skirt billowing out behind her. "We should do it again some time."

Logan pushed his hair back from his forehead. His emotions had been tucked away so tight it was like he didn't have any at all. "It was a solid effort," he said lightly, "but nothing could top the dining hall heist of freshman year."

"Thanksgiving," Cayley said. "I remember."

She led me into Worthington Hall, checking the alarm system and snatching up another handful of chocolates on the way past the front desk. Her face and body were now her own. She wore simple pajamas, her hazel eyes unadorned by makeup, but she looked more alive than I'd ever seen her.

"Hey," she said softly, delicately removing the jar and vessel from my grip, "you just concentrate on making it up the stairs. You're not used to that new power yet. Sometimes you've got to take things slow."

"Nothing's been slow about this," I muttered. "I was human. And then I wasn't. And now my life is fucked. You get to enjoy breaking into the supply closet, pretending to be our teachers, but I have to live with the consequences of what was done to me."

And the knowledge of what I'll do.

Cayley was quiet as she led me to the bathrooms. "Look," she said when the door was closed, "I'm not going to deny that I had fun tonight. I'm a succubus—I love adventure. Excitement. Anything that gets my adrenaline going." She placed the jar and fountain pen down beside the sinks and looked at me in the mirror. "But that doesn't mean I don't know you've had it rough. That you're still going through it." She paused, studying me as her hair curled softly around her shoulders; her lips darkened and her lashes grew, curling up to frame her eyes. "There are so many good things about being a supe. You just have to look for them."

She turned and went into one of the stalls, while I stared into the reflective glass, my gaze catching on the pink and black smudges around my eyes. I leaned forward, trying to look past the fatigue, past the pale skin and lifeless brown hair, searching for something deeper.

Something that might tell me what I had been. What I was. What I was becoming.

This was always supposed to be her life.

I turned on the faucet and splashed cold water on my face, then went and sat down on one of the benches at the side of the room. Resting my head against the wall behind me, I closed my eyes and let my mind fill with memories of my childhood. I'd been happy then—a human girl living a human life.

But I was never really human at all.

"Don't fall asleep," Cayley said as she made her way back over to the sinks. "Ms. Emmerson checks the bathrooms sometimes. Ask me how I know."

I watched the back of her head as she washed her hands. "How do you know?"

"She caught me making out with Vanessa in one of the stalls during freshman year."

"Vanessa? Like, Vanessa Green, Vanessa?" I wrinkled my nose. "Why?"

"She was nicer back then." She dried her hands on a towel and turned around, leaning against the sink. "People change, I guess."

And not always for the better.

"I challenged Thomas tonight," I said, feeling the weight of my own changes settling over my shoulders. "I just wanted to let you know."

Cayley studied my face before asking, "Is he okay?"

I nodded.

"And you're okay?'

I nodded again.

"Then it's nothing to worry about." She sat down beside me and stretched her legs out in front of her. Her black slipper boots were scuffed, the material fraying at the edges. "What was he doing?"

"Walking." I looked down at my hands, wishing I believed her. Because all I'd done since it happened was worry. "He wouldn't tell me where he was going."

"He does that sometimes." She held out her hand and her nail polish faded, leaving her fingernails bare for the first time since I'd met her. "But it's no big deal. He does his thing. I do mine."

"Is that what you want?"

"I don't get a lot of choice. Succubi aren't made for relationships." She pulled her phone out of her pocket and grimaced. "Come on, let's go." Grabbing my hand, she pulled me to my feet. "Don't let Logan keep you up all night. You look exhausted."

"I won't—we don't …" My face burned. "I'm still a virgin, you know."

Cayley's eyebrows shot up. "Are you sure? I've seen the way you look at each other."

I dragged the edge of one shoe against the floor, wishing I was already asleep. "It's complicated. I mean, it's not like we haven't done anything, but we haven't, you know, done … it."

"There's more than one definition of *it*," Cayley retorted, handing me the vessel and the fountain pen. She lifted a hand and began counting on her fingers. "Rebecca

Browne. Ollie Walker. Arnav Patel. Isla Turner. Four very different people—four very different types of sex. None of them right, none of them wrong."

"Oh."

"I mean, don't do anything you're not ready for. But don't get caught up in heteronormative ideals either. Virginity's just a social construct."

She slipped down the corridor to her room, and I hurried back to mine.

"Hey." There was a quiet tap on the window as soon as I closed the door. "I can hear you. Let me in already."

"Sorry," I whispered as I opened the latch. "I was talking to Cayley."

"About me?"

"Uh—"

"I was joking, but …" His breath was hot against the side of my face as his feet hit the floor. "All good things, I hope."

I lowered the vessel and pen down onto my desk. "All good things." *I've seen the way you look at each other.* I bit my lip, dragging the scent of boy and wolf into my lungs. I didn't know if it was the conversation I'd had with Cayley, or the fact that I just didn't want to think anymore, but I suddenly felt wide awake. "Logan, are you tired right now?"

He shook his head.

And then my mouth was on his, my hands slipping under his shirt, pulling him back toward my bed. We fell on the mattress in a tangle of limbs, and Logan's gaze hit mine, his eyes burning with desire.

"Is this okay?" I whispered.

He nodded, and his lips found my neck. I tilted my head, pulling at the hem of his shirt. We were skin against skin, hands brushing faces, fingers tracing ribs. It wasn't until later, when we were curled up against each other, both of us clothed and half asleep, that I realized I'd done what Mr. Green had suggested. I'd let myself *be*.

And maybe I didn't hate it.

Beneath the warm covers, Logan's hand found mine. "Who's going to do the spell?" he asked.

"What?"

"The spell to bind your powers. If Haven's too sick to do it, and the SCC won't let you ..." He trailed off, uncertainty tainting his skin. "How will you find someone you can trust?"

I rolled onto my back and stared up at the ceiling. "I don't know."

"And what if—"

"I don't *know*," I said, pushing his arm off me and sitting up, grabbing Minikins from the end of the bed. "I don't know how any of this works. I don't know if there's some sort of directory for obscure elven magic practitioners. I don't know how to find someone who's not going to betray me. I don't even know if I can get everything I need to do the spell in the first place." I hugged Minkins to my chest, my gaze settling on the vessel and the pen that still sat on my desk. "My mom doesn't have access to any sort of heirloom. And if I can't find one ..."

Dead bodies.

Razed buildings.

Dry, scorched earth.

"What about him?" Logan said, pushing up to sit.

I frowned.

"Your cat. Minikins. He could be your heirloom."

I held him out in front of me, inspecting his patchy fur, his scratched plastic eyes, the lumpy stuffing that always threatened to escape through the holes in his legs. "He can't be. An heirloom's something that's belonged to a family for generations. And Minikins has only ever been mine."

"But what if the depth of your feelings for him cancels out the need for generational ownership? He could be a new heirloom—you're just his first guardian."

"Maybe." I slipped out of bed and placed him down beside the jug and the pen, but it didn't feel right. Minikins was filled with the remnants of my humanity— or what I'd *thought* had been humanity. He didn't belong in this world; he shouldn't be part of the spell.

I spun around slowly, looking for something I was never going to find. *Books, pens, clothes, electronics.* There was nothing even halfway approaching an heirloom.

Wait.

I padded across the room and reached for the small crystal ball that sat on the shelf beside the door. "What didn't I think of this before?"

Logan stood. "What is it?"

I held it out in front of me, staring into its murky depths. It was dense but small—it fitted neatly into the palm of my hand—and I'd had it since I'd left the Paranormal Program. It had been given to me by Laurence, a vampire who'd helped me learn to control my hunger. He'd said it was a gift to connect me to my heritage. I'd thought he'd meant to my vampire heritage, but maybe he'd meant something else.

You'll understand when the time is right.

His words echoed in my mind, a roadmap I didn't understand. "Is the time right?" I whispered, running my thumb across the smooth, glassy surface. "Am I supposed to use this for the spell?"

Logan frowned. "Where did you get it?"

I placed the orb down beside the vessel and the pen, then told him everything. "I'll email Laurence to confirm, but if I'm right about this being the heirloom," I finished, "then I'll have everything I need for the spell. The Blade. The vessel. The anchor. Something belonging to Mr. Olaru. And—" I fished a half-finished rosin cake from my messenger bag and presented it to him with a flourish. "Something belonging to me."

But Logan wasn't listening. His gaze was on the pen. "Shit," he muttered as he picked it up and held it close to the wall, a shimmer of light flicking over the barrel. "This isn't Mr. Olaru's. It's Miss Masefield's. You know, the old lady who used to be his assistant."

I leaned forward. "You said it smelled like him."

"I thought it did. It's musty enough—but I guess it's her scent, not his." He held it closer to the wall. "She used to enchant all her stationery so no one could steal it. Look. See that crisscross pattern? That was the marker of her spell." He drew his hand back, examining the pen one last time before putting it down. "Someone's removed most of it. I guess Haven's enhanced wards are so strong, they've just picked up whatever remnants were left."

I dropped down onto my bed with a thud. "So it's not Mr. Olaru's."

Logan sat down next to me. "It's not."

I lay back and closed my eyes. The sun scratched at my bones and I drew in a breath. Then another. And another. *This is just a setback. Nothing more. Nothing less.*

If I said it enough times, maybe I'd actually believe it.

14

———

IT WAS ALMOST dark outside when I woke, my skin hot and my head fuzzy. I pushed Logan away and shoved the blankets down, rolling over to face the wall. There was a certain comfort in falling asleep beside him, but I still wasn't used to sharing my bed. It was stuffy and cramped, and I stretched my legs carefully, trying not to kick him.

I wasn't successful.

"Go away," Logan mumbled, pulling the pillow up over his head. "It's too early."

I sat, still not sure why I'd woken up. I glanced down at my hands, wondering if it had something to do with the telekinesis, or maybe I'd had a weird dream, when—

There was a bang outside.

A muffled thump.

A quiet curse.

I shuffled down the bed and climbed over Logan, then

peeked out into the hallway. It was quiet, empty, but something didn't feel right, so I tiptoed forward. The floor was cold beneath my feet. Portraits stared down at me from the walls and I shivered, stopping outside Cayley's room.

Another thump.

Another curse.

"Cayley," I whispered, knocking quietly on her door. "Cayley, are you awake?"

Ten seconds later, the door swung open. "I am now."

"Something's wrong." I pointed toward the stairs, wishing for once that Ms. Emmerson or Miss Lassila would magically appear out of nowhere to deal with the situation. "Someone's down there."

My hands shook as we moved toward the noise. Cayley sparked with anticipation. All I could think about was the time I'd been kidnapped—*why had I even decided to check this out? I could be safe and warm in bed with Logan*—but a familiar scent wound its way to the back of my brain and I stopped.

"Vanessa?" Cayley said.

She was disheveled and wobbling, half bent over at the top of the staircase. "What are you looking at?" she slurred, her hair falling over her face. She rubbed her shin, cursing quietly under her breath.

"A walking disaster," Cayley offered.

Vanessa lifted her head and almost toppled back. "I'll give you a—"

"Shhh." Cayley put a finger to her lips. "Do you want

Ms. Emmerson to see you like this? Or Miss Lassila? How did you even get past the chimera like this?"

"None of your business," Vanessa mumbled, staggering toward us on unsteady legs. Her blue eyes were hazy and unfocused. "Get out of my way." It was obvious she'd been partying. Her breath reeked of alcohol, and her blush-colored minidress was wrinkled and stained, her silver heels caked in mud.

"Vanessa," I said, reaching toward her, "do you—"

"Go. Away." She lurched to the side and fell, landing heavily on her arm. Eyes filling with angry tears, she clawed at the wall, trying to pull herself up. "Leave me alone."

"For fuck's sake," Cayley muttered.

"Ohhhh." Vanessa's chest heaved and her hands flew up to her mouth. "Oh no. No no no."

Cayley seized one of Vanessa's arms, signaling furiously for me to grab the other. "Bathroom. *Now.*"

The two of us dragged Vanessa along the corridor, trying to be as quiet as possible, and managed to get her into a stall just before she emptied her stomach. I held her hair back from her face; the ash-blonde strands were soft and fragrant with the scent of artificial perfume.

"Make it stop," Vanessa pleaded, her shoulders shaking violently. "Emily, do something. Make it stop. *Please.*"

"I don't know how." I passed her a wad of toilet paper and wished hyperosmia wasn't a thing. "How much did you drink?"

"I don't know," she wailed. "Does it matter?"

"Maybe." Cayley's voice was sharp. "What were you drinking?"

Vanessa wiped her mouth and stood, tears running down her face. "I don't know." She stumbled to the sinks and tried to splash cold water on her face, but it dripped down the front of her dress. "Beer? And some sort of cocktail with a little umbrella. And beer. Lots and lots of beer." She pulled her phone out of the shiny silver purse that hung diagonally across her body. Swiping across, she unlocked the screen. "Come on," she muttered, cursing as the device slipped from her hands.

Unexpectedly, it rang.

Vanessa scooped it up, her fingers leaving smudges on the unprotected glass. "Hello? Hello, Courtney? Is that you?"

I moved closer to Cayley. "Should we get Ms. Emmerson?" I whispered. "Or Miss Lassila?"

"No, let's just see where this goes."

Vanessa straightened suddenly, grabbing the edge of the sink. "I didn't promise you anything."

Courtney's voice was loud on the other end of the phone. "Stop lying to me, Ness. You told me you wouldn't go there anymore."

"Whatever." Vanessa leaned against the sinks, her cheeks unnaturally flushed. "I just

need a little bit of help. I'm in the bathroom down the hall."

Thirty seconds later, the door burst open and Courtney stormed in. "Never again," she ground out through gritted teeth. "This is the last time, I swear." She hauled Vanessa up by the armpits and fixed us with a glare. "What are you two doing here?"

"Helping your friend," Cayley said.

"Well, you can go now." Courtney pulled Vanessa toward her. "She doesn't need your help."

"Yeah," Vanessa mumbled. "I don't need anyone's help."

We all knew it wasn't true.

"I'm sorry," Vanessa said as Courtney loosened her grip. She slid to the floor, her eyes swimming with tears. "I do need you, Court. I do." Her gloss-smudged lips trembled. "I didn't mean to go there. And I didn't mean to lie to you. It's just … there's something about that place."

"It's called alcohol," Courtney said, grunting as she hauled her friend back up to her feet. "And it's gonna get you locked up."

"Where did you go tonight?" I asked, curiosity getting the better of me.

Courtney scowled. "That's none of your business."

My gaze slid to Cayley. *Please don't kill me for what I'm about to ask.* "Was Thomas there?"

Cayley's expression didn't change. She was a statue, a figurine carved from stone, but no matter how hard she tried, she couldn't control her scent. It whirled around her, wild with spiced impatience and the clouded scent of watercolor; deep down in her veins she was worried, holding onto something I wasn't sure she should.

"Thomas?" Vanessa echoed, pitching forward. She winced as Courtney pulled her back, the strap of her dress catching in her hair. "Of course he was there. We sat under the stars and—"

"Hello?" The door swung open and Mia stepped into the room. "I heard voices and ... oh." She stopped, rubbing her eyes. "What's going on?"

Courtney dragged Vanessa out into the corridor. "We were just leaving. And, Mia, if you breathe a word about this to anyone ..."

"You'll what?" Cayley said. "Start a rumor that Mia's— oh, wait. You won't say anything. Because Mia's one of the few decent people at this school."

I looked at her, surprised at the depth of emotion in her voice. I knew she and Mia were friends, but there was a fierceness in her eyes I'd never seen before, and she stepped forward, ready to fight.

"Of course I won't be saying anything about Mia," Courtney said. "But if this gets out"—her gaze cut to me— "I *will* be telling Miss Lassila there's a boy in Emily's room."

My jaw dropped. "You'll what?"

"I can smell him all over you." Her upper lip curled. "I didn't know for certain he was in there until now, so thanks for confirming it. You've saved me a lot of trouble, Emersyn."

Shit.

For once I didn't even care that she'd messed up my name.

"Enough talking," Vanessa mumbled. "I want to go to sleep."

With one last scowl, Courtney pulled Vanessa toward their room, and I turned to face Mia, who was standing beside Cayley. Her eyes were hooded, her hair standing out in clumps around her head, and she frowned, clearly confused. "Is anyone going to explain what just happened?"

Cayley leaned her head against Mia's shoulder. "Vanessa was drunk."

"That much was obvious."

"That's all we know," I offered, stifling a yawn. "I don't know why Miss Lassila or Ms. Emmerson didn't hear any of the noise."

Mia covered her own yawn with a hand. "Ms. Emmerson's asleep in her office down the hall. I don't know about Miss Lassila though." She put an arm around Cayley's shoulder. "You should go back to bed. Both of you. You look exhausted."

"No," Cayley said. "I'm staying up until I find out where Vanessa was tonight. And what my boyfriend was doing there with her."

Later that night, after classes were done, I sat in my room, scrolling through my essay plan for History. "I'm never gonna get this done in time," I muttered under my breath. Lying my head on the desk, I covered my eyes and groaned. I'd been doing this for hours.

My phone buzzed.

I sat, accidentally knocking a stack of reference books to the floor. "Haven?" I said, leaning over to pick them up. "Is that you?"

"Of course it's me. Where are you? And why am I looking at ... the ceiling?"

"Sorry." I set the books back down beside me and straightened my phone. Haven stared back at me, her image clear on the screen. She was tired and gaunt, but she was sitting up in bed, propped up by a nest of pillows, and her eyes were bright and blue. There were no handcuffs. No sparks burning against her skin. "Is everything okay?"

"No," she said. "I'm bored." She threw a hand up dramatically against her forehead and pouted. "Tell me everything."

"Everything?"

"Yes, everything! What have I missed? Who came first in Algebra yesterday? There was a quiz, right?" She held her phone closer to her face. "What about History? Has Mr. Dufort given our assignments back yet? I think he—"

"Slow down," I said, interrupting before she could go any further. "You're in the infirmary. You shouldn't be worrying about Algebra and History."

"But I'm bored."

"I don't care. You need to rest." I didn't know why she was pretending everything was okay, not after what she'd shown me in the hallway. But I couldn't ignore it; I could still feel the darkness spreading over my skin. "That thing you showed me yesterday ..."

Her smile dimmed.

Bodies.

Darkness.

Cataclysmic pain.

The vision flashed behind my eyes, but I pushed it away. "Was it real?"

Haven nodded, her earlier levity gone. "I don't know when it happens. Only that it will." She pushed her hair back from her forehead, dark roots showing through the platinum tangles. "I could feel it. There was so much suffering. It was—"

"Stop," I said. "*Please.* I just wanted to know if it was true or not. I don't want to think about the details."

"But you have to."

I stood, adrenaline surging through my blood. "You're not an oracle. How could you see what's going to happen? How could you share it with my mind?"

Her swallow was audible, even through the phone. "Because there's something wrong with my aura. It's affecting my magic—enhancing some things, and diminishing others."

"Oh." I leaned against the edge of my desk, my hands shaking. I'd been so busy worrying about myself, that I hadn't even asked how she was. "Are you going to be okay?"

"I'll be fine," she said firmly. "They changed my antibiotics last night—Dr. Owens got some results back that suggested a different one would work better—and the infections are already settling. See?" She held her phone above her arm. The silver marking was irritated, and the skin around it was raised and red, but it didn't look as angry. "The cough is almost gone too. Now they're just figuring out how to fix my magic."

"Is there anything I can do?"

"Yes." Her face reappeared on screen. "Get everything you need for the spell. Because as soon as I'm out of here, I'm doing it."

"But you need time to recover."

"Em." She sighed loudly. "I'm not stupid. I know my limits."

I raised my brows, disbelief clear on my face.

"Fine. I messed up yesterday and did too much, too soon. Even Dr. Owens could tell I'd been using magic." She shifted awkwardly on the bed, her head twisting to the side as she settled back against the pillows. "I didn't tell him about the Blade, though. You know I'd never compromise your safety."

"Yeah, but ..." I drew in a breath, wishing I was with her. Because then I could smell the truth of her words, sense the level of sickness in her blood. I hadn't realized how much I'd come to rely on my vampiric abilities, but they were a regular part of me now—as natural as breathing.

"I can do the spell, Em. I promise." She picked up a glass of water from somewhere beside her and took a long sip. "How many of the items do you have?"

"Four." My gaze cut to the closet. I'd put everything in there, tucking it away neatly where Ms. Emmerson would never see it. *I hope.* "I just need something of Mr. Olaru's. And possibly a different anchor."

Haven yawned, and my phone alarm beeped, reminding me it was time for rehearsal. "Make sure you find them," she said, covering her mouth with her hand. "And keep me updated."

"Of course." Disconnecting the call, I swung my bag over my shoulder and headed for the door. My essay would have to wait.

I hurried downstairs and out into the night, making my way toward the practice rooms. I was almost there when—

"Emily! Yoo hoo! Emily Sanderson."

Crap.

I turned, forcing a smile onto my lips. "Mr. Davis," I said, with what I hoped sounded like genuine brightness. "I'm sorry I haven't emailed you back about—Oh, and Ms. Maguire. Hi."

"Hello, Emily." She inclined her head politely.

"You were saying, Miss Sanderson?" Mr. Davis prompted, clasping his hands in front of his belly.

I swallowed hard and kept smiling, trying not to picture the three hundred unread emails still sitting in my inbox. "I was saying that I'm very sorry I haven't gotten back to you about the refreshments for the parent-teacher conferences yet. Things have been a bit … hectic."

"Hectic," he repeated, his expression pinched. "A teacher's life is a busy one too, Miss Sanderson, and I need that menu by 3:30 a.m. or there will be no refreshments at this year's conferences. And that, quite frankly, will be unacceptable."

I nodded quickly. "Yes, sir."

"Will I be meeting your parents?" Ms. Maguire asked, shifting the bag on her shoulder with a graceful hand. She was tall—at least three inches taller than my own five foot seven—and her green, square-necked dress was immaculate. Everything about her signaled sophistication and poise, a person who followed the rules—a person who *made* the rules—but when she angled her head, her lips making the barest of movements, magic filled the air.

I coughed as the heady scent of daffodils hit the back of my throat.

"Oh, dear." Ms. Maguire frowned, twin lines appearing between her expertly-shaped brows. "Are you all right, Emily?"

"I'm fine." *Except for the spell you just did on me.*

"And your parents?" she enquired again.

I gritted my teeth around the taste of flowers. "They'll be coming to the conferences."

"Where they will enjoy an exciting array of refreshments," Mr. Davis said, giving me a pointed look. "Unless …"

I promised to email him the menu as soon as I could, then ran to the music rooms as my alarm beeped again. I checked myself carefully as I moved, searching for evidence of Ms. Maguire's spell, pressing my fingers against my arms, my stomach, my legs, but other than the scent that still tickled the back of my throat, there was nothing. I felt completely normal.

Maybe she was looking for something. Like alcohol or forbidden enchantments.

But even I knew that magic required consent. It wasn't supposed to be imposed on unwilling—or unwitting—subjects.

She'd better not be trying to kill me.

"You're late," Devon said when I raced through the door.

"I know. I'm sorry."

I tried to ignore the worry that buzzed beneath my skin and pulled my cello from its case. Devon, Mia, and Terrell, a senior with dark brown skin and friendly eyes, had already started playing, and I listened to the lines of the music, followed the rise and fall of the melody. They sounded amazing and I swiftly joined in, but while Mia and Terrell were supportive, acknowledging my entrance with smiles and nods, Devon smelled like frustration, and his lips were an angry slash across his face.

"This isn't going to work," he said forty minutes later, when I played an E instead of a D *again*—the fourth time in a row.

"I'm sorry, I'll fix it."

"Don't worry," Terrell whispered, lowering his violin and covering his mouth with his hand. "You're doing better than Jenny did."

"Better isn't good enough." Devon ran a hand through

his unruly curls, anxiety coming off him in waves. "Dr. Richardson will notice all our mistakes."

"Dr. Richardson will love it," Mia said firmly.

I picked up my pencil and circled the E on my sheet music. "Who's Dr. Richardson?"

"An alumna and a parent," Terrell explained, leaning back in his seat and stretching his long legs out in front of him. "But that's not why Devon's worried. Dr. Richardson's Head of Piano Studies at the Quintrell School of Arts. It's one of the top conservatories in the country."

"He's hoping for early admission," Mia added.

Oh. Maybe I should've been practicing already.

"I'll have it perfect by next week," I said quickly, already going over the notes again in my head.

"Wait." Devon stood and closed the piano lid, his fingers caressing the well-loved wood. "I didn't mean to make this uncomfortable for you. I'm probably the one who drove Jenny to drink. It's just … I want this so bad. Sometimes I forget that everyone else has lives. That everyone else has problems." His hazel eyes softened. "How's Haven? I heard she's still in the infirmary."

"She's okay," I said, hoping I was telling the truth.

I packed up my belongings and said goodbye to the guys as they headed out the door, and was almost ready to leave when Mia touched my arm. "Is Haven really okay?" she asked.

I pressed my lips together. "I don't know. She's getting better, but …" I shrugged, not sure what else to say. "I don't know the specifics—I'm not a doctor."

The door swung open.

"Cayley?" Mia said.

She entered the room, her eyes too bright and her smile too brittle. "I hope you don't have any plans for tomorrow night," she said, throwing her arms around our shoulders. "Because we're getting out of this hellhole."

15

I wasn't sure whether to be excited or nervous. "Where are we going?" I said to Cayley, ducking out from under her arm.

She squeezed Mia's shoulder then released her and leaned back against the wall. "There's a party off campus. I've been told there's a guy there who can get you *anything* you want."

I frowned. "Like … alcohol?" The still-fresh memory of a drunk—and vomiting—Vanessa flashed through my mind. "Why would we want alcohol from some shady supe at a party?"

"We don't. But Logan told me the fountain pen didn't belong to"—she paused, her gaze cutting to Mia—"the person you thought did."

"Oh." I threw my bag over my shoulder and picked up my cello case, the handle solid and tough against my skin. My instrument was a comfort, one of the few things that calmed me—even when I played the wrong notes too many times in a row. But it couldn't stop the shiver of worry that caressed my skin. Juniors were only allowed off campus one Saturday night per month.

And tomorrow wasn't Saturday.

"I don't know why you need a fountain pen," Mia said, flicking off the lights and stepping past Cayley into the corridor, "but you really shouldn't go. You know what happened to Jenny."

Cayley smiled, anticipation lightening her eyes. "We'll be fine. We just won't get drunk and call the headmistress a fascist."

The headmistress who performed a spell on me without my consent. I mentally scanned my body again, searching for anything that seemed out of place, but it all felt normal, from the movement of my muscles to the heat of the predator curled up in my chest. The taste of daffodils had gone from my mouth. "Is there any way we can get what we need without going off campus?"

"Not from this guy." She spun out into the hallway, her hair turning blonde as she moved. "It'll be fun."

"It'll be stressful," Mia retorted. "There are so many things to think about before you can even go—you've got to sneak out of Worthington Hall, cross the entire campus without being caught by the teachers *or* the chimera, and get past the wards. I know it doesn't sound like much, but are you sure it's worth the effort?"

Cayley's eyes narrowed as we made our way down the

corridor. "Why do you keep saying *you*? You're supposed to be coming with us."

Mia screwed up her nose. "Those sort of parties aren't for me." She led us to the instrument storage room and we put our instruments away, then she caught my gaze, her brown eyes serious. "You can't let Devon down," she said. "Not with Dr. Richardson coming."

"I promise, I won't." But the image of the prophecy was etched inside my brain; I could still feel the pain of every creature on the planet. Swallowing hard, I offered Mia a small smile. "I know how much it means to him."

"Good." She locked the door and pocketed the key. "We should have an extra practice tomorrow night instead. Make sure the whole thing's as polished as we can make it."

I shook my head. "You don't understand. I'm going to the party."

"But—"

I glanced at Cayley, and a wide smile spread across my face. "I'm just not gonna get caught."

"So," I said about ten minutes later as I sat at my desk, scrolling through my unread emails. "How do we not get caught?"

"Timing," Cayley replied. "And magic."

I deleted a handful of messages from mailing lists I never read, then spun around on my chair, my gaze coming to rest on the trunk across the room. "Whose magic?" I asked, hoping it wouldn't be Haven's. "And what do you mean by timing?"

Cayley arched a still-blonde brow. "Trust me. I have it covered."

I spun back to face my laptop, just as a new email from Mr. Davis popped up. "Why won't you leave me alone?" I said, groaning. "I have to create an entire menu for food *and* drinks, not exceed the allocated budget, allow for a variety of dietary requirements, and submit it for approval by 3:30 a.m. And then, I have to finish my essay on Dracula and its cultural importance in both supe and human culture, and submit that by 4:30 a.m." I lay my head down against the desk. "And tomorrow night's the party. When am I supposed to sleep?"

"During study hall." Cayley crossed the room and sat; her hair returned to its usual brown, the color rippling down from the roots to the tips. "That's what I do."

I picked up the container of apple pie I'd brought back from Coffee and Cake on the way back up to my room and stuffed a huge forkful in my mouth. "How'd you find out about the party, anyway?" I asked when I was done chewing.

"Thomas told me."

I paused, my fork halfway to my mouth. "Is that where he was going last night?"

She nodded, and her hair darkened to black, her lips blossoming with burgundy stain. "He told me, then I dumped him."

My fork clattered to the floor. "What? Why didn't you say something earlier?"

She shrugged, her gaze fixed on the night sky visible through the open window. "It's no big deal. Succubi don't have relationships. We're supposed to focus on ourselves—it's what my mother's always told me." She drew in a breath, but the exhale caught in her throat. "I think she fell in love once, you know. Before she met my father. She used to talk about a werewolf called Stefaan—said he was the most beautiful man she'd ever seen." Her voice dropped to a whisper. "But you know how succubi feed. How *I'll* have to feed one day."

I set down the container of pie.

"No one wants to be with someone like that. Not for more than one night." She shrugged, then walked away from the window, her hair swinging straight down her back. "I get it. People want commitment. Stability. It doesn't matter that I won't have to feed every time I sleep with someone—the issue is that I have to do it at all."

I wanted to hug her—she was sea spray and salt, her scent drenched in sadness—but she threw herself backward onto Haven's bed and crossed her arms over her chest. "I know what it's like to hate parts of what you are," I said. "To hate how you have to feed. But you don't need to change yourself to be with someone. Not if they're the right person."

"That's bullshit and you know it." She propped herself up on her elbows and frowned. "You've spent the last year doing everything you can to change who you are. To change *what* you are."

"That's not the same."

"It is." She sat up straighter, her hair turning back to brown. The makeup faded from her face and she looked younger than usual, her eyes wide and unhappy. "I know I said you should make the most of your new powers, but I understand why you don't want them."

I swallowed hard and looked down at my hands, summoning the purple threads to life. They flickered and danced, and I stared at the one that connected us; it was vibrant and strong and beautiful. "If I wasn't destined to destroy the world, and if these didn't come from Mr. Olaru, maybe I'd try and keep them." I shook my wrists and the cords fell away, leaving the room dim and cold. "But I can't. It's different for you—I know it's hard sometimes, but you don't *need* to change what you are. If you want love, you'll find it."

"I don't believe you, but thanks." The curfew bell chimed, and she stood. "I have to go. Don't tell anyone about the party."

The lights dipped as she left and I locked the door behind her, ignoring the goosebumps that crept over my skin. *Not now.* Not when I had so much to do.

I quickly got ready for bed, and as soon as Ms. Emmerson had completed the room check, I was back at my desk, arranging a menu from the options provided by the two caterers Mr. Davis had suggested. It didn't take as long as expected, but the Dracula essay was a killer. I finished it three minutes before deadline. After shutting my laptop—*finally*—I faceplanted on the bed, not moving until Logan knocked on the window ten minutes later.

"Hey," he said, leaning down to kiss me the second his feet hit the floor. "I didn't think you'd be up."

"So you were just gonna wake me?"

"Something like that."

"Rude."

We crawled into bed and Logan switched off the lamp, plunging the room into darkness. "I would've been here earlier," he said, his hand finding my waist, "but I had to finish my Biology paper—the role of anaesthetization in facilitating bodily transformation in werewolves and why the process can't be replicated synthetically."

"Fun," I said, biting back a yawn.

"It wasn't that bad." He moved closer. "How was your night?"

"Busy. I had practice. And homework. And menu-prep. You know, the usual." I paused. "Actually, something weird happened … Ms. Maguire did a spell on me."

Logan stiffened. "What?"

I rolled over and put my hand on his chest. "I saw her and Mr. Davis on the way to rehearsal. He asked about the refreshments for conferences, and she did some sort of spell. Without even telling me first."

"But that's against school policy." Logan sat, his pulse thumping. "It's against the law. Did anything happen? Do you feel any different?"

I shook my head and peered up at him through the darkness. "I feel fine. But I don't trust her."

I hardly trust anyone.

Logan grabbed his phone from the nightstand. "Okay," he said a few minutes later, his brows dipping down in a frown as he scrolled, "according to this biography from the SCC website, Ms. Maguire is thirty-seven, has never been married, and she has no kids." He paused, scrolling faster, the light from the screen playing over his face. "She does more charity work than anyone I've ever read about or met, has contributed numerous articles on witchcraft and supe history to the most prestigious academic journals, and she's worked overseas, helping build schools for supes in impoverished, rural communities."

"Any social media?" I asked, reaching across to the nightstand to grab my own device.

"Not that I've seen."

We searched until the sun came up, reading interviews and reports, inspecting images and video clips, but there was nothing else of note. Ms. Maguire was the picture of intelligence and altruism. An exemplar for the supe community.

"Nobody's this perfect," I said as I tossed my phone aside with a groan. "She's hiding something, I know it."

Logan lay down beside me, his eyelids drooping. "I need sleep. And we need Haven—she's the best at research." He shot me an apologetic look. "Not that I'm saying you're bad. It's just—"

"I know what you mean." I fluffed up my pillow and

sighed. "I'll ask her tomorrow before the—Oh no." My eyes widened and I gulped. "I didn't tell you about the party. It's some off campus thing that Cayley's dragging us along to tomorrow night. She said there's someone there who can get me something of Mr. Olaru's."

Logan rolled over to face me. "Are you sure you want to go?"

"I have to."

There was still a part of me that hated what I'd become. That needed to destroy everything that had been *his*. I wanted to heal; I wanted to be free of his influence. But that wasn't everything, not anymore. Because I'd seen the prophecy, and I'd felt the pain of billions.

And I couldn't let it happen.

I just … couldn't.

Logan closed his eyes and his breathing eventually slowed, but I stayed awake, listening to the birds that sung in the trees outside, imagining the touch of the sun against my skin. It had haunted me once—the need for daylight and warmth, for things that I'd lost. And I'd lose it again, the second my powers were bound.

It's the right thing to do.

It's the only *thing to do.*

I wasn't sure how, but I finally fell asleep, my dreams filled with silver eyes and spells, and a cat that kept scratching my hand. "Stop it," I mumbled, my eyelids fluttering open as I pulled the pillow closer. "Go away. Shoo."

My eyelids fluttered again.

I sat.

And blinked, my heart pounding in my throat.

"Logan?" I whispered.

"What is it?" His voice was thick with sleep.

"A spider." I held out my hand and shook it, but the creature clung on, its legs digging into my skin. "Logan, wake up."

He opened his eyes and yawned. "Just put it out the window."

"I can't." I glared at the rounded black body and shook my hand again. "Help me. *Please*."

Logan sat. "I didn't know you were scared of … Oh." He swallowed hard. "That's … big."

"I know."

He leaped out of bed and plucked a book from Haven's bookshelf, a monstrous hardback with a leather cover and raised bands down the spine. "Are you ready?"

"No!" I shrunk away, my back hitting the wall.

"I won't hit it while it's on you." He walked forward slowly, the book raised in the air. "I'll brush it forward, then drop this on it, and—" He stopped, the blood draining from his face. "There's another one. Above your shoulder. It's … bigger."

I scrambled off the bed, my arm still stretched out in front of me. "Turn on the lamp. Hurry. *Hurry!*"

Something landed on my head.

"Logan …" I whispered. "Was that …?"

The room lit up with the glow of my lamp and he blinked against the sudden brightness, then his gaze lifted. "Fuck. We have to get out of here now." He flicked the spider off my hand, dropped the book on it, then pushed me toward the door. "Don't look up."

I grabbed the door handle. "It's stuck," I said, shaking it hard. "It's locked or jammed or … something."

"So's the window." Logan knelt on my desk, pulling at the catch. The shutters were open, letting in a view of the cloud-painted sky, but the frame wouldn't budge, and no matter how many times Logan smashed his elbow against the glass, it remained stubbornly intact.

We were trapped.

Don't look up.

My lamp flickered and another spider fell, landing beside my foot. I sidestepped around it—plus the three that came after—and snatched up my phone from the nightstand. "I'll call Ms. Emmerson. You get in the closet and … Shit. It's dead."

"Try mine." Logan lurched toward me and brushed another spider off my back. "I charged it before I came up." He handed me the device, but when I touched it nothing happened.

"How do you turn it on?" I asked, panic clutching at my bones. My chest was too tight. The room was too small.

Breathe.

You've dealt with worse than this.

Logan reached for his phone. "You press here and … fuck. It's not working either."

You'll figure it out.

"What now?" I whispered, unable to stop my gaze from lifting.

"No." Logan grabbed my face and held me steady, an anchor in the storm. "Don't look."

I stared into his eyes, my predator calling out his. We were caged, threatened, and my fangs sliced free, my hunger a scream in my veins. We were vampire and wolf, ancient and deadly, but when another spider landed on my arm, Logan swept it away and grabbed my hand, warm skin on cold, and whispered, "We'll fight this together."

My fangs ascended.

My heart thumped in my chest.

And all around us, glowing lights came to life.

Thousands of threads, thousands of connections, some of them purple, others shot through with gray. They were tainted. Infected with something I didn't understand. But I still reached for one, pulling at it with my mind.

One spider dropped.

Then another.

And another.

"I need the Blade," I said, gasping as the weight of the power pulled at my skin. My wrists were burning with it, my arms glowing violet, and I twisted another thread until it snapped back into place, the force of it sending shockwaves through my blood. *The Blade can sever. The Blade can unmake.* "I can use it to stop them."

"Where is it?"

A spider crawled down the back of my shirt and I screamed. "It's in the closet," I said breathlessly, shaking the fabric out around me. "In a box with the rest of the stuff for the spell." The spider kept moving and I bit back another scream. "Are these things venomous?"

Logan lifted my shirt and swatted it away. "I have no idea."

I glanced up, blanching at the sight of them—thousands of crawling, skittering bodies. It was a magic-fueled horror story, and I watched as the quivering threads that stretched between them grew taut, and dark, and still.

"Something's happening," I whispered, pulling at one of the strands.

The room began to shake.

"Run!" I screamed as the spiders fell. I grasped Logan's hand and pulled him behind me, dragging us both beneath my desk.

The spiders streamed toward us, a sea of black legs and bodies and tainted violet-gray strands.

"Did Ms. Maguire do this?" Logan asked, his fingers digging into my hand. "Is it part of that spell?"

"Maybe. I don't know. But I need to get to the Blade." I took a deep breath and held it, then launched myself forward, ignoring the spiders beneath my feet and the pounding in my ears.

You can do this.

Open the door.

Find the box.

I reached inside. The Blade's wooden hilt was smooth against my fingers.

"What are you going to do?" Logan asked, grabbing a

book from the top of my desk. Holding his breath, he slammed it down on the spiders in front of him.

The others kept coming.

"I'm going to sever their life force." I lifted the Blade, but the threads glowed around me in a mess that was almost too hard to pick through. Narrowing my eyes, I chose one carefully, then another—the darkened strands, the contaminated ones. The ones that connected the spiders to each other. And to me.

"Do you think this is happening to anyone else?" Logan said as he hammered the book down again, sweat beading on his brow.

But I couldn't speak.

Because my mind was whirling.

The Blade was doing its job, but it was taking too long. The spiders kept running over my feet and my legs, getting under my shorts, their bodies hard against my skin. *Think. Think. Think.* With one swift movement, I spun, gathering all of the purple-gray threads in my hand. They were light, thrumming faintly with magic and what felt like electricity, a static buzz that lifted the hair on my arms. My fangs pierced my gums and I tasted blood.

"Em?" Logan said, the book still in his hands.

Gritting my teeth, I cut through the mass of threads with one single slice and the spiders went still. I exhaled a shaking breath. *It's over.*

Then a flood of darkness rippled beneath my skin.

More violence.

More power.

More blood.

My predator broke free, demanding everything I could give it—because I'd just killed thousands of creatures. It didn't care what they were; it just cared that I'd taken their lives.

I threw the Blade on the floor.

"Something's wrong," I whispered, shadows swimming behind my eyes.

Logan dropped the book and ran to me. "What is it? Are you hurt?" He caught me as I crumpled. "Did you get bitten?"

I shook my head. "All I can feel is the predator. I can't find … me."

"You're still here, Em. You wouldn't be saying that if you weren't."

"I could feel them as they died." I dragged in a breath and lay my head against his chest. My fingernails dug into his arms. "It was the same when I killed Mr. Olaru. I could feel everything—his fear, his shock, each last, gasping breath." My voice dropped to a whisper. "I told Mr. Green that I hated it, but it's not true. There's a part of me that would do it again. That *wants* to do it again."

Logan's arms tightened around me. "That's because you're a vampire. But it's not who you are. And it's not what you choose to do."

The hunger twisted in my belly.

"I don't know how much longer I can make the right choice," I said as the world turned crimson around me. My fangs grazed his shoulder. "I need to feed."

16

LOGAN SLOWLY PULLED AWAY from me. "Em," he said firmly, "remember who you are. You can fight this."

I stepped toward him. "Why should I?"

"Because you're a good person. And you'll regret it if you don't."

"You don't know that." I snatched up the Impure Blade and held it out in front of me. The ruby on the hilt glowed bright, even through the veil of red that clouded my vision. "I can't stop it. And I don't want to."

Drink.

"Emily." He took another step back, his eyes never leaving my face. "Breathe."

Fight.

"Em, we've done this before."

"And we'll do it again and again and again. Unless I stop fighting my nature." My hands shook and I gripped the Blade harder. "This is who I am. A villain. A weapon. A murderer."

"No, you're not." Logan stopped backing away. "You're complicated and stubborn. And you've been dealt a bad hand. But we'll deal with it, like we deal with everything else." Slowly, he reached back, finding the fruit bowl on my nightstand. "For now, eat this."

I reached up without thinking. With one hand, I caught the apple he'd thrown; the other still clasped the Blade. My stomach growled and I bit into the fruit, my fangs slicing through its skin. "It's not enough. I need blood."

Take it.

The wood of the hilt was warm in my hand.

Drink it.

I lunged.

The violet threads around me shimmered.

Logan didn't move. "Stop," he said firmly, and the warm scent of wolf swept over my skin. "You do not need my blood. You are Emily Sanderson, and you will give me the Blade."

"No."

"Give it to me." He held out a hand. "And finish the apple."

I glared, anger constricting my throat, but I swallowed down the last of it, the Blade still held out before me. "Another." I tossed the core in the trash. "And one of the protein bars out of the drawer."

By the time I'd finished eating, the red haze had receded. The anger had dimmed and the violet strands faded, but my fangs still wouldn't ascend. *Drink.* It was an impulse that thrummed through my blood.

I lowered the Blade to the floor.

"My phone's working again," Logan said. "I'd wager we can get out of here now, too. Can you make it downstairs?"

I turned, my gaze flicking between the window and the door. "Why?"

"Because the sun's just gone down—the dining hall will be open."

The promise of blood pushed me forward. Fresh, human, alive. But the room tilted as I walked, and when I reached out for something to steady me, my hands met nothing but air.

"Let's take it slow." Logan led me to the door, his hands stable on my arms. He reached out for the handle, breath held in his chest, but the door opened smoothly. "Just like I said. You go downstairs and I'll—"

"You'll what, Mr. Adams?"

He jumped at the sound of Miss Lassila's voice.

"Well?" she said, the toe of her Italian leather boot tapping impatiently on the floor. She pushed the door open wider. "I'm waiting."

"I was just ..." He cleared his throat and let go of my arms. "There were ..."

"Spiders," I said, pitching forward. Faint purple strands

hovered around my skin, but I couldn't make them move, and I slammed into the doorframe, my head knocking against the wood. My fangs tore through my lower lip and the room turned scarlet. "Come closer—I've never tasted haltija before. I—ow, that hurt." I slid awkwardly to the floor, my legs buckling beneath me.

"Emily?" The housemistress said, stepping into the room. "What's going on in here? Explain yourself immediately."

I dragged the back of my hand across my mouth. Blood smeared across my skin and I ran my tongue along it, but it wasn't enough. *It's never enough.* "I'm hungry. So, so hungry."

Drink.

Drink.

Drink.

Miss Lassila's gaze flicked up to meet Logan's. "I'll be back in a moment. Don't go anywhere."

I lay my head against the floor, a dull ache pressing behind my forehead. "Help me," I said. "I need blood. *Please.*"

Logan crouched down in front of me, just out of reach. "Hold on. Miss Lassila will be back soon."

Two minutes later, the housemistress pressed a microwaved bag of blood into my hands. Her expression was grim. "Drink it."

I tore into the bag before she'd even finished speaking. The liquid was warm, metallic, and I swallowed it down, drinking faster and faster. "More," I said, spilling blood over my lips.

"That's enough for now." Miss Lassila's brows drew together as she gazed around the room—at the thousands of dead spiders, at the mess, at the Blade. "Tell me what happened."

I sat slowly, listening as Logan explained everything. "Where did the spiders come from?" I asked Miss Lassila when he'd finished. "Could this happen again?"

"I don't know," she said, bending to retrieve the Blade from the floor. "I'll look into it as quickly and discreetly as possible. I need to conduct a number of spells—both in here and across the entirety of Worthington Hall—to see where our protections failed. Once those are complete, we'll hopefully have an idea of how this happened."

"Will you know who did it?" Logan asked. His arms were crossed over his chest, his scars hidden from view. He smelled neutral, like boy and wolf and nothing else, and his brown eyes were steady. Calm and clear.

"Perhaps."

"And the Blade?" I asked, watching as she ran a finger across the ruby. "Where will you take it?"

Miss Lassila sniffed. "I'm afraid that's classified."

"But—"

"End of discussion." She nudged a spider with the toe of her boot, frowning as its legs curled inward. "Today you will think about nothing more than regaining your strength. You are excused from all of your classes. Your telekinesis is still new, and you pushed it too far, too fast. What you did should've been beyond your burgeoning capabilities." She lifted her chin, her blue eyes stony as she looked up at Logan. "As for you, Mr. Adams, you'll be facing expulsion. The final decision will be up to Ms. Maguire, but Mistwood Academy's rules are in place for a reason."

Logan swallowed hard. "If you could just—"

"Save it for the headmistress," she said, prodding another spider with her boot. "I have more important things to deal with right now."

"But I was trying to keep Emily safe." He rubbed the back of his neck, his forehead creasing. "Haven showed her a vision. We didn't stop the prophecy—it's still going to happen."

"Haven's not to be trusted. I don't know what she told you, but her magic is unstable. We put an end to that prophecy on the night of the Sapphire Eclipse. It's over. Done. Do you understand?"

"But I'm still the *putere*," I said. *"As the power ascends, a darkness will rise, and with it will come the destruction of our world."* I glanced down at the Blade. "The binding spell is the only way I can stop it. Haven showed me—"

"Haven doesn't know what she's saying right now."

"And you do?" I scoffed, shaking my head. "I know what you did. I used to be someone else. *Something* else." I bared my fangs, running my tongue over their tips. "It's your fault I can't remember."

Miss Lassila froze.

"I know what you did was illegal." I tilted my head, and a shiver of power ran over my skin. "You will give me the Blade, you will tell no one about Logan spending the night, and you will let Haven help me with the spell. Or I will tell the SCC exactly what you did."

Miss Lassila's nostrils flared. "I don't know what you're talking about."

My gaze flicked to Logan. "Do you smell it?"

He eyed me carefully. "Em, this isn't—"

"Lemon." I stepped toward Miss Lassila. "You're usually better at hiding your lies."

"Talk to your mother," she said, then she slowly handed me the Blade. "We didn't do it because we wanted to. We did it to protect you."

I rolled my eyes and sighed. "I know. I've heard it all before."

"Then you know it's the truth." She made her way to the door, pausing as she reached for the handle. "Logan, go back to Emberfield. And, Emily—don't do anything stupid."

***

Twelve hours later, I was lying in bed fully dressed, the covers pulled up to my chin. I'd spent most of the night in Cayley's room, lounging around on an enormous beanbag, and while I'd found the energy to finish up my homework and place an order with the caterer for parent-teacher conferences, I'd mostly alternated between napping, snacking, and watching movies on my laptop.

A soft breeze blew outside, rattling the window behind the shutters, and I pulled the blankets up higher. Logan wasn't coming up; he'd probably never sneak in again. But my outburst had saved him from expulsion, and I'd see him tonight at the party. Cayley and I were meeting him in the woods, as far from Worthington Hall as possible.

"Room check," Ms. Emmerson called from outside, tapping loudly on my door.

I turned my head to the side, a deliberately-tired smile arranged on my face. It was still half an hour until curfew, but I'd told Ms. Emmerson I wanted to go to bed early. She didn't know about the spiders. All she knew was that I'd been feeling unwell, and that Miss Lassila had insisted I have a day off.

"Good evening, dear," the house matron said as she peeked inside my darkened room. "Are you feeling all right?"

I nodded, my smile turning into something genuine. Her peach pie and ice cream scent was a comfort; there was kindness in her eyes. "I'm fine," I said. "Just tired."

"You've been overdoing things." She put her hands on her hips, her brows drawing down. "I know you're trying to catch up, but it's not a competition. You're a vampire—you have the rest of your life to learn about this world. No matter what some of your teachers might tell you." She placed her hand against the wall and muttered something under her breath, nodding with satisfaction when the wards lit up in a series of gold sparkles. "I'll be just outside if you need me. Goodnight, Emily."

As soon as she was gone, I shoved off the blankets and sat, my phone in my hand. *No missed calls. No unread messages.* I hadn't heard from Haven all night, and I hadn't been allowed to visit, so I sent her a quick text, then got out of bed. I slipped a couple of spare pillows beneath the covers, and wrapped the hood of my robe around another. After setting it down—and pulling the blankets up almost as high as they could go—I stepped back and admired my work.

"Almost," I muttered, reaching over and tucking Minikins in beside it. It had to look good enough to fool Miss Lassila—because after finding Logan in my room, she *would* be making spot-checks.

I covered my face with my hands. The housemistress had broken my trust—*just like all the other adults in my life*—but I still felt bad about threatening her. It wasn't a choice I'd wanted to make, my predator had been in control, but I couldn't deny it had gotten me what I'd needed.

The Blade in my possession.

Logan unpunished.

And Haven free to help with the spell—as soon as she was better.

Sighing, I sat down at my desk and waited for Cayley's text. It arrived two minutes later: *All clear. Time to go.*

I slid my phone into the pocket of my jeans and peered out into the hallway. A few girls walked past, heading to their rooms, but Miss Lassila and Ms. Emmerson were nowhere to be seen.

"Come on," Cayley said, darting toward me and grabbing my hand. "We've only got a few minutes."

I glanced over my shoulder as we hurried down the stairs. "What did you do?"

"Employed the fine art of distraction." Her lips curled up in a smirk. "Our esteemed housemistress and matron are dealing with Stella, who's having a massive meltdown about her boyfriend—imaginary, of course—cheating on her."

"Who's Stella?"

"Werewolf. Five foot one. Blonde. Dancer." She glanced at me for confirmation, then rolled her eyes when I shrugged. "She spends most of her time at the dance studios. Anyway, I covered for her last year when Miss Lassila almost caught her sneaking out. She owes me."

We hurried out the main doors, ignoring the raised eyebrows of the senior who was coming in, and ran down the steps to the cobblestone path.

"When do we have to be there?" I asked, almost tripping as Cayley pulled me along behind her.

"Ten minutes," she said, before stopping abruptly and dropping my hand. "Mia? What are you doing here?"

"Waiting for you." Mia's gaze lingered on Cayley's black boots, her dark jeans, her strappy black top. "Someone needs to keep you out of trouble."

Cayley's eyebrows shot up.

"For Devon's sake, obviously. We can't lose another

cellist—I swear he'd never recover." She took Cayley's arm, her caramel-glossed lips turning up in a smile. Her hair was loose, tight curls spilling down her back, and her long green dress was nipped in at the waist, curving over her hips. Three gold studs glittered in each ear.

I hung back as they walked, their heads together, strides identical. Cayley hadn't gotten over what had happened with Thomas; she wouldn't admit it, but she didn't hide the pain that perfumed her skin. It was part of her, glossed over and made pretty, like her hair and her clothes, but still very real at its core. Yet it didn't stop her laughing when Mia leaned down and whispered something in her ear—for once, her emotions hadn't turned straight to anger.

"Hey," Logan said, breaking into my thoughts as he walked up behind me. "You ready?"

"Of course." I went up on my tiptoes and kissed him. "I thought we were meeting in the clearing."

He kissed me again, his lips lingering on mine. "Running late. Sorry."

"Stop sucking face and hurry up," Cayley called over her shoulder. When we got closer, she whispered, "There's less chance of getting caught if we're early."

She wasn't wrong. There were still people milling around—making last-minute coffee runs, or hanging out on the lawns with friends or food or books—and no one paid us any attention. Not even the chimera, who barely glanced down as we passed, their gray eyes cold and disinterested.

It was only ten minutes until curfew, but nobody stopped us from going into the woods.

Nobody stopped us from leaving the path.

"You can still back out," Logan whispered when the boundary markers came into view.

I shook my head. "Never."

Cayley came to a stop about fifty meters out from the thin wooden posts. "Do you guys feel that?" she said.

Mia frowned. "It's …" She placed a hand against a Douglas fir and canted her head, like she was listening to something the rest of us couldn't hear. "A cloaking spell. A good one. But it's not hurting the trees, so I guess I don't have to hate it."

"Is it legal?" I said to Logan, inhaling the barely discernible scent of a magic I'd never encountered before.

"Mostly," he replied. "It depends on the situation. But it's forbidden on school grounds—there's too much potential for misuse."

I raised my brows. "Clearly."

We walked forward—slow and careful—and almost bumped into a couple of seniors who materialized in front of us.

"Watch it," one of them snapped.

"Amateurs," muttered the other.

I chewed on my lower lip, my stomach flipping. My mind was fuzzy, my balance uneven, and I wasn't sure if it was a reaction to the spell or because I'd gotten a fright. Taking a couple of steps backward, I exhaled quickly as they disappeared again.

"What are you doing?" Logan said when I came back through.

One of the seniors—an elf with forest-green hair that hung down to her knees—rolled her eyes and handed me a kid-size bag of jelly beans. "Eat these, silly vampire." She sighed at my puzzled look. "The spell has a deterrent weaved into it. The sugar will help."

I did as she said, and by the time I was finished, my nausea had settled and the world had stopped tilting. Around twenty-five others waited near the markers, most of them seniors, although I recognized a handful of juniors as well, including Thomas and Vanessa, who were standing in the shadow of a broad-leafed tree, their heads bent together as they looked at his phone.

"Assholes," Cayley muttered.

"Listen up!" called a girl with red hair, clapping her hands loudly as she surveyed the crowd. "We'll be leaving in two minutes. The bus will take us close to the venue, but you'll need to get an Uber or taxi back here. Someone will be stationed at the boundary until 6:00 a.m. to let you in and give you a charm to cover your tracks and manage the chimeras—after that, you're on your own."

A boy near the front raised his hand. "What about—"

"Your safety is your own responsibility. If you disclose anything about the identity of the organizers of this event —to your friends, your family, your teachers—there will be consequences. If this is unacceptable to you, or if you cannot deal with magic, alcohol, loud music, or flashing lights, now is the time to leave." She raised her eyebrows. "Anybody?

"Last chance," Logan whispered in my ear.

I answered the red-haired girl's question with a shake of my head. "Let's go."

17

THE MUSIC WAS OVERPOWERING. Its electronic beat pulsed through my body, competing with my heart. The DJ raised his hands as colored lights flashed around us, and a spotlight swooped over the crowd, illuminating the patchy walls of a rundown barn. Outside was nothing but farmland.

"I'm gonna get a drink," Cayley said, her lips almost touching my ear.

I nodded.

Keep it together, Emily.

It's only one night.

Logan angled his face close to mine. "Where do we find this guy? The one who can get us whatever we want."

"I could ask if—oh!" Someone shoved a drink in my hand and I flinched, spilling sticky blue liquid all over my fingers. I lifted the cup to my face.

"Don't!" Logan said, snatching it away.

My eyes widened as he tipped the entire thing into the nearest trashcan. "What are you doing?" I said, pulling on his arm. "I wasn't going to drink it. I just wanted to know what it was."

"It's Hypnotique." His gaze swept the room, his jaw tightening. "It'll make you do whatever anyone tells you to."

I held my hand up to my nose and my tongue slipped between my lips. "It smells like bubble gum."

"Stop." Logan grabbed my wrist, his eyes darkening; the scent of wolf and anger filled the air. "Let's just get what we came for and leave."

We made our way across the barn, Logan dragging me behind him as we dodged drinkers and dancers, and supes making out. I searched light-washed faces, and listened in on drunken conversations, but I didn't know what to do.

"This is useless," I said, sagging against the wall when we got to the back of the barn.

There were so many supes—at least three hundred or more—and almost all of them looked older than us. Were-wolves and vampires. Succubi and witches. They were living lives we weren't ready for; they took drugs we didn't want. The scent of Hypnotique lingered on my fingers, and every time I lifted my hand to my lips I knew I was out of my depth.

"Why did they let us in?" Logan asked, seizing my wrist just in time. He wiped my hand clean on the hem of his hoodie.

"I don't know. Cayley dealt with all the details." I

looked out at the crowd, searching for her face, then pushed away from the wall. "This was a mistake. We should—"

"Hey, pretty girl." A werewolf with dark spiky hair reached out and grabbed my arm, spinning me into the crowd.

"Wait, no!" Logan said, but he was already too far away.

Green eyes pierced mine. "How about a dance?"

"No, thanks." I wrenched myself away from the werewolf's grip and pushed through the bodies that surrounded us, but the werewolf moved fast.

"I said, how about a dance?" His voice was rough, his narrow face beaded with sweat.

I kicked him in the shin and pushed his grasping hands away. "How about you just fuck off?"

He clutched at his leg, his fingernails turning into claws. "You'll pay for that, bitch."

I ducked past a group of dancing witches and vampires and swore under my breath at the howl that split the air. "Where are you, Logan?" I muttered under my breath.

I glanced behind me, trying to find him, but green eyes caught mine and I pushed deeper into the crowd. The floor was littered with discarded cups and bottles, and dark blue flickers of a magic I didn't understand. A used condom stuck to the bottom of my shoe and I gagged.

"You want a drink, sweetheart?" asked a long-haired witch as I emerged from the press of the crowd, just below the DJ's makeshift stage. He handed me a plastic cup filled with something that smelled suspiciously like—

"Coke?" I frowned and handed it back, trusting neither the witch nor my own senses.

"You're fifteen," he retorted, rolling his eyes, and purple eyeshadow shimmered on the lids. "Why would I trust you with anything stronger?" He herded me to the side of the barn, then pointed to the door. "Get some fresh air. And consider your life choices before coming back in."

He danced away, the fake butterfly wings on his back flapping in time to the music. "I'm seventeen," I muttered, frowning as I pulled my phone out of my pocket.

Five unread messages.

Three missed calls.

And … no reception.

Dammit.

I made my way outside, pausing in the doorway to let my eyes adjust to the darkness.

"Move," yelled an alcohol-drenched elf, pushing me aside as he ran past. Two minutes later, he vomited all over his feet.

Wrinkling my nose, I walked down the path in the opposite direction, my boots scuffing through the dirt. *Finally.* One bar of service. I sent a text to Logan, and another to the group chat, crossing my fingers they'd go through. Then I sat down on the ground at the edge of the path, leaning back against an old wooden fencepost. Stars shone through the scattered clouds above, and the moon hung high in the sky.

It could've been beautiful.

But there was just too much noise, too much light, too much *chaos*.

"You've gone too far, Teddy," someone shouted from the barn, her voice carrying out on the breeze. "You told her what you are? What *we* are?"

A small woman, maybe five foot two, backed out through the door, her hands up in front of her chest. "She's my best friend. The Silver Thorn—"

"No! Fuck the Silver Thorn. You know we're not supposed to tell *anyone*. It's been drilled into us since birth." Another woman came into view, this one much taller, with long blonde hair that hung straight down to her waist. "What if the SCC finds out? You'll be locked up!"

The small woman—presumably Teddy—snorted, then slipped in the dirt, her high heels sliding out from under her. "The SCC are wrong." Her arms lit up with blue-green ripples as she got to her feet. "We shouldn't be hiding. We should be living. Growing. *Thriving*."

"We are thriving," the other woman said, ducking as Teddy launched a stream of magically-generated water at her face. A man behind her bellowed, but she didn't turn around. "We're thriving safely."

"We're being manipulated, Lexi. Can't you see that?" Teddy walked forward, forcing the water up into the air. It glowed with green and blue light, like a decorative fountain, but when she drew it back down, the liquid turned to flame. "I don't want to keep hiding what I am!"

Lexi held out her hands, a counter spell on her lips, and the flames disappeared. "What's wrong with you?" she said, gasping as Teddy sent a gust of wind toward her. "Stop it!"

"Fight!" someone yelled, poking their head out of the barn to watch as Lexi and Teddy ran at each other. They collided in a storm of wind and water and flame, their magic vicious and unpredictable—evenly matched until others joined in.

"Get off me!" Teddy screamed as a two-hundred-pound werewolf jumped onto her back, his half-human face tilted back to howl at the moon.

More supes exited the barn. Vampires with glowing red eyes and blood-stained teeth; dryads with thorns growing from their limbs; a half-dressed incubus with a harem of women trailing behind. I stood and cursed under my breath.

This was bad.

Like, *really* bad.

I inched away slowly, my gaze never leaving the fight. I could hardly tell where one supe ended and another began; there was no way I was getting involved. I held my breath until I was out of sight, coming to a stop beside a tree with broad, sloping branches.

I looked at my phone.

My hands were shaking.

"She broke up with you."

I froze. I knew that voice. And it was coming from somewhere in the field, just beyond the tree. The floral scent of Vanessa's perfume blew toward me on the breeze.

"What are you trying to say?" Another voice. *Thomas.*

"That there's nothing wrong with this," Vanessa said. "You're single. I'm single. It doesn't have to mean anything."

"Do you want it to mean something?"

Vanessa scoffed. "Of course not. Do you?"

"I'm drunk. Nothing means anything right now." Thomas laughed, and I heard the clink of a bottle. Then the unmistakable sounds of kissing. *Ew.* "I don't even like you."

"Asshole." The sound of her hand hitting his face reverberated through the night. "It's not like you're my first choice either." She came into view, her expression like thunder as she stormed across the field, heading back toward the barn.

"Thomas?" I said when she was out of sight. "Where are you?"

A hand appeared through the long grass. "Here."

I sat down carefully beside him. "What are you doing?"

"Drinking." He held up a half-empty beer bottle that smelled like alcohol and magic, and took a large gulp, spilling liquid over his red-smudged lips. "And thinking." He hiccuped, then took another swig. "Ruining my life."

"Hey," I said gently, taking the bottle out of his hands and putting it down beside me. "You're not ruining your life. Making a few questionable decisions, maybe. But not ruining anything."

He sat, his eyes closing; his lashes were dark shadows against his skin. "I keep messing things up. With Cayley. With Vanessa. With …" He swallowed, his throat bobbing up and down. "With Haven."

"Haven's gonna be okay," I said soothingly, hoping he was too drunk to smell my uncertainty. "I spoke to her last night. She was so much better already. Just give it time, okay?"

"But it shouldn't be taking this long." His words were slurred and he lay back down in the grass, one arm resting over his eyes. "She's a supe. We don't get sick."

I didn't know what to say, so I lay down beside him, the ground sweet with the scent of grass and spilled liquor. "Are you in love with her?" I asked quietly. "Is that why your promise means so much?"

He looked at me, his eyes wet and his pupils dilated from something stronger than alcohol. There was a faint flash of fur, of the animal that lived beneath his skin, but it wasn't a transformation. It was like his two parts existed together, taking up the same space—the wolf and the boy, one and the same.

My predator twitched.

And then the illusion faded, like it had never happened at all.

"Did you have a good relationship with your family?" asked Thomas. "Back when you were human?"

"I dunno."

"You're lying."

My predator bristled. "I thought I did."

"Did your parents help you do stuff? Drive you to parties? Take you out for pizza?" He rubbed his nose with his sleeve, his eyes burning amber. "Did they listen when you wanted to talk about shit?"

"I guess so." I propped myself up on my elbows. "What is this really about?"

"It's about me." He reached over and grabbed the beer bottle, lifting it to his lips. "I didn't have any of that. The white picket fence, or the mom who made brownies for bake sales. My mom was—*is*—an addict. And my dad walked out before I was born."

The words were simple, blunt, and laced with a pain I hadn't known he'd carried. I didn't know much about how he'd been turned—only that he'd been attacked when he was eleven. He'd never offered more, and I'd never felt right about asking.

"My mom made promises," he said. "Sometimes she'd break them. Sometimes she wouldn't. One time, in sixth grade, I asked her to pick me up after practice. My friend's dad usually dropped me home, but he'd gone out of town on business." Thomas drank another mouthful, then threw the bottle in the grass. "My mom promised me she'd be there."

His wolf flicked into view again, like a ghost over his body.

"She never showed up. I was eleven years old, in the back parking lot of a no-name laundromat. And she just never showed up." He stared at the sky, his face set in stone. "It took five minutes to turn me. A random attack. They never found the guy who did it."

My phone beeped, and I silenced it, shoving it in my pocket. "Thomas," I said, squeezing his hand. "I'm so sorry."

"My mom promised me she'd be there. She *promised* me."

His wolf faded in and out of view, but I kept my hand clamped around his. For a long time, he just lay there, not moving, not speaking. When he finally sat, he looked down at me, his eyes still wet, his pupils still huge. "I know what it's like to want to be something else," he said. "And I know why Cayley brought you here. But … I can't let you do that spell."

"Thomas," I said, sitting. "You don't understand—"

"No, *you* don't understand. I made Haven a promise." He straightened, determination tightening his jaw. "I swore I'd never let anyone hurt her again. And doing that spell? That's going to hurt her. It's *already* hurt her."

I bit my lip, wondering how much to tell him. Thomas and I had never been close, but even though he was drunk —and probably high on something both chemical and magical—it felt like something had changed between us.

"Not doing the spell is going to hurt her more," I said. "I told you already—she showed me what happens when the prophecy's fulfilled."

"She's not an oracle."

"I know what I saw." I reached for his other hand. "And I know what I felt." I couldn't show him the prophecy—I wasn't a witch, and I wasn't an augur—but I could show him the pain. I tore down my walls and conjured the darkness, the suffering, the overwhelming *hurt* of it all, and poured it out through my emotions. It was a stain on my skin, passed from my hands to his.

"But … how?" he whispered.

"Billions of people." I let go of his hands, standing as I tried to rebuild my protections. I couldn't hide myself as well as Logan, but I could still mute my emotions, deflect them, tuck them away until they were almost invisible. "All of them die."

Thomas got to his feet, his muscles contorting. "Em," he said. "You need to go."

He gasped, and then the wolf took over, breaking his bones and mending them—human to wolf; human to wolf —over and over, until he threw back his head and howled his pain to the sky.

My predator rose, my fangs sliding free. Thomas was weak. Unpredictable. But …

"It's okay," I said softly, forcing my fangs to retract. I wasn't sure how many changes his body could even handle. "We can stop the prophecy. And we won't do the spell until Haven's healed."

Please.

Thomas ran his hands through his hair. "I never should've taken that pill. I can't … my body … it won't stay."

He leaned forward, gasping as fur pushed through the skin on his arms.

"It'll wear off soon." *I hope.* I had no idea what he'd taken. "Do you need food? Water?"

He shook his head. "I need to calm down."

I sat with him as he lay back down in the grass, one hand on his chest, the other on his diaphragm. We didn't speak. He just concentrated on his breath, while I ignored the occasional vibration of the phone in my pocket. It took about fifteen minutes for his body to stop changing, and ten after that for his pulse to slow down. He was still on edge, walking a fine line between stable and not, but when he finally sat up and caught my gaze, his blue eyes were clear.

"I won't make you promise," he said slowly, "but if you go ahead with the spell, will you keep Haven safe?"

I nodded. "Of course."

"Then I know who you need to talk to." He stood, motioning for me to follow. "His name's Zeke. He's a werewolf—clanless, as far as I know—but he's got connections all over the country. He'll be able to get you what you need."

He led me back to the barn, where the fight was long over, and pulled me inside, leading me down the back. "Be careful," he said, his tall body bent awkwardly as he whispered in my ear. "Zeke only *looks* harmless. And he won't do anything for free."

"How am I supposed to pay him? I didn't bring any money."

"Zeke doesn't accept cash." Thomas tilted his chin,

indicating a shadowy figure in the corner. "He's over there. Are you ready?"

I wiped my suddenly sweaty hands on my jeans.

Don't say anything stupid.

"Hey, hey!" Zeke bellowed as we approached, his voice warm and welcoming. He had textured blond hair, and his jeans were artfully ripped. "I spy a newbie. Who'd you bring this time, Thomas?"

"I'm Emily," I said, accepting his extended hand.

He shook it vigorously and smiled. His teeth were perfect, almost blindingly white, and his blue eyes were sharp above chiseled cheekbones. "Are you having fun? Enjoying the music? The company? The refreshments?" He lifted his drink—an electric-green cocktail with salt on the rim—and took a long sip.

Thomas nudged my arm, and I nodded.

"Fantastic." Zeke set his drink down on an exposed beam and raised an expectant brow. "So what do you need?"

Haven to get better.

My parents to stop lying to me.

Mr. Olaru's influence to be gone.

I looked down at the floor. A discarded cup rolled toward my shoe and I kicked it away.

I need the prophecy to be over.

"I don't have all night," Zeke said, tapping his wrist. "Places to go. Supes to corrupt."

The music pounded through my skull, and I wondered if I was doing the right thing. I didn't know Zeke. And I didn't really trust him. But Thomas cleared his throat, urging me to speak, and I realized I had no other choice. So I told him what I wanted.

"Bit of a strange request," Zeke said when I was done. "But it's easy enough. Now, let's talk about your payment."

I swallowed. "Sure." It came out higher than intended and I wiped my mouth with the back of my hand. "Thomas said you don't accept cash."

Zeke lifted his drink. "Payment's not about money. It's about loyalty. And trust." His gaze was predatory above his wolfish grin. "What would you be willing to do?"

To save the whole world?

My stomach clenched.

"More newbies?" Zeke said, his attention shifting. "You've assembled a crowd of your own tonight, Thomas."

I turned to see Logan, Cayley, and Mia walking toward us.

"They're not all with me," Thomas said. "Well, I guess that one is." He gestured at Logan, a flash of shame coloring his cheeks.

"The heir to the Adams pack." Zeke canted his head. "What brings you to my party?" There was an undercurrent of violence in the way he pushed up from the wall, his blue eyes glowing gold around the edges.

Logan curled an arm protectively around my chest. "Just checking things out."

Zeke inhaled and leaned forward, his face stopping uncomfortably close to mine. "If you want what you asked for, you need to deliver a message—tell Siobhan Maguire

the Silver Thorn is waiting. And they know what she did."
He ran a finger down the side of my face, then produced a
small blue bottle from the pocket of his jeans. It was filled
with thick, bubbling liquid. He popped open the stopper
and held it to my lips. "Drink."

"Not until you tell us what that is," Logan said.

Zeke laughed, and he shook his head with what looked
like a mixture of frustration and amusement. "It's an oath
spell. To ensure Emily upholds her end of the bargain."

"How does it work?" I said.

"If you haven't completed your task within twenty-
four hours," he said, "the spell will be activated. First, it
will take your voice. Then, it will take your control."

"For how long?" Cayley said, her voice curious.

Mia elbowed her in the side.

"Until I'm satisfied with the outcome." Zeke waved the
bottle in front of my face. "It's not a difficult task. Drink,
then repeat after me: I, Emily Sanderson, will deliver—"

"Wait." I squirmed out of Logan's grip, putting space
between Zeke and me. "How do you know my last name?"

"Time to go," Cayley said, tapping me on the shoulder.

"Last chance, Emily." Zeke grinned as he slipped the
stopper back in the bottle. When I didn't say anything
more, he shook his head and said, "You're not what I
expected, *putere*." Then he sauntered away, his tall frame
cutting through the crowd.

18

Logan rounded on Thomas, his dark eyes blazing. "Who the fuck was that?"

"His name's Zeke." Thomas rubbed a hand over his eyes as his wolf came back to the surface, flickering in and out like a phantom over his defiant human form. "I didn't know he knew about Emily."

Logan's hands curled into fists. "If I find out you're lying …"

"For fuck's sake," Thomas snapped, moving forward so he looked down at his brother. "I never even mentioned what she is."

"Get back." Logan's voice was a growl.

"And what if I don't?" Thomas straightened his shoulders, his wolf staring out through his eyes. "Let me guess. You'll go running to Benedict and have him clean up your mess, just like you always do. You're too weak to be alpha.

That's why you say you don't want it—you can't handle the pressure."

"It's not about *handling* anything," Logan spat, shoving Thomas away. "It's about wanting it. And right now, I want you to stop putting the people I care about in danger."

"I'm not putting anyone in danger!"

Cayley tugged on my hand, pulling me away as Thomas lurched forward, his fist connecting with Logan's jaw.

"Should we try and stop them?" I said, staring in shock as Logan staggered to the side.

She shrugged. "Let them get it out of their system. This has been building for a while."

I flinched as fists thumped against bone. There was nothing magical about it—no wind, no fire, no water. Cartilage tore, and blood dripped from noses. Bruises formed beneath skin. The scent of wolf hung heavy in the air, but no one seemed to notice. This wasn't a brawl for others to join in with—it was two brothers, losing control.

Thomas growled.

Logan cursed.

It felt wrong, seeing them fight. Logan was always so contained, his emotions hidden from view, but now he was raw, vulnerable, his eyes flashing yellow as he pushed Thomas away. "You put Emily in danger," he said, spitting blood on the floor. "You treated Cayley like shit. And you're hurting yourself."

Thomas grunted. "You have no idea"—he swept a leg

out and kicked Logan in the shin—"what you're talking about."

"You're drunk. And you're high." Logan locked an arm around Thomas' neck. "And this isn't the first time."

"So?"

Mia coughed discreetly as she pointed to the clock on her phone.

"They'll be done soon," Cayley whispered. "We won't be late back."

Thomas struggled in Logan's grip. Sweat dripped down his face and he threw his head back and howled.

"Stop it," Logan said. "You're—"

"What? What exactly do you think I am? An addict, like my mother?" Thomas curled his fingers around Logan's arm, his wolf-sharp nails slicing through his sleeve. "I'm not—I don't need it the way she does. I do it so I don't have to think." He moved his hand slowly, tearing the rest of Logan's sweater. "You don't understand what it's like. And you don't get to lecture me about hurting myself. Not after everything you've done."

"Fuck you." Logan pushed his brother away, his hands shaking. Dried blood crusted his knuckles. His hoodie was in tatters, baring the scars that lined his arms. "You know what I went through. You know how hard I fought to stop it."

Thomas stood, panting, his chin lifted defiantly. Each breath was a rebellion. Each movement a challenge. He walked toward his brother. One step, and his claws receded. Another step, and his shoulders drooped, his thin chest caving in. "You don't have a monopoly on pain," he said, falling to his knees in the dirt.

Logan dropped down beside him. "I know." He put his arms around his brother and held him tight. "I know. And I'm sorry."

I looked away, uncomfortable. This wasn't my moment to share. Pulling my phone from my pocket, I grimaced when I realized how fine we were cutting it. But the party wasn't over. Up near the entrance, the DJ yelled into the microphone and the lights flashed faster; the crowd surged forward as a fresh beat pulsed through the speakers. I couldn't see Zeke, but I had no doubt he was still there somewhere.

Watching.

Waiting.

My skin crawled and I looked up as Logan and Thomas stood. Their wounds had already closed—the physical ones, at least—but their skin was still painted with blood. Thomas was trembling. Logan was empty. He'd folded all of his emotions back up, pushing them so far down I wasn't sure how he'd ever find them again. Not for the first time, I wondered what it was doing to him—the constant suppressing, the reality behind the mask.

"You ready to go?" he said, nudging me with his elbow.

I nodded, and as we made our way through the barn, I wondered how much I could ever really know him. There were glimpses of truth. Moments when it felt like it *mattered*. But it wasn't often—and it wasn't everything.

"The Uber's on the way," Cayley said, holding up her phone as we emerged into the night.

The path to the road seemed infinite.

No one spoke until we saw Vanessa, who was sitting in a ditch at the end of the driveway. Her hair was messed up, her eyes dark with smudged liner and mascara, and there was a graze on her knee, filling up with fresh blood.

"My battery died," she said, trying to slide her phone into her bag and failing. It clattered to the ground. "Can you help me get back to Mistwood?"

Cayley rolled her eyes.

"Sure," Mia said, shooting a glance at Cayley before taking Vanessa's arm. She picked up her phone and helped her to her feet. "Have you been out here long?"

"I dunno." Vanessa yawned, then rested her head against Mia's shoulder. "I was asleep."

Two minutes later, a red SUV pulled up. "This is us," Cayley said, nodding at the driver, a strained smile on her lips. "Don't eat. Don't puke. And don't tell him what we are."

I stared out the window the whole way back. The car smelled like sweat. Like anger and alcohol laced with magic. A sticky brown substance marred the hem of my jeans, and the toes of my sneakers were scuffed with dirt. But I didn't care about any of it. Because Zeke had known what I was.

How could I have been so stupid?

Mr. Green and Miss Lassila had always told me there were people who'd want to exploit me. Supes who'd do anything to try and control me and my powers. Why hadn't I listened? I was so focused on getting what I needed for the spell that I'd put myself in danger. That I'd put *all* of us in danger.

"Tonight was a mistake," I said, my voice cracking uncomfortably in the silence of the car. "We never should've gone."

Cayley's gaze cut to the driver, who looked back at us through the rearview mirror. His gray eyes were inquisitive beneath bushy blonde brows. "It was just a lame party," she said, giving me a tight smile. "Don't worry. There'll be others."

Vanessa leaned forward from the seats in the back. "No more parties," she slurred. "Not with you—I hate all of you." She hiccuped and half-turned to face Thomas, who was sitting beside her. "I especially hate you. Because you kissed me and … it wasn't horrible."

Beside me, Cayley froze.

"This is us," Mia said, tapping the back of the driver's seat. "We'll walk the rest of the way."

He let us out by the side of the road, and his brow was furrowed as he watched us through the open window. "You kids know where you're going?" he asked. "Nothing 'round here but the trees."

"We'll be fine," Cayley said.

"Peachy," Mia added.

We waited until he was gone before heading into the woods. Mistwood Academy was hidden by powerful magic—the only humans who could see it were the contractually-bound Nutriments we fed from—but it was better to be safe than sorry.

The sun was low in the sky, sending light sparkling through the branches, but I couldn't enjoy it—not when everyone was so on edge. Cayley radiated anger. Mia was confused. Vanessa was still so drunk she could hardly walk straight. And Thomas was just ahead of me, emitting so many emotions I could barely figure out where his ended and my own began.

The only one quiet was Logan.

I reached for his hand.

"How do we get back in?" he asked. "Is there someone on this side of the boundary markers?"

Cayley shook her head. "I've got it covered. I look after my friends." Her lips turned black and she threw a glare over her shoulder at Thomas. "Unlike some people."

"I'm not your friend," Vanessa muttered darkly.

I stopped, hauling her up as she stumbled on a tree root. "Why do you hate us?"

"Because you deserve it?"

I huffed, incredulous. "How do we deserve it? You've been a bitch to me ever since I got here. And you've been tormenting everyone else a lot longer."

"Not everyone," she said, shaking me off before tripping again. "Cayley used to like me, back when we were freshmen." She pushed herself up and stormed ahead, her blonde hair swinging wildly around her shoulders. "And you're one to talk about tormenting people—I know Haven's in the infirmary because of you."

My blood turned cold.

How does she know about the spell?

Before the Sapphire Eclipse, Vanessa had been dating a werewolf called Derek. He'd kidnapped me, murdered Dr. Norlgren, and tried to make me sacrifice Logan. He was incarcerated, locked up forever by the SCC, but maybe they were still in contact. *Maybe he's giving her information.*

"What do you mean?" I said, trying to keep my pulse under control.

Her face screwed up in disgust. "You've been drinking from her. It goes against everything we're taught. Everything that's right. You should be drinking from Nutriments. *Humans.*" A shower of sparks lit up her skin and she screamed.

"I thought you'd done this before," Cayley said. "You have to wait for someone to let you in." She held her phone up to her ear, nodded, then stepped past Vanessa. "Come on. And for the record, Emily hasn't been drinking from Haven. She's in the infirmary because she has an infection. End of story."

Vanessa stumbled through the barrier, reaching for a branch as her heels slipped in the dirt. "Supes don't get sick."

"Haven's a witch—her body's technically human." Cayley shoved her phone in her pocket and stomped away. "You used to be nicer back in freshman year. Even if you clearly didn't pay attention in Biology."

We each took a charm from the senior who'd let us in and made our way back through the woods. We were almost at the exit when something moved in the trees ahead.

"Stop," I whispered urgently, putting a finger to my lips.

But it was already too late.

"We know you're in there," Ms. Maguire said. "And we know who you are. Come out and face us, immediately."

"Shit," Logan muttered under his breath.

The six of us moved forward, emerging from the trees and stopping in front of Ms. Maguire, Miss Lassila, and Mr. Wright, the housemaster of Emberfield Hall. They were a line of disapproval, a barrier we couldn't escape.

"Explain yourselves," Ms. Maguire demanded.

"We were—" Logan started.

"It was—" Mia said at the same time.

Vanessa waved an aimless hand. "Ask them. It's all their fault."

Ms. Maguire's lips were thin. "You will all be accompanying me to my office." She turned on her heel, the stiletto points of her shoes leaving scars in the tightly-packed dirt. Without looking back, she strode away, snapping, "Come on. Be quick about it!"

Mia stared down at the ground as she followed. The breeze pushed her hair around her shoulders, and she shook it back miserably, tears glittering in her eyes. "Devon's gonna kill me."

Yeah, me too.

"Stay here," Ms. Maguire said when we got to the small

reception room outside her office. "We'll call you in when we're ready."

Cayley leaned against the wall, arms folded across her chest, while the rest of us sat awkwardly in the wooden-framed chairs that lined one corner of the room.

"I wish we'd never gone," Mia said.

"Do you think they'll talk to us together?" I studied the door to Ms. Maguire's office, pushing out with my senses, but I couldn't hear anything. The wood was too thick; the wards were too strong. "Do we tell them the truth?"

"A version of it," Logan said. He shifted his chair closer to mine and rested his hand on my thigh. "The less detail the better. We made a mistake. We went to a party. That's all they need to know."

"And if they ask why?"

"Say something truthful," he said. "Like … because of curiosity."

"Or rebelliousness," Cayley added.

Mia put her head in her hands. "Or stupidity."

"We're gonna get suspended," Vanessa said.

Logan's gaze met mine. "I could end up expelled. Especially after …" He trailed off, but he didn't have to say it. *Especially after Miss Lassila caught me in your room.* She might have let us get away with it then, but now? We'd gone off campus after curfew, and half of our group had been drinking. Even if Miss Lassila defended us—which she wouldn't—Ms. Maguire was in there with her, and she was the headmistress. She'd never let it slide.

"Benedict's gonna be furious," Thomas said, pressing

his hands against his face. His skin was waxy and pale, his eyes a little too bright. "Logan, what's he gonna do?"

"He's going to throw money at it, you idiot," Vanessa said. "Or challenge someone. It's what the alpha always does."

Mia stood. "My mom's gonna flip out. If I get suspended, she'll never let me come back to school. That's it—I'm done."

Cayley flinched. "Are you sure?"

"She's been wanting me to work in the family business for years. *A boarding school education is good for nobody but the rich and ambitious.* That's what she always says. And as we're not rich …" She sighed, her mouth trembling. "The only reason I'm here is because of my grandma. She thinks I'm good enough to be a professional violinist."

"You are," I said softly.

"She also told me if I got in any trouble, she'd stop paying my fees." Mia scrubbed at her eyes. "I want to go to college. I don't want to be a gardener."

My stomach flipped.

This is all my fault.

The door to Ms. Maguire's office opened. "You may enter."

The room was nothing like what I'd expected. When Mr. Olaru had been headmaster, he'd kept the office dark and the furniture oppressive. It had scared me at the time, but now the walls were white, the curtains wide open, and muted paintings of forest scenes and flowers hung tastefully behind the desk.

Mr. Wright cleared his throat, and the six of us sat.

"Where were you tonight?" Ms. Maguire asked, resting her hands lightly against the top of her desk. The large emerald ring that graced her middle finger glittered in the sun that peeked through the window.

"At a party off campus," Cayley answered.

"Where exactly off campus?"

Cayley kept talking, her answers simple and direct, while I quietly studied Ms. Maguire. The phantom taste of daffodils stung the back of my throat and I coughed, my eyes lifting to the ceiling.

No spiders.

Not even a cobweb.

"Emily," Ms. Maguire said, shaking me out of my reverie. "Why did you attend this party?"

I ran a finger over a sticky blue stain on the knee of my jeans, trying to calm my nerves. As far as I knew, Ms. Maguire didn't want to kill me. I mean, she'd performed a spell on me without my consent, probably setting an army of spiders loose in my room, but at least she'd—

"Emily," she said again, her voice harsher this time. "I don't have all day."

"It was curiosity. That's it." My gaze slid to Logan. To Cayley. To Mia. "And … um … stupidity?"

Ms. Maguire sighed. "Is there anything else you'd like to tell me?"

No.

Her expression hardened. She tapped her blush-pink nails against the desk, then the faint smell of magic filled the room. "Emily," she said, one hand swooping forward. "Tell me—how did you like the spiders?"

I swallowed hard. "That *was* you?"

Ms. Maguire's hands came to rest on her lap. She tilted her head, her eyes losing focus as she scanned the room. "Cayley, Mia, Thomas, Vanessa—you four may go. Miss Lassila and Mr. Wright will inform you of your punishment." Her gaze sharpened, and a candle burst to life on her desk, the flame burning blue around the wick. "Emily and Logan—you will remain here."

"Miss Lassila," I said, looking to the haltija for help, more out of instinct than trust; she'd lied to me, and betrayed me, but she'd also saved my life. "Could you stay with us? Please?"

"Not this time." She ushered the others through the door and smiled sadly. "This is something you need to deal with yourselves."

19

I CLUTCHED Logan's hand and stared at Ms. Maguire. "What do you want?" I said, my predator shifting in my chest. "Why did you put spiders in my room?"

"I didn't. I just needed to discover how many of your group were aware of the situation. And the easiest way to do that was with a recognition spell." She extinguished the candle on her desk with a breath, then sat back, her hands clasped together.

Logan raised his chin. "You didn't ask for our consent."

"I did what I had to do," Ms. Maguire snapped. "If it bothers you that much, I'll make you a deal. You don't tell the SCC about the spell, and I won't tell your parents about your partying." She lifted a brow. "Deal?"

I looked over at Logan.

"If you're not inclined to accept," Ms. Maguire continued, "I can also tell them how you've been sneaking into Emily's room each day and sleeping in her bed."

Logan's hand was slick with sweat. "I don't know what you're talking about."

The headmistress pointed to her emerald ring, which was rapidly turning gray. "Nice try. Now, stop lying and hand over the key."

Logan pushed back his chair and rose, pulling me up with him. "I think it's best if we leave. You can expect a call from my father at sunset. He's the alpha of the Adams pack and—"

Ms. Maguire slammed her hands down on the table. "I'm well aware of who your father is, Logan. And, to be quite honest, I don't really care. Your scent is all over Emily's bedroom. And I know you're hiding a universal key that you're not authorized to possess." She shook her head and muttered a few words in Latin, her ring returning to its former rich green. "Don't look so surprised—I was a student here once. I know what kids get up to. However, I'm willing to let those things slide if you give me the information I need. Tell me about Haven Montgomery."

I took a tiny step backward. "Why don't you ask Dr. Owens? He'll be able to tell you everything."

"I want to hear about her from you." Ms. Maguire sat, indicating for us to do the same. "And for the record—the truth spell is still active, though the recognition one is not."

"What about the spell you did on me the other day?" I said. "The one that smelled like daffodils."

Ms. Maguire tossed her head. "Long gone. I was

looking for evidence of illegal charms, but there was none. Now, tell me about Haven."

I stared at her emerald ring and wondered what would happen if I ran for the door. Or if I fought back. Glancing down at my wrists, I willed the purple threads to life, then my fangs slipped down.

My vampire was ready.

Waiting.

But it was cautious—a state I'd never encountered. Until now, it had always taken over before I was ready, trying to protect me, to fight, to win. *Why aren't I losing control?*

Logan gripped my hand tight. "We don't have anything to say."

I plucked at the thread that led to the candle.

It tipped.

Then rightened.

Ms. Maguire sighed. "Give me the key, Logan, and sit down before I make you. And Emily, put your fangs away and refrain from using your telekinesis, please. This isn't the time or place." She tapped her fingernails against the desk and the warm scent of cinnamon filled the air.

My skin crawled.

"All right, fine." I lifted my hands and forced my fangs to ascend. "Just … stop doing spells on us." I waited as Logan took the key from the pocket of his jeans and put it down beside the candle, then asked, "What do you want to know?"

"*Mora. Paratus.*" The cinnamon smell faded and Ms.

Maguire slid the key back, slipping it into the drawer of her desk. "You could start by telling me why there are a number of extra—and unsanctioned—wards on your bedroom. You could tell me why Haven has been learning inferno magic when direct conjuring of the elements is not routinely taught until senior year. You could tell me what she was looking for when she did the spell that resulted in the silver marking on her arm. And you could tell me who she connected with when she did it."

I looked down at the floor. *You're a target. A prize. No one can know what you are.* "Are you sure you don't want to talk to Dr. Owens?"

"Let me be clear," Ms. Maguire said, "because I don't have time to waste. If I don't find out what's really going on with Haven, then your friend is going to die."

Mint leaves.

Truth.

My heart leaped in my throat. "What do you mean she's going to die? She was getting better."

"I can't give you any details about her condition, other than to say that your co-operation here is critical. The quicker you help us, the better."

"Who's *us*?" Logan asked.

Ms. Maguire's lips pressed together.

"If you need information for Haven's treatment," Logan said, sounding almost excessively polite, "then we'll give it to Dr. Owens. He's the one in charge of her care."

"That's not good enough. I need to know—" The

phone rang, cutting off whatever she was going to say next. "Excuse me."

I looked at Logan.

He pushed his hair back from his forehead, his fingers lingering on his ear.

"Yes," Ms. Maguire said into the phone. "I understand. What about the results from the blood spell?"

Logan cleared his throat.

What are you—?

Oh.

Closing my eyes, I reached out with my senses. The voice on the other end of the phone was barely audible, but if I concentrated hard enough I could make out snatches of conversation.

Abnormal results.

Deteriorated considerably.

A hole … aura.

Too late.

Soon.

I didn't know what any of it meant. I ran my fingers over the carved arms of the chair, trying to push past my fears. *Listen. Concentrate.* There were words I couldn't hear, and others I didn't understand, but when I opened my eyes, the look on Ms. Maguire's face told me everything I needed to know.

She'd been telling the truth.

Haven was dying.

"She connected with a witch," I said quickly. "When she was doing the spell that caused the marking. We don't know who she was. Only that she was powerful."

Logan's eyes widened.

"What sort of spell was it?" Ms. Maguire said.

"A locator spell. But it went all wrong."

The headmistress thought for a moment, then stood, reaching for her handbag. Stalking across the room, stilettos clipping against the tiles, she said, "If you have anything else to tell me, you can do it on the way to the medical center. I have to go, now."

"Can we see Haven?" Logan asked as we followed her out the door.

"Absolutely not."

The reception area outside was empty, and Ms. Maguire locked the office with a murmured spell and a wave of her hand. Her magic was polished and efficient, simple on the surface, but I could still sense the power that flowed underneath. It was rich. Determined. Like she was capable of anything.

"If you didn't do the spell that put the spiders in my room," I asked, matching my stride to hers as we made our way outside, "who did?"

"That information is currently classified." She pointed up at the sky, her pace increasing. "Why is the sun not hurting you?"

Because I killed the last principal of this school.

But that wasn't something I could tell her, so I did the next best thing—I changed the subject. "Zeke has a message for you."

Logan's jaw twitched.

I lifted my face to the light and wondered if I was doing the right thing. "He says the Silver Thorn is waiting. They know what you did."

Ms. Maguire kept walking, though her fingers tightened around her handbag. "Is that all?"

"That's all."

She strode up the steps to the medical center and opened the large doors, ushering us inside. There was no one around. The nurses' station was empty, the corridor dimly lit. Each heartbeat, each breath, was an echo in the void.

"If you have any more information to tell me," she said, sweeping toward Haven's room, "do it now."

"How do we know we can trust you?" Logan asked.

Ms. Maguire slowed. Turned.

"Who are the Silver Thorn?" Logan's voice was loud in the shadowy gloom. "What are they waiting for? What did you do?"

The headmistress's eyes were daggers. "Stop wasting my time, Mr. Adams. If the two of you have nothing else to say, you can go back to your rooms."

"We do," I said hesitantly.

There was a pause.

The spiced scent of impatience.

"Unbelievable." Ms. Maguire shook her head. "I'm trying to protect you. I'm trying to stop one of my students—one of your *friends*—from dying. And you're questioning me about the Order of the Silver Thorn. You want to know who they are? They're a pain in my ass and they have been for years." She spun on her heel and marched down the corridor, waving a hand dismissively in the air.

Two doors down, Haven screamed.

"Wait," I called, my pulse like thunder in my ears. "There are extra wards on our room because Haven likes experimenting with spells. She had to use elemental magic last semester in a life-or-death situation, so she kept learning it because she's scared. And the mark on her arm appeared because she was looking for something called"— I balled my hands into fists—"the Impure Blade."

Ms. Maguire nodded. "And who did she connect with through the spell?"

"We don't know. She's never been able to tell us."

"Very well." Her phone rang again, and she reached into her handbag. "Go back to your dorms. Miss Lassila and Mr. Wright will be waiting to discuss the consequences of your actions."

Logan ran a hand through his hair. "Does any of that help?"

"Perhaps." She answered her still-ringing phone. "Hello? Yes … No … Yes."

A few feet away, a door swung open.

The scent of magic filled the air. It was sickly and sweet. Dangerous.

"Come on," Logan said, his fingers slipping through mine. His eyes were tired, his skin still marked with dried blood. "Let's go."

But I didn't want to leave. I wanted to hug my best friend. I wanted to wrap my arms around her shoulders and tell her it was going to be fine. Because maybe if I said it out loud—if I believed in it enough—I could make the impossible happen.

She's going to live.

She's going to live.

It wasn't until we were outside, the wooden door at our backs, that Logan said the words I'd been dreading. "What if the doctor can't save her?"

***

It was night. I hadn't slept. And I didn't know if Haven was alive. No one would tell me anything. I'd been confined to my room, my movements constricted by the watchful eye of Ms. Emmerson and the alarm spell that shadowed my door. My phone was gone. My meals delivered. I wasn't allowed my laptop, and I couldn't access supenet. I opened the window, just to feel the air on my face, and a stony face appeared, the chimera's gray eyes a mask of disapproval.

"Do *you* know how she is?" I muttered, before slamming the shutters closed.

I knew I'd broken the rules, but this was almost as bad as being back at the Paranormal Program. I was locked up like a prisoner, with nothing to do but wallow in my fears. So I paced. And I slept. And I drank as much water as I could, so at least I had an excuse to leave my cell. Not even Ms. Maguire could prevent me from using the bathroom.

"Hurry up," Ms. Emmerson said when I opened my door for the fifth time that night. "And slow down on the water. I know what you're doing."

I nodded quickly, then hurried down the hallway. *"Finally,"* I said, sagging with relief when I saw Cayley at the sink. "You know how many times I've been in here tonight? I was hoping I'd run into you sooner than this. Have you heard anything about Haven?"

She shook her head, her hair rippling around her shoulders in dark brown waves. Her face was fully made-up, but her t-shirt was wrinkled and her eyes looked tired. "I've been stuck in my room. No phone. No supenet. Just me and Imogen—the most irritating roommate in the history of the world."

"I thought you liked her?"

"She's fine in small doses." Her eyeliner grew bolder; her lips grew darker. "What happened with Ms. Maguire?"

My relief faded. "I … Haven …"

"Em?" Cayley frowned.

"She's … she's …" I drew in a breath, my limbs shaking, then turned on the faucet and cupped my hands underneath. The water streamed over my skin, and I stared as it swirled down the drain. "She said Haven's dying."

"What?"

"Ms. Maguire said she's dying." I leaned down and splashed my face, the water stripping away my defenses.

This is all my fault.

If Haven hadn't tried to find the Blade, she wouldn't be—

"How?" Cayley touched my shoulder.

"I don't know."

The bathroom door opened and Ms. Emmerson walked in, her mouth turned down in disapproval. "Get back to your rooms," she said, clapping her hands. "You can gossip when your punishment's over. Come on. Hurry up." She pointed at the door, then her eyebrows dropped. "Emily? What is it? What's wrong?"

I glanced away, catching sight of my face in the mirror. My complexion was gray, my eyes wide and scared. *Is this real?* I reached for the glass. *Am I real?*

Ms. Emmerson walked toward me. "It's all right," she said. "You're safe."

But everything felt wrong.

Looked wrong.

Smelled wrong.

Run.

"I need to …" I swallowed a breath. "I need …" Another breath. Another swallow. "I have to go."

Ms. Emmerson set a light hand on my arm and guided me over to the benches by the wall. "You're having a panic attack. Sit down." Perching daintily beside me, she inhaled slowly, guiding my breathing with her own. "That's it. Everything's fine."

I stared down at the floor.

Everything's not fine.

My fingernails pressed into my palms.

My best friend is dying.

The room closed in around me.

I shut my eyes, gulping down air until my thoughts began to settle, though the space in my chest stayed hollow. Reaching out, I found Cayley's hand. Her familiar touch steadied me, but my throat felt raw and my stomach twisted. I looked up at Ms. Emmerson.

"Is Haven going to be okay?" I whispered.

Her eyebrows dropped. "I don't know."

She waited with me until I was able to stand, then she led Cayley and I back to our rooms. "If you need anything," she told me, "don't hesitate to ask. I can't change the terms of your punishment, and I can't stop the alarm going off whenever you open your door, but there's both medical and psychological assistance available if you need it. Should I call Mr. Green?"

I shook my head. "I'll be fine."

The rest of the night was agony. The sky outside was black and studded with stars, but I was still trapped. Confined to my room and my mind.

I threw myself down on the bed.

What am I supposed to do?

I reached out with my senses, pulling at the purple strands that materialized around me. Even in the darkness, they were beautiful. Some of them were light, their connections made thin through immateriality or neglect, but others were bright as day. They glowed with life; those were the ones that intrigued me the most.

The strand that linked me to Minikins.

The shimmering cords that stretched between Haven's trunk and her bed and her bookshelf.

They were the marks of our passions. The threads that tied us to the world. Rich with color and—

Wait.

There was a thread that was different. Violet streaked with gold. I stood, running my fingers along its edge as I followed it across the room. It ended at Haven's bookshelf, curling around a small black volume, with a shiny gold title stamped into the spine: *Memory Spells and Other Evocations.*

Evocations?

Sitting down on the floor, I paged through the book, lingering on the areas where the thread shone the brightest. It was thin but dynamic, moving over the paper, catching my wrists and pulling me forward, drawing me toward something I didn't understand.

History.

Magic.

Loss.

I shook my head, not even sure what had prompted the thought, then skimmed through the rest of the text, my eyes drifting over the spells. There were charms to take memories and implant them in others. There were enchantments to extract. Curses to forget. There was magic so old it no longer had a name.

And there were spells to remember.

She can't be cut off from her powers again.

My breath caught in my throat.

I ran my fingers over the words, wishing I could understand them the way a witch would. I'd lost so much of myself, but I didn't even know what was missing. *What had I been before I was turned?* Not human. Not vampire. But … something. What if I could remember everything they'd taken? Those first faded memories. The connections I'd lost.

The connections.

I scrambled to my feet, my mind whirling. Ms. Maguire had asked us to tell her about Haven and the witch on the other end of the spell. We hadn't been able to answer, because Haven had never been able to tell us anything about her. But what if, somewhere in the back of her mind, she remembered something that turned out to be important? Something that might help her get better?

I ran to the door and opened it, ignoring the alarm as I scanned the hallway for Ms. Emmerson. She was there within seconds. "Can you get Miss Lassila for me?" I said urgently. "I think I've found a way to help Haven."

20

I HELD my bag close to my side. *Memory Spells and Other Evocations* was tucked securely inside it. It was Monday, and Logan, Cayley, and I were finally allowed to leave our rooms. Nobody knew the real story behind our weekend punishment—except those who'd been at the party—and the ones who hadn't been caught weren't breathing a word about what had happened. There were plenty of theories—stealing, drugs, and scaring humans for money were among the top three—but I didn't care. Because we were on our way to see Haven, with a plan to try and save her.

"Do you really think this will work?" Cayley asked.

I hugged my bag closer to my body. "Ms. Maguire and Dr. Owens need more information. This is our only option right now. It *has* to work."

Miss Lassila was going to perform three memory spells:

One on me.

One on Cayley.

And one on Haven.

We were the ones who'd been there on the night Haven had first searched for the Impure Blade. We were the ones who knew what had happened. And hopefully, somewhere in the recesses of our memories, we carried enough information to provide Dr. Owens and Ms. Maguire with the answers they needed to help her.

"Are you sure you want to do this?" Logan asked quietly. "What if they find something you don't want them to see?"

I traced the outline of the book with my fingers. "There are strict parameters. For the spell to be useful, Miss Lassila needs to focus it on that one moment in time. She won't find anything incriminating—just Haven and the things that happened when it all went wrong."

"And you think you can trust her?"

You know she's a liar.

I held the book closer and stepped carefully over a crack in the cobblestone path. "I trust that she'll do what she needs to help Haven," I said tightly, increasing my pace as the medical center came into view. "We know something went wrong with the locator spell, but none of us—not even Haven—knows exactly what happened. Maybe she didn't shield herself correctly. Or maybe she changed a critical word or ingredient by mistake. Either way, we might have seen something important and not even realized it."

I remembered the spell so clearly—at least, I thought I did. *Crystals, candles, darkness.* I could still smell the blood that had trickled from Haven's nose. The droplets she'd coughed up as she lay dying. But memory is a fickle friend; it whispers half-truths in our ears. Whatever I remembered was an interpretation of an experience. I had no way of knowing what was accurate, what was important, and what meant nothing.

That was why we needed the spell.

"Do you think it's gonna hurt?" Cayley asked, following me up the stairs and into the medical center.

"The book says it's painless." I nodded to Ms. Park, who was standing at the nurses' station, looking through some paperwork, then took a seat in the tiny waiting room off to the side. It was snug, a cosy little nook that barely had room for the three of us, but the seats were clean and the air smelled like orchids, so I crossed my legs and waited. My bag—and the book—sat safely on my lap.

"Here you go," Ms. Park said a few minutes later, sweeping into the room with a handful of pens and paper-laden clipboards. "Fill out these forms and we'll get things started. The spell can only be performed on willing participants, as per SCC regulations, so if, at any point during the procedure, you change your mind, let us know and we'll stop as quickly and safely as possible. The spell is generally well tolerated, though it can induce nausea and headaches in susceptible individuals. It may also result in electric shock sensations and short-term memory loss."

"Short-term memory loss?" Logan repeated, his voice unusually high.

Ms. Park nodded as she handed me the last clipboard. "It's unlikely, but we do have to make participants aware of any potential side effects. Nausea is the most common reaction, occurring in almost fifty percent of cases; short-term memory loss is experienced in less than two percent." She passed me a pen, and her lips turned up in a reassuring smile. "There's really nothing to worry about."

Logan pulled at the cuff of his sweater, the faint scent of smoke edging its way past his protections. "What if it does happen? How is it identified and treated?"

Ms. Park's voice was gentle. "We've done this before, Logan."

"But what if there are long-term effects?"

"The literature says there are none. Do you want to come and watch? Or would you be more comfortable staying here? There are magazines in the corner and a coffee machine in the kitchen."

Logan's fingers fell still and his back straightened, the acidic smoke fading. When he looked at me again, his face was calm. "I'll stay here."

Disappointment flowed through me, but I lifted the clipboard, my own expression neutral. Logan had come with us for moral support, but it was fine if he didn't want to come in. *Fine, fine, fine.*

The bell rang in the nurses' station and Ms. Park hurried away, leaving Cayley and I to fill out our forms. It was all standard stuff—name, age, student ID, allergies, emergency contacts—followed by an explanation of the spell, the potential risks, and a section covering reasonable alternatives.

"Who writes these things?" Cayley said, her nose wrinkling as she pointed at the list of other options. "Why would we want to do a truth spell instead? We volunteered for this—it's not like we're gonna lie."

But I wasn't really listening. Because filling in my parents' names as emergency contacts reminded me of another life. Of a relationship I could never have back. Still, I scribbled down their numbers and finished off the form, my foot hitting Logan's as I uncrossed my legs.

"Are you ready?" he said.

I nodded.

"What if it messes with the memory spell that's already affecting you? The one your parents did when you were little?" He reached for my hand. "You don't know what the rebound effects could be. It might—"

"Logan," I said, pulling out of his grasp. "Miss Lassila's already looked into it. She knows what spell was done on me as a kid—she helped perform it."

"Just chill out, okay?" Cayley said. "It's gonna be fine." She moved over to the small table in the corner and picked up a magazine. "The book says the spell works better when you're calm. It makes it easier for the spellcaster to focus on the correct memories. Otherwise they have to filter through various layers of shit to find them."

Logan stiffened.

"Oohhh, look." Cayley held up the magazine, open to a

double page spread featuring the ten best drum brands of the twenty-first century. "Do you guys think I should learn to play?"

"I think it's time to go." I looked at Logan and tried to ignore the nervousness that fluttered in my stomach. "See you when it's done."

We dropped our forms back to Ms. Park in the nurses' office and went down the corridor to room five, as directed. The room was empty when we entered, but the scene had already been set. Four white candles marked the cardinal points, their flames already lit, while fragrant herbs marked out the perimeter of a circle. A single quartz crystal lay in the center.

"Do you think we should sit?" I asked, eyeing the chairs by the wall, but the door swung open before Cayley could answer.

Ms. Maguire walked in, followed by Miss Lassila and Dr. Owens. "Good evening, girls," the headmistress said. "We'll begin shortly, but before we do, I have to let you know we've had an issue regarding parental consent."

Cayley rolled her eyes. "My mom forgets this stuff all the time. She won't care if you do the spell. She'll just—"

Ms. Maguire cut her off with a raise of her hand. "Your mother emailed back her confirmation yesterday," she said to Cayley. "You, however,"—she turned her attention to me—"will have to sit this one out."

"What?" Confusion pulled my brows into a frown, then I whipped my phone out of my bag and pulled up my mom's number. "She must've made a mistake. I'll call her and …"

Ms. Maguire shook her head. "There's nothing else I can do. Your mother was very clear. And you're a minor, so her word on the matter is final." Looking at Cayley, she pointed to the circle in the middle of the room. "Go and sit behind the crystal, and Dr. Owens will do a cleansing spell. Then we'll begin."

I stepped in front of her. "You've broken the rules before."

"And you've outstayed your welcome." She walked past me, moving toward the circle, each movement precise and controlled. "See yourself out."

Cayley folded her arms. "I won't do it if Emily has to go."

Dr. Owens looked up from the desk at the back of the room, where he was skimming through the pages of a leather-bound book. "Let me be frank," he said. "Haven is dying. I've done as much as I can to slow it down, but something is draining her life force through a hole in her aura, right at the top of that silver marking on her arm. We don't have time for petty games."

Cayley's face grew pale.

"I'll go," I said quickly. "Here's *Memory Spells and Other Evocations*. You can—"

"Stay." Dr. Owens crossed the room, his long white coat flaring out behind him. "Hearing Cayley's answers during the spell may spark memories of your own."

Miss Lassila guided me to one of the seats at the side

of the room. "Keep your book," she said. "We have our own copy. And be quiet."

I closed my mouth and gripped the book tightly as they began. It was an unremarkable spell—at least, from the outside. There were no sparks, no lights, no pretty smells. Just a smattering of Latin, then Cayley, sitting in a circle with a crystal in her hands, answering questions about what she'd seen.

"What did you say before the lights went out?"

"Who tried to open the door?"

"When did you notice the silver mark appear on Haven's arm?"

It went on and on. I listened as closely as I could, picturing that night in my mind and wishing I could participate in the spell. I hated that my mother hadn't given permission. *Focus.* Why wouldn't she let me do it? Didn't she know it was to help my best friend? *Stay calm.* I glanced at my phone and exhaled, listening to Cayley as she described how Haven's heart had stopped. How we'd helped her to the infirmary. How she'd been scared of the power displayed by the supe on the other side of the spell.

Ms. Maguire frowned.

Miss Lassila kept asking questions as she strolled around the perimeter of the circle. She smelled like concentration, like the bitter aftertaste of an over-brewed coffee. There was care in each step, each thought, each word, and when she finally bent down to extinguish the candles, a light breeze lifted the herbs from the floor.

"The spell is done." She leaned forward and retrieved

the crystal from Cayley's hands. It was smoky and gray, the once clear facets clouded with the strength of her memories.

"Was that enough?" Cayley asked as she stood, wiping her hands on her jeans.

Miss Lassila nodded. "You did very well."

Dr. Owens moved toward the now-broken circle. "I need to perform a few simple tests before you go." He put a small plastic contraption on Cayley's index finger, nodding as he read out the numbers. "Your oxygen and heart rate are perfect. Do you have any nausea? Headaches? Tingles?"

Cayley shook her head.

"Very good. Can you tell me what day it is today?"

"Do I have to?"

Dr. Owens narrowed his eyes. "Fine. You will tell me today's date, your phone number, and your mother's contact address."

Cayley sighed, but she answered, her voice flat. "I'm fine," she insisted when she was done.

"Very well. If Dr. Owens is satisfied, the two of you may leave." Ms. Maguire opened the door and gestured to the corridor beyond. "We'll be in touch if we need anything else."

My bag banged against my thighs as I rose from my seat. "What about Haven? Can we stay for her spell?"

"I'm afraid not," Miss Lassila said. "We need to keep her calm—with the condition she's in, we can't risk any distractions."

"But we'll be quiet. I promise."

Miss Lassila sighed. "The answer is no, Emily."

Cayley and I were halfway down the corridor, trying to figure out a way to see Haven, when Dr. Owens called us back. "Girls," he said, "we've been informed that Haven will not participate in the spell without the two of you present. It seems you and she have a lot in common, Cayley. And while I wouldn't normally acquiesce to the manipulations of teenage supes, as I mentioned earlier, we don't have time for games. So come back, sit down, and don't get in the way."

Five minutes later, Haven entered room five. Her shoulders were curved, like her body couldn't support her weight, and her skin was pale and covered in goosebumps. "Hey," she said, giving us a shaky smile.

My vision blurred.

"Hi," Cayley said.

"We've missed you," I added, quickly wiping my eyes.

Haven followed Dr. Owens to the center of the re-made circle. Her nightgown swamped her thin frame; her collarbones jutted out sharply above the collar. Purple shadows bruised the hollows beneath her eyes, and when she breathed in to cough, her chest gave a high-pitched wheeze. She held onto the doctor's arm as she lowered herself to the floor, then she crossed her legs and said, "Let's get this over with."

The spell began as Cayley's had, with a recitation of words I didn't understand, followed by questions and questions and questions. Haven's eyes were unfocused as she answered. The crystal in her hand grew cloudy.

"What did you do when you saw the woman on the other side of the spell?" Miss Lassila asked, sprinkling herbs between the candles as she walked around the circle.

"I pushed myself harder. I put … everything I had into that spell." Haven shook her head, like she was trying to clear something away. "But the woman was strong. And angry. She wanted to fight."

"What did you see? Was she young? Old?"

"I don't … I don't know."

Dr. Owens moved closer to the circle as Haven coughed again, blood spattering her nightgown. He pulled a small leather pouch from the pocket of his coat and shook a handful of herbs into his hand. He lifted it to his mouth. And blew. As the particles scattered, a sense of calmness washed over the room.

Haven's breathing slowed.

"When did you start hearing her in your mind?" Ms. Maguire said, stepping toward the circle.

"What?" Haven blinked. "I don't understand."

"The woman's voice. When did she start speaking to you?"

"I haven't … I don't … She doesn't speak to me. I haven't heard her voice since I did the spell to find the Blade."

Miss Lassila glared at Ms. Maguire. "Do you remember

anything else from that night that might be of use?" she asked Haven gently.

"No, I …" She shook her head, her forehead creasing. "My head … it hurts. There's something blocking me. It's blocking my thoughts."

Dr. Owens looked down at his watch. "It's time we wrapped this up. Haven, if you could—"

"No," Ms. Maguire said. "One more question." She bobbed down so she was eye-level with Haven. "I want you to think about that spell. Put yourself back there. Remember everything you can—the smells, the sounds, the textures."

Haven nodded.

Ms. Maguire closed her eyes, murmuring softly to herself as she sorted through Haven's memories. "There," she said finally. "That's where she attached it."

"Attached what?" Haven said, her voice hazy.

"What's she talking about?" Cayley whispered.

I shrugged, putting a finger to my lips.

"Come out," Ms. Maguire said, her eyes snapping open. "I can hear you. Come out and talk to me."

Haven laughed. "Siobhan Aisling Maguire. You always were good at putting your nose in where it doesn't belong." She turned her now-silver gaze toward me and smiled. "You've got something I want, *putere.*"

I shrunk back in my seat. I didn't know what was happening, but I knew this wasn't Haven. There was someone else looking out at me from behind her eyes, and I wondered why I hadn't recognized it before.

"Who are you?" I said.

Ms. Maguire rose, staring down at Haven. "We've met before. Is it … Yvonne? Abigail?" She leaned forward, as if she could draw her out. "Darcy Blake?"

Haven scrambled to her feet. "I can break this circle."

The lights dimmed and the crystal shattered.

"No you can't—not with this body," Ms. Maguire retorted. "Get out of my student and go back to where you belong. If you want to talk to me, you'll have to do it with your own face on."

Haven grinned. "This isn't about you." Her mouth stretched wider, distorting until she screamed, and her skin sparked with electric shards of yellow and blue. Her hands went rigid, and a low-pitched buzz filled the room. She turned to me, her eyes—now pale blue and shining—filled with horror. "She's coming," she whispered.

"Haven!" I shot forward as she fell to the floor.

Miss Lassila grabbed my arm. "Don't touch her!"

"You can't break the circle," Dr. Owens said.

Trapped behind the line of herbs, Haven lay impossibly still. Her eyes were closed and her breathing shallow; sparks crackled over her skin. I inched toward her. The sharp scent of magic and fear filled my lungs, but beneath it all … she was just Haven.

"She's scared." Cayley's shoulder grazed mine as she crouched down beside me.

I know.

Ms. Maguire hissed as sparks scattered on the floor beside us. "Get back," she said. "Quickly."

Miss Lassila herded us across the room, but my gaze never left Haven's face. I didn't want to be stuck on the sidelines. I wanted to do something. To *fix* something. But I didn't know how to help, so I stood, my spine pressed into the wall, and watched from the back of the room.

"Aidahr," Ms. Maguire said to Dr. Owens, "you and Maarika keep things under control. I'll be back as soon as I can."

The door banged shut.

Haven didn't move.

A few minutes later, Ms. Maguire returned with a large potted plant in her hands. It was a strange-looking thing—spiky leaves and red tubular flowers erupted from the dirt, and it smelled almost like vinegar. Ms. Maguire gritted her teeth, then tore it from the pot.

"Is she going to eat it?" Cayley whispered. "Because I read about a spell once where the witch casting it had to eat a cactus and it didn't end well."

I shrugged. Somewhere across the room, my phone was ringing. *Is that my mom? Calling to tell me it's not enough to destroy my life—she has to ruin Haven's too?* I stepped forward, but Cayley put a hand on my arm, holding me back.

Dr. Owens tossed my bag into the corridor.

Miss Lassila locked the door.

Then Ms. Maguire cast the plant aside and began to walk slowly around the perimeter of the circle, tipping soil from the pot onto the floor as she went. It criss-crossed the barrier into the space around Haven, causing the candles to flicker and the herbs to rise. *"Terra, vis, terra, potestas."* The headmistress spoke softly, her voice rich with power.

Haven screamed.

"Terra, vis, terra, potestas."

Haven's eyes flew open.

"Terra, vis, terra, potestas." Ms. Maguire's voice grew louder. She swept out a hand, forging a path through the herbs and candles. Moving slowly forward, she came to a stop at Haven's feet. *"Exire."*

"No," Haven said, lightning sparking across her teeth as she rose up horizontally in the air. Her body was weightless, untethered. "I. Will. Not. Leave."

"Exire!" Ms. Maguire stamped her foot so hard the tiles cracked, and her entire body shook as she repeated the spell like a mantra. *"Terra, vis, terra, potestas. Terra, vis, terra, potestas."*

Haven shrieked and I covered my ears with my hands, but even then, I couldn't escape it. It was fingernails scraping on a chalkboard, metal sliding against glass. It was the sound of power. The sound of pain.

"You have so much potential," she whispered, her silver gaze hitting mine. "And you don't even know how to use it."

"WHAT DO YOU MEAN?" I demanded. "Who are you?"

"Someone who's trying to do what's right." Haven's voice was lower than usual. Serious. The sparks around her body faded and she rose up vertically, her feet hovering above the floor. She was a specter, a stranger, her eyes still silver and her fury muted; she was dangerous and real. "You could do so much with the power you've been given. You could help us."

Ms. Maguire drew a symbol in the dirt. "*Exile.*"

"Stop trying to get rid of me—you've never understood what I want, Siobhan." Haven raised a hand, her fingers extended. "You're rejecting your history. Our history." Her gaze shot to me. "*Your* history."

Ms. Maguire straightened.

"You're one of us," Haven whispered.

Miss Lassila glowered. "Emily will never be like you. You're a coward, hiding behind a seventeen-year-old girl, using her as a vessel. The next time you want to talk to us, do it in person. The SCC will be waiting." She snapped her fingers and the symbol burst into flame.

Haven screamed.

Then she dropped to the floor, her body crumpling in a heap.

"Haven!" I ran across the room and pushed my way into the broken circle, gasping as residual magic arced across my skin. "Haven, wake up. Wake up!"

Her eyelids fluttered.

"Haven, are you in there?" I shook her shoulder, glaring at Ms. Maguire as she crouched down beside me in her four-inch heels, her profile icy and perfect. "You told someone to get out of her. Who is it?"

The headmistress ignored me and drew two velvet-covered pouches from her pocket. She handed one to Miss Lassila, who knelt at Haven's head, then nodded briskly. Opening the small, brown bags, they scattered herbs—green and yellow and fragrant—over Haven's forehead and wrists.

"*Redeo*," Ms. Maguire said.

Haven coughed. "Em? Is that … is that you?" She raised her head and looked around, her forehead wrinkling. "What's happening? Why am I … on the floor?"

Ms. Maguire brushed her hands together and stood, slipping the pouch back into her pocket. "There was a complication with your memory spell. Do you remember where you are?"

"The infirmary?" Haven raised herself up on her

elbows. "I've been here for … I don't know. A week or two? But I came in here—to this room—for the spell." She paused to cough, the sound a deep rattle in her chest. "You wanted Emily and Cayley to leave, but I said I wouldn't do the spell if they did. And then … I can't remember. Why can't I remember?" She sat taller, leaning against my shoulder. Running a hand across the floor, her fingers grazed a piece of darkened, shattered crystal, and she picked it up slowly. "Did I do that?"

Ms. Maguire nodded.

"How?"

"We'll discuss it later, when you're back in your room." She nodded to Dr. Owens, who stepped into the circle and offered Haven his arm. "You need to rest."

"I don't want to rest." Haven coughed again as she pushed the doctor away. "I want to know what's happening to me."

"You've had an infection," he said. "Do you remember that?"

"We all remember that," Cayley retorted as she strode toward us. "But we all know there's something else. Anomalies in Haven's test results. A hole in her aura. An entirely different person inhabiting her mind." She came to a stop in front of the circle, smudging a line through the littered remains of dried herbs and dirt with her shoe. "Tell us what's going on. And tell us the truth."

"This is most irregular," Dr. Owens said, his gaze flicking to Ms. Maguire. "I need to perform the post-spell tests. We could tell them and they'd—"

"No," she said immediately. "Emily and Cayley, get to class. Second period begins in ten minutes. Detention if you're late."

"No." Cayley drew back her shoulders. "Haven deserves an explanation."

The room fell silent. Ms. Maguire scooped up the shards of broken crystal, cradling them in her hands. A thin strand of hair escaped her chignon and grazed the side of her cheek. She smelled like conflict, like she was waging a battle within herself, and when she lifted a fragment of crystal to the light, it cast a shadow across her eyes.

"If Haven wants to know what's going on," she said, "the two of you will have to leave."

It was a command, issued by a witch who'd never seen what Haven could do. Who'd never experienced her intelligence and insight. Who'd never felt her loyalty.

"We'll do what's best for Haven," I said, my hands shaking. "Have you even asked her what she wants?"

Ms. Maguire's lips were thin.

"Do my parents know I'm sick?" Haven asked.

Miss Lassila shook her head, compassion lining her face. "I've left messages for them on their cell phones, emailed their business and personal accounts, and sent a letter via the postal service to their home address. So far, I haven't had a response."

Haven squeezed my hand, then looked up at Cayley. She was hurting, a different kind of pain than I'd smelled from the witch inside her head, but no less debilitating. It filled her with the scent of sea spray and carnations, of sadness and shame, and I wished I could take it away.

"It's okay," she said softly. "My real family's already here." She turned her head, confusion marring her brow. "Except … where's Logan?"

I couldn't meet her gaze.

"He's in the waiting room," Cayley said. "But he loves you. And he's worried."

Haven yawned and closed her eyes. "I hope he's all right."

Dr. Owens swooped forward, helping Haven to her feet. This time, she didn't resist. He led her to a chair, then shone a penlight in her eyes. She was weak, her body slouched backward, but she answered his questions without hesitation. When he was done, she raised her head up and met his green gaze with her own.

"Now, tell me what's going on," she demanded.

Dr. Owens turned his back on Ms. Maguire, ignoring her furious face. "There's a hole in your aura," he began, his tenor voice soft. "It was skillfully made, almost impossible to perceive, but when the tests we performed for dark magic residue kept returning weak positives, we knew there was something peculiar going on. It was more than an infection. And more than a simple curse. Your body had been infiltrated through the silver marking on your arm; it was like a pinprick in your defenses that let someone through."

Haven nodded slowly. "So the witch I connected with when I was looking for the …" She swallowed, her wide-eyed gaze meeting mine. "Is she in my head? Can she control me?" She gripped the edges of the seat and her knuckles turned white. "Does she know everything I know?"

"We don't have any definitive answers—none of us have come across a spell of this nature before—but from what I've seen, and from what Ms. Maguire and Miss Lassila have told me from their own investigations, it appears that this witch, the one you connected with, can enter your thoughts at will."

My stomach lurched.

"But …" Haven ran her fingers over her forehead. "I did that locator spell months ago. Why is this happening now?"

Miss Lassila looked up from the circle, where she'd begun sweeping the debris into a pan. "We have three theories. One—that the infection in the marking weakened you enough for the witch to gain access to your mind. Two—that she's been quietly dipping in and out of your thoughts since you performed the locator spell, incapacitating you slowly from the inside out. Or three—that she's a permanent passenger in your mind and body, somewhat akin to a parasite."

Haven blanched. "Ew. No. Not the last one. Anything but the last one." She squeezed her eyes shut, though I could still see them moving beneath her eyelids like she was searching for something in her mind. "Come back," she said suddenly, her raspy voice echoing around the room. "Come out and face me!"

Nothing.

Just the silence of heartbeats and breath and blood humming in veins.

"Can you get rid of it?" Cayley asked.

Dr. Owens pressed his lips together. "We're working on it. In the meantime, we'll examine the information from your memories and see if there's anything in them which will lead us to a weakness in the other witch's spell. Right now, it's like she's got a magical hook in Haven and we can't quite pry it out." He rocked back on his heels and looked at Ms. Maguire. "Is there anything you'd like to add?"

"Yes," she said bluntly. "Does the name Darcy Blake mean anything to any of you?"

I shook my head.

Cayley shrugged.

"Never heard of them," Haven said. "But I need to lie down. The room won't stop spinning."

She was bustled away, and Cayley and I were left alone in the room with Ms. Maguire. I headed for the door as quickly as possible. Why would I want to stay with an adult who kept performing illegal spells? Who was ruthless, and untrustworthy, and … crying?

"Ms. Maguire?" I said, uncertain.

"Get to class," she snapped, turning away.

"Why are you so upset?" Cayley asked. "And who's Darcy Blake?"

The headmistress whirled around, her arms falling to her sides. "I'm not upset. A tiny shard of crystal just went in my eye." She blinked furiously. "Darcy Rose Blake was a student who used to be a pain in my ass. Nothing more. Nothing less." Waving a hand in front of her face, she tipped her head back and muttered a long phrase in Latin. The thin, black crystal floated free and she grimaced. "Thank you for the memories, Cayley. And Emily—I'm not the bad guy in this situation. You'd both do well to remember that."

We walked out into the corridor, and when Cayley pulled the door shut, she stared at me, eyebrows raised. "She put that shard in there on purpose."

"I know. I saw her do it as she was turning around. But what I don't get is why?"

Cayley shrugged. "To hide what she perceives as weakness. She's a strong witch—extremely strong, from what I've seen—but we live in a world of predators and prey. And she occupies a position of authority. Have you noticed how she curates her persona? How her makeup and clothes are always perfect? How she expects others to move out of the way when she walks?"

I picked my bag up off the hallway floor, where it was crumpled from being tossed out of the room, and tried to slow my thoughts. "I can see how she manipulates people and situations to get what she wants. And how she's careful with her image. But ... I guess I just thought it was an ego thing."

Cayley shook her head. "Part of it might be, but mostly it's about the success of the strongest. That's why she's fine with showing anger, but not fear or uncertainty or frustration. It's old-fashioned and messed up, but change takes time." Her hair darkened around her shoulders. "But it means we can't trust her. And we can't count on her to do what's right, only what serves her own interests."

I tightened my ponytail and sighed. "Tell me something I don't know."

I can't trust any of the adults in my life.

It was one of the hardest things I'd learned since being a supe—how much everyone manipulates the truth to fit their own agenda. You'd think being able to smell the scent of a lie would make things easier. Somehow, it only made things worse.

"Hey," Logan said when we got back to the waiting room. "How did it go?" His hands were in his pockets, but his face was relaxed and he smelled neutral. Normal.

No.

Not normal.

I tilted my head. "Why do you smell like blood?"

"I …" He looked down at his shoes, his face pale. "Maybe I stood in something?"

It wasn't a proper answer. I breathed in, searching for something true, and my hand tightened around the strap of my bag. *Maybe it's not just the adults who lie.*

"Why did you stay?" I asked. "You said you were coming to support us, but you spent the entire time out here by yourself."

He didn't say anything.

"I wasn't even able to do the spell," I continued, my

voice rising in the face of his silence. "My mother wouldn't give me permission."

"I didn't know," he said softly.

"Of course you didn't know. You weren't there!" I shook my head, anger and distrust pressing in on all sides. "I needed you, Logan. *Haven* needed you."

"You had to stay calm for the spell," he said. "And I wasn't in a place where I could help with that. I would've made things worse." He pulled at his sleeves and winced. "I'm sorry, okay? I didn't mean to abandon you."

"Yeah, well …" I turned away, bristling. "That's not good enough."

"Em," he said. "Come on. You know it wouldn't have worked if—"

His words disappeared as I strode out into the night. Pulling cold, spring air into my lungs, I scrubbed my hands over my face. I knew I was being unfair; I should've let him finish. But I had so much to deal with already.

Haven.

The binding spell.

My parents.

The quartet.

I couldn't handle Logan as well.

So I dragged myself to class and pretended everything was normal. Because magical disasters and emotional baggage? Apparently that *was* my normal.

My room was quiet. It was an hour before curfew and I'd gotten through an entire night without bumping into Logan. My hand hovered by my phone and I wondered if I should text him, but in the end I drew it away.

"Focus," I muttered under my breath.

I'd been trawling through Haven's books and then supenet, searching for anything I could find about damaged auras and magical parasites. It wasn't that I thought I could do any better than the adults. I just wanted to do *something* to help. Because Haven never would've done that locator spell if it wasn't for me.

My phone rang and I answered it without thinking. "Hello?"

Logan's voice was echoed through the speaker. "I didn't think you'd pick up."

Dammit.

"What do you want?" I snapped. "I'm busy."

"I want to explain."

For a moment, I wanted to hang onto the anger. But he sounded so earnest, and I knew I was being unreasonable —at least, my human side did—so I lay my head down on the desk and sighed. "You don't need to explain anything."

"I should've been there for you."

"So why did you stay in the waiting room?"

"Because I was … scared, all right? They were talking about side effects, and memory loss, and Miss Lassila was going to go into your *mind*. Don't you realize how horrifying that is?"

I sat up and shrugged, though he couldn't see it

through the phone. "It wouldn't be my favorite activity, but the spell was controlled. And I didn't even get to do it." I paused, thinking back to what had happened in the infirmary and the waiting room. "Why did you smell like blood?"

There was silence. Then Logan cleared his throat. "Because I did something stupid."

"What did you …?" *Oh.* It wasn't something I'd expected. He hadn't self-harmed in a year—he'd told me he had strategies to manage it, that he'd figured out ways to cope. "Are you okay?"

"I'm fine. But Mr. Green wants me to try medication again."

"Are you going to?"

"I don't know. Maybe."

I leaned back in my chair and lifted the phone closer to my face. "Maybe it's a good idea," I said softly. "I'm not going to judge."

"I know." His voice was quiet, and I wished I could see his face. "I just wanted you to know."

We talked for a little while longer, but both of us seemed lost in our thoughts. "I'm sorry you can't come up," I said, picking up the books I'd left on the floor and putting them back in Haven's bookshelf. "It's weird up here by myself."

Logan sighed through the phone. "I know."

I sat on the edge of my bed and picked up Minikins. "Call me," I said. "You know, if it happens again. If you get the urge … or if you do it. You've been here for me through all of my … issues. You don't have to deal with this alone."

"Okay," he said. "Thanks. So … we're good now?"

"We're good. I promise."

He disconnected the call, and five minutes later I was lying on my bed when Cayley came bursting through the door. "Delivery!" she said, setting a large cardboard box down on the floor in the middle of the room.

"What is it?" I said, using my telekinesis to close the door behind her.

She raised her eyebrows, then shook her head, turning her attention back to the box. "I don't know. There's no return address. Ms. Emmerson said it was delivered to the admin building earlier this evening."

"And you offered to bring it up?"

She snorted. "Ms. Emmerson insisted."

The box was sturdy, securely taped though it clearly hadn't gone through the postal system, and it smelled like rose-scented perfume.

"Maybe it's a care package," Cayley said. "From your parents. Or maybe you have a secret admirer."

I grabbed a pair of scissors off my desk and sliced through the packing tape, then frowned. "This doesn't look like the sort of thing an admirer would send." Bracing the sides of the box with my legs, I lifted out an antique lamp with a ceramic base and a dark, textured shade. "Why does this look so familiar?"

"I don't know. It's hideous."

"Whoever sent this must hate me." I stood back, tilting

my head to examine the lamp from another angle. It was ugly, a relic from another era, and when I ran my fingers along the top of the shade, the musty scent of ancient vampire filled my senses.

Holy shit.

Zeke.

"I know what this is," I said. "This vase belonged to Mr. Olaru."

22

Cayley's eyes widened. "I remember it now. He had terrible taste."

I put the lamp back in the box and carried it to my closet. My lungs filled with the scent of roses, undercut by the decay of ancient vampire, and I exhaled through my mouth. Was this a glimpse of my future? Was I destined to become a husk of a creature, desperate to cover it up with perfumes and potions?

No.

You're going to destroy the world.

I shivered, goosebumps rising on my skin.

Pushing the box behind a pile of shoes, my fingers brushed something taped beneath the top flap of cardboard. It was a square piece of paper filled with neat, black letters. I pulled it off, accidentally tearing the corner, and began to read: *I know you kept your end of the bargain, so here's what you needed. Next time, I won't be so accommodating. – Zeke*

I wasn't sure whether to be grateful or intimidated.

"What is it?" Cayley asked.

"A note." I balled it up and tossed it toward her. "From Zeke."

She blew out a low whistle as she read. "You'd better hope he actually considers you even. Otherwise he's gonna hit you up for a favor when you least expect it. Supes like him always do."

I shut the closet door and grimaced. "Do you think he'll go away if I ignore him?"

"He knows what you are. He's keeping tabs on you whether you like it or not."

I sat down at my desk and pulled my laptop toward me. "We need to do the binding spell as soon as we can then. I have almost everything—something of Mr. Olaru's, something of mine, the Impure Blade, and the vessel. I just need confirmation about the anchor."

"You haven't heard back from Laurence?"

I flipped open my laptop to check my emails. "Nope. Maybe the first one went to his spam folder." My fingers flew across the keyboard as I sent him another message, then I turned back to Cayley. "Do you think this will ever get easier?"

She shrugged, her t-shirt changing color as she paced around the room. "That depends on your definition of *this*. I mean, do I think you'll get more used to being a supe? Yes. Do I think Laurence will eventually reply to your emails? Maybe. Do I think being the *putere* will always be a source of conflict? Definitely." She sighed, coming to a stop beside me. "But you don't have to manage it alone."

A ghost of a smile crossed my lips. "I know. You were there for me on the night of the Sapphire Eclipse. And you were there for Haven today."

She leaned down and hugged me.

"What was it like?" I asked. "The memory spell? Do you think you saw anything that might help?"

"I don't know. But I remembered things I hadn't even realized I'd seen. Like the way the pendulum sparked before the room went dark. And the sound of Haven's scream. It wasn't fun—the spell made me feel weird, like my mind wasn't under my control—but I'm sorry your mom didn't give permission for you to do it."

"Yeah," I said softly. "It sucks."

The curfew bell rang and Cayley went back to her room, leaving me to get ready for bed. I was exhausted but I couldn't sleep—not even when the sun was high in the sky, its heat a low hum in my blood. I wanted to go outside and feel it, to pretend I wasn't being held hostage by a hundred thousand emotions I couldn't even name, but Miss Lassila still had extra wards on my room, so I just opened the shutters and gazed out at the sky.

It wasn't supposed to be like this.

I wasn't supposed to be like this.

I'd been born something else. Not human. Not vampire. But I was always supposed to be here at Mistwood. I just didn't know why—my heritage, my memories, had been stripped away.

Do it now before you lose your nerve.

A cloud dipped across the sun and my fingers twitched.

Do it.

I picked up the phone.

Do it.

I pressed the name in my contacts. "Mom?" I said when her face popped up on the screen.

"Emily?" Her brow wrinkled. "What is it? What's wrong?"

I swallowed past the sandpaper in my throat, the phone gripped tight in my hand. "Tell me."

"Tell you what's wrong?"

"No. Tell me what you are."

Tell me what I am.

She blinked, holding the phone farther away from her face. "I'm your mother, Emily." Her words were soft. Simple. "You know that."

"I don't know anything," I said, hot tears prickling behind my eyes. "Why didn't you let the school do the memory spell? What are you hiding from me? Why did you lie to me?"

She shook her head. "Not over the phone. Not like this."

"Tell me now. Or you'll never see me again."

Her face paled. I could see it, even through the tiny screen. Through the tears that blurred my vision.

"I'll just …" Her breath wavered. "Wait there a moment, okay?"

The image tilted and I propped my phone up on my desk as I stared at the ceiling of a once familiar room. It was white, painted crisply from the light fixture to the scotia, except for one small place where it had cracked, a line of shadowed color that cast a spear through my heart. Because no matter what my mother said, it would never be my home again.

"Emily?" my mother said, her face reappearing above the screen. She picked up the phone and straightened it, the blurry image settling into focus as my father came to stand at her shoulder.

"We missed you, kid," he said.

I swallowed a sudden sob. "I missed you, too." My fingers dug into my palms, and the copper-fresh scent of blood filled my senses. "But it doesn't change what you did."

My father looked down.

Mom reached toward the camera, then drew her hand away. "Every day I look back and wonder if we made the wrong decision. Even more so, now that you're at Mist-wood." A melancholy smile brushed across her lips. "It was lovely to see you play your solo all those months ago, when we last came to visit. You look comfortable at the Academy. You look like you belong."

"That's because I *do* belong. But I never should've been here as a vampire. Or as the *putere*." I lowered my voice, whispering the word, even though no one was around to hear it.

"We never wanted the prophecy to happen," Mom said. "You have to know that."

My father nodded in agreement. "We did everything we could to try and stop it."

"Everything except trust me," I muttered.

"It was never about trust," my mom said firmly. "It was about responsibility. And love. We did it for *you*—for your life, your autonomy, your safety."

I ran my finger along the surface of the table, leaving a thin trail of blood on the wood. "How did you even know about the prophecy? And how was not telling me about it supposed to keep me safe?" I stood, my throat constricted, each word a battle. "You deprived me of my heritage. My truth." I locked eyes with my father. He looked older than I remembered, with wrinkles feathering out around the corners of his eyes. "I know you're not my dad," I whispered.

His stricken expression was a knife to the gut.

"He's always been your father in every way that counts," Mom said. "He drove you to practice, tended scraped knees and bruised emotions, taught you how to ride a bike. He—"

"I don't need a history lesson." The building's resident chimera came into view, and I slammed the shutters hard, closing myself off from the sun. From the memory of humanity. "Tell me what you are."

My mother sighed, and everything about her deflated.

"I am a witch, Emily. And you are—*were*—the same. That is your heritage."

A witch.

I picked up my phone and leaned against the desk, letting it take the weight of the revelation. On some level, I wasn't surprised. There were times when I'd felt magic against my skin, felt the breath of its power like a half-remembered song, like a memory buried deep within my bones. I'd never pursued it. It had seemed too fragile, too superfluous—especially when I already had a host of very real problems in front of me.

"Emily?" Mom said.

I clasped the phone tighter. "What about my father?"

"You dad is a dryad," she said, glancing back at the blond-haired man whose blood I'd thought I'd shared. "But your biological father—well, he was a man I met at a magical retreat one summer. A short-term thing. He was … a decent man, a warlock, but not the right person for me."

"And his name?" I said.

"Marcus Webber."

Finally.

The missing piece of the puzzle. I didn't know what it meant for me yet, whether I'd find out more about him, or whether I'd let his memory rest, but at least now I knew who he was.

"Did he know about me?" I asked.

Mom shook her head. "He died before you were born. He was out partying one night and there was some sort of altercation. A brawl, really, from what I was told. He took a bolt of elemental magic—fire magic—to the chest." Her expression softened. "I'm sorry you never got to meet him."

I sat, my shoulders slumping forward. I'd known he was dead—I couldn't have become the *putere* if he wasn't —but to hear it said out loud felt different. I'd never get to know if our laughs were the same, or if he'd loved music, like me. I'd never hear the sound of his voice, never inhale the scent of his favorite aftershave. They were a lifetime of experiences—and I'd never get to have them.

"So why did you lie?" I said, trying to steady my voice.

My mom sighed. "I told you, we were trying to keep you safe." She moved her phone closer, her blue eyes shining with unshed tears. "We always knew you were going to be a witch—there wasn't anything else you could be, given your genetics—but you were even more powerful than we'd anticipated."

I looked at my father. "Were you around then?"

"I was there for everything. Even your birth. Your mom and I met not long after she called things off with Marcus."

"He's always been your dad," my mom said softly.

He nodded, lifting a mug of something—probably coffee—to his lips, and I realized his hands were shaking.

I wanted to ask if he was okay.

I wanted this all to be over.

My mom smiled thinly. "We knew something strange was happening when you mentioned the prophecy."

"What?" I said, tipping forward in my chair.

"We didn't know what you were talking about, at first," she said. "You'd only just turned three, but you kept saying the word *putere*, usually without any sort of context, although sometimes you'd say it at night and point up at the moon. We figured it was childish gibberish. A made-up word. But one day you very clearly mentioned the Sapphire Eclipse."

I didn't know what to think.

"Was I psychic?" I managed to say.

Mom shook her head. "We don't use that term. It's too imprecise. You were, however, a witch with the gift of foresight. You could see things before they happened."

I gripped the edge of the table. *This is insane.* "I don't …" The room started to dim and I dipped my head. *Breathe. Breathe. Breathe.* "Why don't I remember this?"

"Because I did something terrible." My mother's voice was brittle.

"It took us months to find out anything about the Sapphire Eclipse," Dad said. "And even when we did, we weren't too worried. It was thirteen years in the future. It had nothing to do with us."

Mom's expression hardened. "Except it did."

I pulled my phone toward me. "Go on."

"I found out about it from a book," she said. "Not one of our research books. But from an old picture book Marcus had given me when he found out I was pregnant."

My phone beeped with a low battery warning, but I

felt around in my drawer for the charger and nodded for Mom to keep going.

"I was reading it to you one day when the dust jacket fell off. Behind it was a family tree printed on a folded piece of paper. Marcus' family tree. He'd added a little space for you—the only one left alive."

My phone beeped again, but I couldn't find the charger so I sat back and kept listening.

"He'd traced his lineage right back to the warlock who'd performed the original spell," Mom said. "And he'd left a message beneath it, encoded in magic, telling me what you could become, and telling me to keep you safe."

"Suddenly, thirteen years didn't seem very long," Dad said.

Mom put a steadying hand on his arm. "During the course of our research, we'd found out there were at least two other people interested in the prophecy. They'd tracked down Marcus, and they knew of your existence. They just didn't know your name."

"That was when we decided to do it."

Purple threads rose all around me.

Somewhere on my desk, a pen began to shake.

"I took your memories," Mom said. "And I suppressed your abilities."

Dad put an arm around her shoulder. "We thought we were doing the right thing. We went into hiding. We left our jobs, our families, our friends. For thirteen years, we lived as humans."

My phone beeped another warning.

"And my abilities?" I said, searching deep down within myself for something that felt like magic. "Can you give them back to me?"

My mother shook her head. "They're gone. Erased forever when you were turned."

The pen rose up.

My phone case shattered.

Purple light glowed around me, ethereal and enchanting, each strand perfectly positioned. It was mystical and powerful, but it wasn't what I wanted; it wasn't the magic I was born with.

"You took my powers," I said, ripping the broken case from my phone and tossing it behind me. "You took my memories. You stole everything from me."

My father winced. "You were a child. You didn't understand that you couldn't talk about it. If the wrong people had found out ..." He trailed off, his knuckles white where he clutched my mother's shoulder.

I didn't care if they were sorry.

I didn't care if they'd done it for the right reasons.

They'd taken *everything.* My past and my present. The future I'd deserved. They hadn't even warned me. Sam and I had grown up without—

Shit.

"Does Sam know?" I asked.

My brother.

He was blond and blue eyed, just like our dad—*his* dad, I guess—and he was a pain in the ass, annoying in a way that only younger siblings can be. But we'd also been close. Our family was so small we'd only ever had each other.

"He knows," my mom said. "We told him before we came to see you perform. It's been hard for him, losing you, and then finding out you're a vampire and he's a dryad, but we've enrolled him at Mistwood for the next academic year." Her brow furrowed. "You'll look out for him, won't you?"

I almost laughed. *Look out for him? Whose been looking out for me?* But I nodded and muttered, "Of course," because that's what older sisters do.

My dad—*Sam's* dad—smiled. "I knew we could count on you."

"We'll discuss this some more when we see you at the conferences," Mom said. "We're still meeting up before-hand, aren't we?"

I exhaled slowly. "I don't know. This has been … a lot." The battery bar on my phone flashed red, and I still hadn't found the charger. "I'll see you guys later. I just … I have to go."

My phone went dead.

I stood, tossing it down onto the desk. I didn't know what to do. My skin was cold; my blood burned hot. Pacing over to the door, I reached for the handle. *No. You can't.* I couldn't go out there. Not when Miss Lassila was still watching my room to make sure Logan didn't come up.

Breathe.

I turned, the purple threads shimmering around me.

Concentrate.

I dragged in a breath and dropped to the floor.

One ...

Two ...

Three ...

The ground rose up beneath me as I did push ups until my arms shook. There was no room in my mind for anything else—just the burn of my muscles and the sensation of movement. When I stood, twenty minutes later, my lungs still gasping for air, I felt calmer than I'd been in ages.

I considered going to bed, but I was still wide awake, so I searched for my phone charger—which I found beneath my pillow—then sat down at my desk and opened my laptop. *Marcus Webber.* Carefully typing each letter into the search bar, I tried to hold onto my hard-earned composure.

The search results were dismal.

"Unrelated, unrelated, unrelated," I muttered.

There was an unexpected *ding!* and I frowned and switched tabs. A message had just come through: *Are you awake?*

Pressing the green button beside it, I started up a video call. "Are you okay?" I asked as Logan came into view.

He pulled a hoodie over his head, the image going fuzzy for a moment with the movement. "I couldn't sleep."

"Me neither." I pushed my hair back from my face, fear twisting my stomach. "You're not ... you haven't ... you know, have you?"

"You can say the word," he said. "And no, I haven't cut myself. I'm not planning on doing it again."

"Okay."

"Why can't you sleep?" he said, leaning back against the wall behind his bed.

"I talked to my parents."

His eyes widened. "Yeah? What did they say?"

"My mother's a witch. *I* was a witch." I rubbed my eyes, exhaustion washing over me. "My dad—the one who's not really my dad—is a dryad. And so is my brother." I explained everything else while I looked through the rest of the search results, clicking on links that all lead to dead-ends. "There's nothing here."

"We could try the library," Logan said. "Tomorrow, during study hall. There might be something in the old newspapers there."

"Maybe."

We talked a little while longer, our silences growing longer as we both began to yawn. I was just about to log off when an email came through, the notification popping up on the screen.

"It's Laurence," I said as I clicked on the message, my eyes skimming quickly through the text. "I was right—the orb is an heirloom." I looked at Logan, my heart racing. "I've got everything I need for the spell."

23

———

MY STOMACH CHURNED. This was everything I'd wanted—a way to remove Mr. Olaru and his influence forever—but now that it was finally within my reach all I felt was fear.

"What does this mean?" Logan said, his voice thick with apprehension.

My predator stirred. "It means we can do the spell."

"Are … are you sure you want to?" Logan looked down and the shadows in his room obscured his face. "Remember what Mr. Green said about the risks—there's a fifty percent chance of injury or death. That's … don't you think it's too dangerous? What if you—"

"Stop, Logan. Just … stop." I pressed the heels of my hands against my eyes. "I can't deal with this right now."

My predator uncurled, slow and sinuous, ready to defend us against a threat that wasn't there. *You're safe. You're in your room. You're in Worthington Hall.* But the pounding of my heart, the fear in my blood, the goosebumps on my skin—everything about the anxiety that pressed in on all sides was a signal of danger. The predator didn't care that the threat came from my mind. All it cared about was keeping us safe.

"Em?" Logan said. "Do you need me to come up?"

When I looked at him again, the world had turned red. "This is all his fault," I said roughly, tearing open the bag of Skittles that lay beside me on the desk. I stuffed half of them in my mouth and chewed slowly, trying to find my center. *Push ups. Music. Running.* I thought about everything that made me calm. "If I didn't have his powers, if I didn't have his blood in my veins, I wouldn't feel like this. I wouldn't keep losing my grip on my humanity."

"Do you want me to call Miss Lassila?" Logan said. "Ms. Emmerson? Mr. Green?"

"I want to be myself again. I want …" Tears burned in my eyes and I wiped them away as they slid down my cheeks. "I want what I should've had. I've spent so long trying to get back to being human. And for what? I wasn't even human in the first place. Not really." I blew out a breath and wiped my eyes on my sleeve. "I had magic, Logan. *Magic.*"

"You still have magic," he said. "Just a different sort. Your vision, your hearing, your telekinesis—all of that *is* magic."

I sniffed, swallowing hard. "It's not the same. I should be casting spells, and learning the history of witchcraft, and working towards being whoever *I* want to be." I picked up my laptop and candy and crossed the room, lowering myself onto my bed. "Everything should've been different. I should've known about the prophecy—seen it through my *own* visions of the future—and maybe I would've been able to stop it. We wouldn't have had to fight Mr. Olaru." My voice dropped to a whisper. "I wouldn't have almost killed you."

"It happened—"

"If you say 'it happened for a reason' I'm going to *actually* kill you."

Logan huffed out a breath. "What I was going to say is that it happened, but we can't change the past. We can only move forward. I know it hurts—and I'm not saying you have to get over it, or that you have to forgive your parents, or that you have to like any of it—but you have to stop hating yourself. Please."

"I don't hate myself."

Logan sighed. "All you've wanted since you got here—no, all you've wanted since the day you were turned—is to be human again. You hate being a vampire. And you've hated it even more since the Sapphire Eclipse."

"That's not fair," I said, shaking another handful of Skittles from the bag. "I was attacked. I was taken away from my home, from my family. You don't get it, because you've always been a werewolf. You can't expect me to love what I've been through."

"This isn't … that's not what I'm trying to say."

"Well, what are you trying to say?" I shoved the Skittles in my mouth, then lifted Minikins out from beneath the blankets and held him to my chest. *Breathe.* "I was turned into a monster. Everything's heightened—my senses, my emotions, my hunger. I don't hate myself, but I do hate what's in me." My voice cracked. "I hate *him*."

"I know," Logan said. "And I'm sorry—I shouldn't have said what I did. It's just … when I look at you, I don't see a monster. I see someone who's brave, who's strong, who's been through so much and still keeps fighting every day. I know what it's like to hate yourself, but you have so much about you that's incredible. And I want you to see that." He looked down at his hands, his lashes falling against his cheeks. "I love you, Emily."

I pulled the laptop closer, dropping Minikins to the floor. "You do?"

"Of course I do. And you know it."

He was right. I did know it. It wasn't hard to miss—the scent of vanilla when he touched my hand; the sweet smell of roses before we fell asleep—but neither of us had actually talked about it.

Because saying it was different.

Vulnerable.

There was an unspoken rule among supes that you didn't discuss what you learned with your powers. When you could smell feelings, hear pulses, see the smallest dilation of someone's pupils, it was almost like hearing their thoughts. And while we all tried to hide our emotions, it was impossible to manage all of the time.

So we pretended not to know.

"I love you too," I said softly.

Logan lifted his head and grinned. "I know."

I picked up the empty bag of Skittles and pretended to throw them at the screen. "Can't you ever just be serious?"

"I've spent the last thirty minutes being serious!"

"Fine." I lay down, my laptop beside my head. "That's more than enough for one day."

"I wish I could be there with you," Logan said, his image blurring as he moved his phone. "If Ms. Maguire hadn't taken my key …"

I stifled a yawn with the back of my hand. "We'll have to steal it back."

"Tomorrow," Logan said.

"Yeah," I murmured, my eyes drifting shut. "Maybe tomorrow."

———

"Hey," Cayley whispered, leaning over to tap my arm. "Look at this."

I shook my head, my gaze darting to Mr. Dufort, who was walking slowly around the class. "Later."

"Ms. Rodriguez," the history teacher said, "do you require assistance with the assignment?"

"Nope." Cayley straightened, knocking her textbook to the floor. "I'm good. It's all good."

Mr. Dufort smiled, white teeth against grayed-out skin. "Very well, do not let me prevent you from doing your work then. Carry on." His pale eyes flicked to mine. "Emily, is there something you would like to ask me?"

I forced my gaze forward. "No, sir."

We worked in silence for a few minutes, then Cayley tapped my arm again. "I'm serious. You need to look at this," she whispered.

"Ms. Rodriguez," Mr. Dufort said, his voice rising. "You know I can hear you."

Cayley's teeth snapped together, and thirty seconds later a new email popped up on my laptop. We were supposed to be working silently on our latest History assignment, a comparison of the working conditions of Nutriments in Renaissance Italy and present-day America—a topic I was actually fascinated with, for obvious reasons—though Cayley had clearly drifted off-course.

She cleared her throat.

I kept writing my introduction.

Another email popped up, this one with the subject line: *just read it already!!!!!*

With a half-suppressed sigh, I clicked on the link Cayley had sent. It took me to an article entitled *The Order of the Silver Thorn: A Genuine Push for Change or A Dangerous Game?* I skimmed through the text, forgetting about my essay. According to the article, the Order of the Silver Thorn were a group of supes who wanted to over-throw the SCC, describing the Paranormal Program and council-governed prison system as "barbaric." They were a nationwide movement, though the location of their headquarters was a closely-guarded secret, and they believed the SCC weren't doing enough to support the rights of supes in the community.

"So?" Cayley whispered, her gaze boring into the side of my head. "What do you think we should do?"

"About what?" I glanced over at Logan and frowned. "Why did you toss a pen at my arm?"

"Because I want to know what's going on," he said.

On Cayley's other side, Thomas leaned in. "That doesn't look like the assignment."

"Cayley, Emily, Logan, Thomas," Mr. Dufort said, suddenly appearing behind us. "The four of you have earned yourselves detentions for three days. Congratulations." He peered at the screen of my laptop as he handed us all yellow cards. "And we will be discussing the contents of that article after class."

"But Mr. Dufort," Cayley said. "We weren't—"

The vampire lifted his hand and gave a world-weary sigh. "Nothing you can say will make me change my mind."

Cayley pouted, and I stuffed the yellow card in my pocket and minimized the article. How was I going to explain to Devon that I'd be late for practice again? It was only three days until the conferences and we *still* weren't sounding as perfect as he'd like.

From somewhere behind me, Courtney laughed softly. "Your parents are going to have a blast on Friday night, Emmeline," she whispered, the words still reaching my ears. "Remind me, why are they visiting Mistwood again? I thought you grew up human."

I swallowed hard.

I didn't have an answer.

"Ms. Beckett, you may have a detention as well. If I had known they would be in such high demand today, I would have replenished my collection of yellow cards before class." Mr. Dufort surveyed the class, his head tilted in a way that might have seemed predatory on anyone else. He was slight, his jaw defined and his pale eyes sharp, but his voice was mild, and when he caught me staring, he grinned. "I have only good things to tell your parents," he said.

For the rest of the period, we worked in silence. I could feel Courtney's eyes on my back, taste her curiosity in the air, and I almost emailed my parents to ask them how I was supposed to explain their presence at Mistwood. What happened when someone asked about them again? There was still so much I didn't know. Like, where did everyone think they'd been all these years? Did I have any other family? Was I supposed to keep my heritage a secret?

"Time to finish up," Mr. Dufort said, clapping his hands. "I hope you all got a good start on the assignment, because I expect no less than three thousand words in my inbox by Monday night."

Everyone groaned, then the bell rang and the class descended into chaos. Cayley swung her backpack over her shoulders, her lips curled up in a hopeful line as everyone jostled past on their way to the door. "So ... I guess I'm off now. Can't be late to Photography."

"You will stay, Ms. Rodriguez. You, and the rest of your friends." Mr. Dufort leaned back against his desk. His pose was relaxed, but the muscles in his fingers were tight where he gripped the edge of the wood. "Why were you reading about the Order of the Silver Thorn?"

"Curiosity," Cayley said.

"And you?" Mr. Dufort's grayed-out eyes met mine.

"Because Cayley sent me the article."

"What about you two?" he said to Logan and Thomas.

They glanced at each other, then at Cayley and me. I still wasn't sure what to expect from Thomas after the other night—I hadn't really seen him since the party—but his eyes were clear, a sharp, crystalline blue, and he gave me a brisk nod. "I haven't read anything about them, sir," he said.

"Me neither," Logan added.

It was technically true—the scent of mint swirling around us confirmed it.

"I don't know how much you know about them," Mr. Dufort said, shaking out his hands and folding his arms over his chest, "but every generation or two, someone will decide we should all be out in the open. It might seem like a good idea at the time—to them, and to others —but it never ends well. Think witch burnings. Vampire hunters. Werewolf patrols. We might outrank humans on strength, but they always triumph through sheer numbers alone."

It was a lesson that had been drilled into me at the Paranormal Program—always keep your species a secret. It was the law, a rule to keep all of us safe, but ...

"Would it really be so bad if humans knew about us?" I

asked tentatively. "Things are different now. People might be more understanding. If they knew what we—"

"It *never* works." Mr. Dufort's voice was forceful. "I've seen it time and time again. And it's not just about the humans. How could you even suggest that, knowing what the Order of the Silver Thorn believe?"

I stepped back, wilting under the strength of his gaze. "I don't … I didn't finish the article."

What had I just aligned myself with?

"Em!" Cayley said, elbowing me in the side. "I sent it to you for a reason. The Silver Thorn don't just want us to stop hiding what we are. They despise humans—they want to subjugate them, control them, use them for food."

Mr. Dufort raised his brows. "So you do know how to examine and interpret a text."

"Of course I do," Cayley said. "But I only do it when it interests me."

"And why are you so interested in the Order of the Silver Thorn?"

Cayley paused for a moment, clearly thinking. "Because they're a threat. They're well-organized and their reach is growing. They've got at least one enemy all of us know. And because I don't understand their motivation."

Mr. Dufort glanced down at his watch as students from his next class started trickling into the room. "You may go now," he said to the four of us, "but do not be drawn in by the rhetoric of the Order. Keep your research broad and your eyes wide open. And Cayley? If you put as much effort into your assignments as you do on your outside"—he paused, searching for the word—"interests, you could easily be an A plus student."

She nodded. "I know."

We made our way out of the room, dodging a group of freshmen who were arguing over who should get to eat the last chip in the bag they were sharing.

"Give it to me," Mr. Dufort said loudly, taking the bag and putting the chip in his mouth. "And do not bring food into my classroom again."

Logan grinned.

We walked out into the corridor and Thomas bumped my arm. "I heard you have everything you need for the binding spell," he said quietly. "Just … be careful, okay? I should never have introduced you to Zeke. If I'd realized he knew what you are …" He shook his head, his thin shoulders curling forward. "He sent me a message yesterday. He wants you to come back."

My fingers tightened around the strap of my bag.

"Don't go," Thomas said. "Please. I told him he won't be seeing me again either." He held open the doors as we made our way outside. "And don't mention anything about him to Benedict if you see him on Friday, okay?"

"I won't. I promise. I don't even know what Benedict looks like."

A few minutes later, we walked into the library. It was almost deserted—the only people in there were the librarian, who stood at the front desk scanning in books, and two freshmen girls who were looking through the stacks.

The space was enormous, with soaring arched ceilings and stained glass windows, and we headed to the back of the room. It was the only free period the four of us had together all week, and we sat at one of the big desks by the windows, pulling out our laptops.

"I'm bored," Cayley said, less than five minutes later.

Thomas shook his head.

"We're not together anymore," she called over her shoulder as she headed into the stacks. "You don't get an opinion on my choices."

"Harsh," he said under his breath. "But … fair."

Logan patted his brother's shoulder. "You'll find someone else. Eventually. But I swear, if you've destroyed our friend group …"

"I haven't," Thomas said, ducking away from Logan. "Cayley and I talked last night. We're good. We both agree that we're better off friends."

Logan looked dubious, but he didn't say anything else. The two of them went back to their assignments, while I tried to concentrate on my History essay. But I couldn't make myself focus. My thoughts kept wandering, lingering on anything other than Renaissance Italian Nutriments, so I minimized my tabs and clicked on my emails. There was one from Devon—*rehearsal after last period classes today. Don't be late!!* And another from the caterer, telling me that the fresh raspberries she needed for the muffins hadn't arrived and that we'd have to make do with boysenberry.

"It's just one thing after another," I muttered.

Still, at least these issues were straightforward. I just had to email Devon and tell him I had detention first, then follow up with the caterer about the change in menu. It was simple. Easy. Not like—

"The binding spell," Logan said, his eyes narrowing as he glanced at the screen of my laptop. "How did Laurence know the orb was an heirloom?"

"I … what?" I shook my head. "Are you reading my emails?"

Logan's cheeks turned pink. "Not on purpose. I just saw the subject line. Anyway, wasn't Laurence some random guy who helped out at the Paranormal Program?"

I closed my laptop and folded my hands on top of it. "That's what I thought, but apparently he was friends with my great-great-great-plus grandfather in the 1700s. According to his email, they went to parties together and wrote poetry and traveled through France and Germany, being fabulous and young and irresponsible. I think they might have been lovers."

"And you trust him because …?" Logan asked.

He was kind. And genuine. And I never would've passed the Program without him.

"Laurence wouldn't lie to me. Not about something like this."

Thomas looked up from his laptop. "Does he know what you are?"

I shrugged. "I don't think so. He recognized the orb when he found it in a market in Europe a few years ago, then he spent a while trying to track down any heirs. Eventually, he came across me."

Thomas frowned. "That's so … weird. Maybe I could ask …" He stopped. "No, I can't. I'm sorry."

I had a feeling he'd been about to say he could ask Zeke.

"I trust Laurence," I said firmly, looking up as Cayley came striding toward us, a huge stack of books balanced precariously in her arms. "Everything's gonna be fine."

Beside me, Logan's leg started shaking.

"Sorry," I whispered, putting a hand on his knee.

He offered me a smile, but it didn't reach his eyes. "You don't have to accommodate my … issues."

"You're my boyfriend," I said quietly. "And I love you. I *want* to accommodate your issues."

Cayley dropped the books on the desk in front of us, killing the conversation. "I don't know what you guys are talking about," she said, "but shut up and look at this."

24

I EYED THE BOOKS WARILY. "What are we looking at?"

"I was searching for information about Haven's 'passenger,'" Cayley said, making quote marks with her fingers, "and it turns out Darcy Blake went to school here about twenty years ago. I found a picture of her in one of the old yearbooks. There was a cryptic comment scrawled under it—*she used to be a rose, but now she's a thorn*—so I kept digging around for a bit and found ..." She paused as she flipped open the red-covered book on the top of the stack. "... this."

I stared down at what looked like pages from an old newspaper, my eyes skipping up to the date in the corner. "Twenty-one years ago," I said, realization slowly dawning as my gaze settled on a black-and-white photograph of a dark-haired teen in school uniform. "This is Darcy?"

"The one and only," Cayley said. "Read it."

I pulled the book closer, angling it so Logan and

Thomas could see. It was from what looked like a national supe newspaper, and the story and accompanying image were splashed across the top half of the front page. The headline was straightforward: *Mistwood Academy Student Expelled After Spell Goes Wrong.*

"She did a compulsion spell on one of the kids in her year?" Thomas said, his eyes widening as he read. "'Samantha Harris was unable to resist the effects of the enchantment, transforming into a werewolf in the middle of the courtyard. A number of students attempted to restrain her, but the spell rendered her uncontrollable, and by the time reinforcements arrived, she had almost disemboweled Lucy Fisher, a freshman witch who was passing by. Lucy remains in critical condition in the hospital wing of the SCC offices in Seattle. Harris is currently undergoing both physical and psychological testing.'"

"And Darcy?" Logan asked, shifting as he tried to see the newspaper better.

"She was locked up." I pushed the book toward him, uneasiness seeping into my bones. "It says she was incarcerated at the same facility I was at when I went through the Paranormal Program."

"Is she still there?" Thomas said.

I lifted my shoulders. "How would I know? It's not like I knew I'd need to look for her."

We fell quiet then, browsing through the rest of the yearbooks and bound newspapers, searching for anything else we could find about Darcy. The clock on the wall ticked loudly, and my eyes glazed over as I skimmed past photos of smiling faces. Debate team and chess club. Orchestra. Rock band. Kids with their arms around each other on sports day, colored stripes painted across their cheekbones. They were snapshots of lives, brief moments caught in time. I dragged my fingers across the page, wondering what people might see if they ever found my picture, years from now, just a face in a yearbook.

They'd never know what I'd been through.

They'd never know what I was *going* to do to protect them. To save the lives of everyone on the planet.

"Look at this," Cayley said, shoving a book across the table.

The blue-bound volume was opened to the front page of another newspaper, the headline proclaiming: *Mistwood Academy Declares Unsupervised Magic Off Limits to Minors Following Near-Fatal Consequences of Compulsion Spell.*

"She's the reason no-one's allowed to perform unsupervised magic in schools anymore," Cayley said. "Darcy targeted Lucy Fisher on purpose. It says here they'd had a disagreement earlier that night and Darcy had timed the spell perfectly for Samantha to attack her."

"And now she's inside Haven's mind." Thomas turned a sickening shade of gray. "She's controlling her thoughts. Her actions. Looking through her memories." He stood, his hands trembling. "What are we even doing here? How is this supposed to help?"

"We could tell Ms. Maguire what we've found," Logan said. "Maybe it would—"

"Ms. Maguire already knows." Cayley snapped the book closed and dragged the next one across the table toward her. "They went to school together. They were in debate club. The softball team. And Ms. Maguire was roommates with Samantha Harris."

"Then what's the point of all"—Thomas waved his arms around aimlessly—"this?"

"Knowledge," Cayley said.

Even Logan looked confused.

"You can't fight your enemy if you don't know anything about them." Cayley flipped over a page. "Their strengths, their weaknesses, their secrets and lies." She turned another page. "It would've been easier if the library had this all digitized though."

Thomas shoved his laptop in his bag. "I'm leaving."

Cayley didn't even look up as he walked away.

"Have they digitized anything?" I said, my gaze skipping across the room. I wasn't sure if my dad had gone to Mistwood or not, but Logan had suggested looking through the old newspapers for information about my dad. Maybe I could find an article. Or a picture. *Did we have the same eyes?*

"Em." Logan tapped me on the arm. "Your phone's ringing."

"What?"

"Your phone," he repeated. "It's ringing."

I swiped at the screen without even looking, then lifted the phone to my ear. "Hello?"

"I heard you got detention," Devon said, his voice tinny

through the speaker. "We need to practice—the performance is in three days. Dr. Richardson—"

"Dr. Richardson will love you," I cut in. "And I can squeeze in an extra practice at lunch today if you want. Or we can do it after detention."

"Fine," Devon said. "I'll see you at lunch."

He hung up and I blew out a breath, staring down at the book in front of me. In the center of the page was a photo of the school orchestra. They were arranged neatly on risers and dressed in performance clothes, their instruments held at their sides.

"I bet none of them had to deal with a prophecy or mind-controlling witch, let alone deal with phone calls from highly-strung pianists," I muttered.

Cayley glanced up, her hazel eyes unreadable. "Everyone's got problems."

* * *

By Friday night, I still hadn't solved any of my issues, though the most pressing one—aside from the fact I was supposed to be seeing my parents in less than an hour—was the highly-strung pianist.

"You're not even dressed yet," Devon said as he hurried into the auditorium. "Dr. Richardson can't see you like that!"

"She won't." I took him by the shoulders and led him toward the chairs at the side of the room. "Sit. Relax. I'm not ready yet because I was setting out the refreshments. See?" I gestured toward the large, food-laden tables that lined the other side of the room. Plates were stacked at one end, and a selection of drinks were available at the other. Round wooden tables had been set out around the auditorium for those who preferred to sit and socialize, and takeaway containers were on hand for those who wanted to eat on the run. Everything looked perfect.

"But we still have to set up," Devon said. "And tune. And—"

"It'll be fine," I said firmly. "Get yourself a muffin. I'll be back—dressed, made-up, and ready to perform—in fifteen minutes. Maybe ten if you're lucky."

"And what if Dr. Richardson gets here early?"

"Then you'll talk to her. Tell her who your favorite composers are or something. You can do this, Devon—I believe in you." I swiped a mini quiche from one of the tables and stepped out the door just as Terrell was coming in. "Distract him," I said, taking a bite and nodding toward Devon. "I'll be back soon."

It was twenty-five minutes until the evening's events were due to begin, but there were already more adults outside than I was comfortable with. I passed dryads admiring the gardens and witches standing and chatting. Some of them were with their kids, but most of them weren't.

They all seemed to know each other.

I swallowed the last of my quiche and coughed as a crumb got caught in my throat.

What do I say if someone asks me where my parents have been?

I'd meant to email my mom and find out what the "official" story was after Courtney had taunted me about it the other day, but I'd been so busy with … well, everything, that I hadn't gotten around to it.

Head down, I walked quickly toward Worthington Hall, only turning when a familiar smell filtered through my senses. "Logan?" I said.

"The one and only." He came to a stop in front of me, adjusting the collar of his shirt. "Do I look okay? Is this too big?"

I stepped back, taking him in. His shirt was heather gray, with halfmoon cufflinks securing the sleeves, and he wore freshly-pressed trousers and shiny black shoes. For once, his hair was almost tidy. "You look perfect," I said as I went up on my toes to kiss him.

"Break it up," Cayley said, walking up beside us. "You're giving the parents a show."

Logan's face flushed red as we broke apart. "I thought succubi didn't care about that sort of thing."

"You're right," Cayley said, smiling. "I don't care. But I thought you guys might."

I ignored the pointed glare of a parent walking past and looked down at my phone, sighing. There were already three new messages from Devon:

Dr. Richardson's here!

Hurry up!

We need one last practice before we perform.

"I have to go," I said, giving Logan another kiss. "Devon's having a meltdown."

"I'll see you at the auditorium then." He tucked a lock of hair behind my ear and smiled. "I'll be the one at the door, handing out information sheets and timetables and pretending like I'm enjoying it."

"And I'll be the one avoiding the entire thing," Cayley said. "I'm spending the night in the infirmary with Haven. I don't know if her parents are coming, but if they do, she's gonna need a buffer. You know what they're like …"

Logan grimaced. "Call me if she needs anything, okay?"

"I'll be taking care of her. She'll be fine."

Logan's shoulders tensed and I kissed him one last time before the two of them left. I was walking back to Worthington Hall when my phone beeped again. *Devon.* I wished I could go and see Haven before the performance, but Devon would never forgive me if I was late.

I swallowed a sigh and increased my pace. At least Haven was finally getting better. We'd visited her the night before and she'd told us Dr. Owens and Ms. Maguire had figured out a new treatment, based partly on what she and Cayley had recalled during the memory spell, and partly on what Ms. Maguire knew about Darcy Blake and how she operated. Did I understand what that meant? Nope. Was I extremely hopeful anyway? Of course.

I'd just looked down at my phone to text her, when a

witch in a sumptuous red coat stalked past, her elbow brushing mine. "Excuse me," she said sharply.

I spun around to watch her. "Sorry. I didn't—"

"You should look where you're going," said the tall, well-dressed man beside her. His lips turned down at the corners. "What are you doing, walking around with your eyes on that device? You could cause an accident."

"I was just—you know what? Never mind." They'd already left, muttering under their breath about the "dangers of technology" and the "insolence of youth."

I made it back to my dorm without annoying anyone else and went straight upstairs, barreling into my room and kicking off my shoes. I picked up my sheet music off the bed and—

"Haven?" I said, lifting my head.

The scent of antiseptic and witch invaded my senses.

"Surprise!" She bounced toward me, her arms stretched wide. "Dr. Owens let me out!"

"Does that mean …?" I paused, waiting for Haven to fill in the blank.

She nodded and flung her arms around me. "I'm only allowed out tonight, but I'm getting better. Like, *actually* better."

I closed my eyes and squeezed her tight. "I've missed you."

"I've missed you too. I've missed *me*." She stepped back and ran her hands through her hair. It was longer than usual, her dark roots showing, but her face wasn't so drawn and the dark circles beneath her eyes were fading.

There was still a faint red ring around the silver marking on her arm, the last remnants of the infection. She smiled when she caught me staring. "The hole in my aura's closed. Or closing. I can't quite remember. But it's fine—Darcy can't get through anymore."

"Are you sure?" I inhaled slowly, searching for anything out of place. "Wait … why can't I smell your emotions?"

"It's a side-effect of the treatment. Dr. Owens said it shouldn't last long—no more than a week or two." Something in her expression turned sour. "And then it's back to shielding and suppressing, just like everyone else."

I watched her from the corner of my eye as I slipped my performance clothes out of the closet. "I'm not an expert at hiding my emotions," I said. "Not like Logan. But it's not as bad as I thought it would be—it's just part of being a supe."

Haven opened up the trunk at the end of her bed. "I know. But I'm not talking about emotions. It's just … don't you hate having to hide who you are? *What* you are?" She held up a small jar or herbs, examined it closely, then set it back down in the trunk with a frown. "We have so much power. Why can't we use it freely?"

A chill trickled over my skin. I thought of Teddy and what she'd said outside the barn that night before she'd attacked her friend: *The SCC are wrong. We shouldn't be hiding. We should be living. Growing. Thriving.*

"You know why we can't use our abilities around humans," I said. "It's not safe—for them or for us."

My phone interrupted us with a beep. Then another.

Haven's eyes narrowed. "Who is it?"

"It's just Devon. He's nervous about our performance."

"You should go then." She looked down at my jeans, her nose wrinkling. "You're not wearing that, are you?"

I shook my head and quickly got changed. "Will I see you at the conferences?"

"Maybe."

I slid my feet into a pair of chunky Oxford shoes and laced them up. "Why don't you come with me?"

"You go," Haven said. "I'll come down later." She offered me a bright smile. "I won't miss your performance. I promise."

I bit my lip, tasting only the uncertainty of my own emotions.

My phone beeped again, and this time it was my parents: *We're at Coffee and Cake. Are you coming?*

"Go on," Haven said. "Leave. I'm not ready yet, and you'll be late if you wait any longer."

I could tell by the set of her jaw that she wouldn't come with me, no matter how many times I asked, so I went out into the corridor, dodging students and parents as I searched for Miss Lassila. Something wasn't right. *Something I don't have time to deal with.* I was being pulled in too many directions—with Haven, with the performance, with my parents—and I didn't know what to do. But I couldn't find Miss Lassila anywhere.

"Dammit," I muttered.

I pulled out my phone and messaged Cayley: *Haven's in*

my room. Something's wrong, but she wouldn't come with me. Check on her!!

Ten minutes later, she still hadn't replied, and I was stuck standing at the side of the stage in the auditorium, Ms. Maguire's speech like a drone in my ears.

Mia nudged my arm. "Everything okay?" she mouthed.

I forced myself to smile. "Fine."

Balancing my cello against my body, I sent my parents an apology text, then messaged Cayley again, hoping she'd already found Haven.

"And now," Ms. Maguire said, throwing an arm out to the side, "I'm delighted to introduce four of our most talented students—Devon Williams, Mia Dubois, Terrell Barton, and Emily Sanderson."

The audience applauded as we walked onto the stage. Devon took his place at the piano, and Mia, Terrell, and I sat, adjusting our sheet music on our stands. Looking out into the crowd, I saw my parents near the doors, Logan standing behind them. Butterflies swooped in my stomach, the way they always did before a performance, and I exchanged a glance with Mia, then with Devon and Terrell.

Then we began to play.

The music soared and the world disappeared, each note precise, each moment connected. I forgot about my parents. I ignored Haven and Darcy. I was nothing more than movement and sound, perfectly present in this one moment in time.

When we finished and stood, the bright lights shining

down on us, we grinned at each other, hearts pounding. Devon's face was flushed, his hands shaking from adrenaline, but he nodded and we bowed, then walked offstage.

"That was incredible," Mia said as soon as we were out of view.

"We were amazing," Terrell added.

Devon flung his arms around our shoulders, pulling us into a huddle. "Thank you," he said, his voice cracking with emotion. "I know I've been difficult the last few weeks. High maintenance, demanding—"

"Go on," Terrell cut in.

Devon shook his head and laughed. "What I'm trying to say is, I appreciate you all for putting up with me."

"You know we love you," Mia said. "Even when you're a pain in the ass."

Terrell covered his laughter with a hand and pulled away, pointing at the stage, where Ms. Maguire had stepped back up to the microphone.

"What a beautiful performance," she said, smiling broadly. "Now, please make yourselves at home and enjoy the food provided. Mistwood Academy is—"

"Where's Haven?" The interruption was demanding and loud and I peeked around the side of the curtain and saw the woman in the red coat, the one who'd walked into me earlier. She swept down the center of the room, her blonde hair bouncing around her shoulders. Her lips were a crimson line, and her blue eyes shone colder than the diamonds that sparkled around her throat. "What have you done with my daughter?"

25

"THAT'S HAVEN'S MOM?" Terrell said, letting out a low whistle. "She looks fierce."

I don't care what she looks like.

"Where's Haven?" she demanded again.

Ms. Maguire descended the stairs at the side of the stage, her gaze skimming over the watching crowd. "Mr. and Mrs. Montgomery," she said, stopping in front of Haven's mother and the tall, well-dressed man who now stood stonily beside her. "We'll discuss this in my office. Follow me …" She walked toward the door, her back straight and confident.

"No."

Ms. Maguire slowed.

"I'm not going anywhere until you tell me where my daughter is." Haven's mother lifted her chin and glanced around the room. She was about the same height as her daughter, though her beige pumps gave her an extra five inches, and she spoke with the confidence of someone who always got her own way. "I pay an exorbitant amount of money to this school. I want to know where my daughter is."

Ms. Maguire's smile was chilly. "I've been trying to get in contact with you both for weeks. Perhaps if you took the time to answer your voice messages and emails, you'd be more aware of what is going on with your child."

Mr. Montgomery's face turned red. "How dare you!" He took a step toward Ms. Maguire, but his wife put a hand on his arm, her painted-red nails bright against his navy suit jacket. "We were away on assignment. Do you not understand what we do for a living?"

"I understand very well," Ms. Maguire said. "You both hold positions of influence—positions which necessitate, at minimum, uninterrupted access to communication devices. Correct?"

"You don't understand the pressure," Haven's mom started. "It's why we—"

Ms. Maguire lifted a hand. "As I said earlier, we will continue this in my office."

Whispers formed behind hands as a room full of people watched the three of them leave. Food sat abandoned on plates; schedules were forgotten. Logan stared at me from the doorway, his eyes wide, a bundle of flyers hanging limp in his hands.

"Look after my cello for me," I said to Mia.

"What are you—" she started, but I was already halfway across the room.

"Emily!" Mr. Davis waved to me from one of the food-laden tables, panic shining in his eyes. He hurried toward me and thrust a platter full of pastries into my arms. "Circulate. Circulate!"

"I can't." I dumped the platter down on the nearest table, managing to knock a steaming cup of tea over the pristine white tablecloth, which earned me a glare from the parent whose drink I'd just ruined. "I'm sorry. I have to go."

I dashed toward the door.

"What's going on?" Logan said as he came up beside me. "Do you know something?"

"I'm not sure. Maybe? Haven was in our room when I went up there to get changed." A parent turned and stared, and I lowered my voice. "Something was off. She was saying we should be able to use our powers freely—like, around humans."

Logan hissed out a breath. "That's not Haven. Learning about the Salem witch trials in fourth grade gave her nightmares for months. She'd never do anything to jeopardize any supe's safety."

Shit. Shit. Shit.

I knew I shouldn't have left her.

I reached in my pocket for my phone. "Where's Cayley? I sent her a message but she didn't—" I stopped abruptly as my hands came up empty. "Dammit, I left my phone backstage. Anyway, I asked Cayley to check on Haven, but I don't know if she did."

"I don't know either," Logan said, his focus shifting to

someone behind me, "but there are two parents coming this way and they clearly want something." He pasted a smile on his face. "Leave now, while you still can."

I kissed him on the cheek without thinking. "I'll keep you—"

"Emily?"

"—updated," I finished, my heart jumping at the sound of my mother's voice.

"Who's this?" she said. "Your boyfriend?"

I spun around slowly, wishing I'd done what Logan had said. At least then I wouldn't be having this conversation. I swallowed hard and lifted my gaze. *You know what you are. You know what she is.*

"Hey, Mom." I swallowed again. "Hey, Dad."

My dad reached forward and shook Logan's hand. "Christopher Sanderson," he said. "And you are?"

"Logan Adams, sir." His voice was polished, but his eyes held a flicker of alarm.

"You're Benedict's son?" My mom's brows tilted as she considered my boyfriend's face. "Ah yes, I can see it now. Same hair. Same nose. Your dad and I used to work together, Logan, a long time ago, before he became alpha. I'm Jessica Sanderson."

"A pleasure to meet you," Logan said.

Mom looked down at the schedule in her hands. "We're due to meet Mr. Dufort in five minutes, Emily. If you could—"

"Sorry." I shook my head. "I have to do something first. Logan can give you a map, and I'll meet you there."

Ignoring my parents' exclamations of protest, I ran through the foyer and out into the night. My shoes slapped against the cobblestones as I headed down the path toward the administration block—toward Ms. Maguire's office. I had to tell Haven's parents that she'd been in our room. That she wasn't missing. She'd been through so much already, and no matter what she'd said about getting better, I was pretty sure she still had Darcy Blake in her mind.

"Em! There you are!" Cayley hurried toward me, a white slip of paper in her hands. "Why aren't you answering your phone?"

I came to a stop, pausing to catch my breath. "I was … performing. Then Haven's parents came in. They said … she's missing." Leaning forward, I put my hands on my knees, waiting for the stitch in my side to subside. "But she was … in our room … earlier."

"I know. I got your text." Cayley waved the piece of paper in front of my face. "She left this for you."

"You saw her?"

Cayley shook her head. "She was gone by the time I got there. You know she wasn't discharged from the infirmary, right? Dr. Owens has been looking for her for the past hour."

I straightened. "Shit. Does this say anything useful?" Grabbing the paper from her, I smoothed it out and read.

Emily, meet me in your favorite clearing in the woods. I have something for you—you'll love it, I promise. But you have to be there by 1:00 a.m. It's a time sensitive surprise. xx

"This is … strange." I read the message again, looking for anything—a misspelled word, an awkward turn of phrase—that could tell me what was really going on. But the note was brief. Simple. "There aren't any exclamation points."

"That's because it's from Darcy."

I balled up the note in my hands.

You have so much potential and you don't even know how to use it.

You could help us.

You're one of us.

I looked up at the clouds and sighed.

"I'm coming with you," Cayley said. "Darcy's unpredictable, but she's smart. One of the yearbooks had her listed as coming first in her year in almost every class. The only thing she was even slightly less than perfect in was Art and Design. And she still got a 'highly commended.'"

"Darcy's not going to control me. Or steal my powers." I stuffed the note in my pocket and started walking toward Ms. Maguire's office.

"Where are you going? The woods are that way," Cayley said, pointing behind us.

"You want to walk right into her trap? Darcy's dangerous—she was incarcerated for years, and none of us know if she was legitimately released. We need to get Haven back to the infirmary so Dr. Owens can continue her treatment. But we need help."

"It's almost 1:00 a.m."

"Then we'll hurry."

I didn't trust Ms. Maguire—she'd already proven herself willing to bend the rules to get what she wanted—but I didn't think she'd try and harm us. She was an enemy of the Order, she'd helped Dr. Owens with Haven's treatment regime, and she was willing to do anything to maintain her image of strength and perfection. She'd never let Darcy win.

But … she wasn't in her office.

Or anywhere in the administration block.

"Come on," I said to Cayley as I started running toward Worthington Hall. "Maybe Miss Lassila can help."

We knocked on every door in the entire dorm. Most of them were empty—aside from one room on the second floor where a vampire was showing her collection of pinned butterflies to her parents, and a room on the top floor where a werewolf was playing computer games with her girlfriend.

"You're almost out of time," Cayley said.

I bit back a growl of frustration. "Fine. I guess we do this ourselves."

We ran toward the woods, taking a shortcut through the science building. The classrooms were brightly lit, filled with parents and kids meeting with teachers, and I wished I was one of them. I should've been talking about my progress with Mr. Dufort; I should've been ducking my head when he mentioned my detentions; I should've been glowing with pride when my parents were told I'd gotten the top mark in our last assignment. Instead, I was running into danger.

Again.

"Incoming," Cayley said under her breath.

I looked up as Vanessa and her parents exited one of the classrooms. Her parents were tall—they smelled like money and power—and their faces were uncomfortably grim. "Your grades are slipping," her mother said sharply. "Do you want to go to summer school? Because that's where you're headed, young lady. We will not have you ending up like—"

"Angelica," warned Vanessa's dad. "We have an audience."

Vanessa cheeks flushed red.

"Don't look at them." Angelica pulled at her daughter's arm as they passed us. "Just because the alpha lets his son fraternize with witches and vampires, it doesn't mean you have to."

"Those are Logan's friends, Mom." Vanessa's voice was tight. "And I don't *fraternize* with them."

"Good," said her father. "But we still need to talk about those grades."

"And your hair," her mother added. "Why are you wearing it tied back like that? You know it makes your ears look big."

They carried on down the corridor, and I almost felt sorry for Vanessa. She was obnoxious and rude, and nothing excused the way she treated other people, but maybe there was more going on in her life than I knew about. Maybe there was more going on in *everyone's* lives than I knew about.

Thomas and his drinking.
Logan and his self-harm.
Haven and Darcy.

I turned to Cayley as we ran out the doors and into the night. "Is there anything happening with you that I should know about?"

"What?"

"Like … things going on in your life."

Her forehead wrinkled. "I think you have more important things to worry about right now. Like finding Haven —or Darcy—as soon as you can."

"Fine," I said, "but we're talking about your issues as soon as we're done."

Cayley just shook her head.

It didn't take long to get to the woods. We kept to the paths, sprinting across the leaf-brushed dirt, and while both of us were expecting something to go wrong—we were dealing with Darcy, after all—neither of us had anticipated the sudden appearance of Zeke. He emerged from the clearing, his blonde hair carefully arranged and his sneakers suspiciously clean.

"You're late," he said, looking down at his phone.

Cayley lifted her nose. "It's only five minutes past the hour."

"Which means you're late. Anyway, that note wasn't meant for you." Zeke pulled a small glass bottle from the pocket of his jeans and tossed it toward her.

I grabbed onto my powers with everything I had. The bottle shimmered. Purple threads reached around it. "You don't get to hurt us," I said as I pulled it toward me. "It's bad enough that—shit!"

Zeke laughed as the bottle shattered.

Cayley lifted her arms and darted away.

Too late.

Glittering white powder flew toward her, covering her face and her still-rising hands. I tried to grab onto it, to pull it away using the purple strands that clung to each speck, but it just dispersed faster, soaring away from me and clinging onto Cayley.

"What the hell?" she said weakly as she fell to the ground.

"Cayley!" I moved toward her, but Zeke grabbed the back of my shirt, pulling me away.

"That's not your damage," he said.

"Get off me, Zeke." I elbowed him in the gut and lurched backward, yanking at the violet strands that glowed around the branches above us. *Snap.* Three branches. Thick. Solid. Heavy.

"Stop!" Zeke yelled. "Or Haven will die."

I paused, the branches hovering two inches above his head. "Go on."

"Darcy has her. In the barn where I first met you." He crept toward me. "If you come with me—and do what Darcy says—she'll let Haven go. She'll let *you* go." He glanced up, his jaw tightening when he saw the branches following along. "She doesn't want to kill you."

"But she wants to take my powers?"

"Last I heard, you wanted to give them up anyway." At

my surprised look, he shrugged. "Darcy spends a lot of time in Haven's head. She knows what Haven knows."

I bit my lip and looked over at Cayley. She lay in the dirt, her white-powdered hair spread out around her. Her eyes were hazy. Limbs frozen.

"*Transformare,*" Zeke whispered.

Cayley sat, gasping loudly, then her body shrunk in on itself, each muscle and tendon shifting and changing. It took less than a minute, and then there was a rabbit sitting in a pile of clothes, nose twitching, its brown fur glossy and smooth.

"Cayley?" I said.

The rabbit lifted its head and hopped away.

"Come back!" I whirled around and poked Zeke in the chest, the branches still hovering menacingly above his head. "What did you do?"

"What I had to." He glanced up, his expression hard. "And get rid of those things. If you hurt me, you—"

I let go of the threads.

"Dammit." Zeke growled as the branches crashed down onto him, knocking him to the ground. He pushed himself back up, his eyes glowing amber. "Darcy's not gonna kill you, but if I don't deliver you to the barn in the next thirty minutes, she'll happily get rid of your friend."

"You're lying."

Zeke grabbed my arm. "You need me."

"Why do you care if Darcy murders Haven?"

"I don't. I *do* care that I'll be next."

"I don't," I muttered as I wrenched myself away and

started to run. *Don't look back.* I kept watch for Cayley as I dodged trees and bushes, sharp leaves scraping against my skin. *Get to the auditorium. That's all you have to do. Then you can—*

The ground rushed up to meet me.

Pain shocked the air from my lungs and I winced, disoriented, as I rolled through the dirt. *Zeke.* He loomed over me, yellow eyes watching, his predator close. "Get up."

"Fuck you."

He backhanded me across the face. "Get. Up."

I snarled, showing my fangs, then stood, my gaze locked on his. "I'm not going with you."

"If *I* don't turn up, Haven will die. If *you* don't turn up, Haven will die. And if neither of us turn up, Darcy will find me and *I* will die. So we're both going to the barn. Understand?"

An owl hooted in the distance and I resisted the urge to look. "Fine," I said, my voice cutting out like a growl. "We'll go together."

"I knew you'd see sense."

I stomped through the woods behind him, my eyes never leaving his back. *Don't let him smell your fear.* Thomas had warned me about Zeke—I knew I couldn't trust him.

"What's going to happen to Cayley?" I said. "How do I get her back?"

"The succubus? She'll be fine—the spell should wear off in a couple of hours."

That, at least, smelled like the truth.

By the time we got to the edge of the woods, the boundary markers standing like sentinels in the dark, I was tired and angry. I wanted my friends. I wanted my phone.

"This way," Zeke said, walking right past the markers.

"Another spell?"

He laughed as I crashed into the wards. "Universal key."

"Dammit," I muttered, my body bent double from the force of the blow. "Why didn't you say something sooner?"

He was still laughing when we got into his car; it was parked on the shoulder of the road, hazard lights flashing. Like Zeke, the car was shiny on the outside and dark on the inside. Blue metallic paint coated the body, and black leather covered the seats. There were stains on the carpet, leftover marks from whatever Zeke did when he wasn't threatening teenagers, and the air smelled like burnished metal.

"Buckle up," he said before slamming it into gear.

I hate you.

I put on my seatbelt and held my breath.

Ten minutes later, Zeke turned down the long driveway to the barn. "Now the fun begins," he said. "Darcy's been waiting long enough."

"Darcy can bite me," I muttered.

Zeke laughed, long and low, before bringing the car to a stop in front of the barn, tires kicking up clouds of dirt.

Stepping out into the night, he lifted his face to the moon and howled.

My fangs slid free.

No.

I couldn't lose control. Not here. Not now.

"Hurry up," he said, slamming the door. "It's a beautiful night for chaos."

I dragged in a breath, then slowly got out of the car. I needed more time. I needed a plan. My predator was ready to fight—and I'd let it raise hell if I had to—but I had to be realistic. Haven was weak; she was sick from months of Darcy's incursions. I couldn't run the risk I'd see her as prey.

"This way," Zeke said, heading around the side of the barn.

I followed him to an open field out the back, still trying to figure out what I was going to do. Maybe I could grab Haven and run.

"Thank you for joining us," said a voice from behind me.

I whirled around. "How did you...?"

It was a woman. She was small, with dark brown hair and pale skin, and she smiled at me, her gray eyes crinkling at the corners. "Magic," she said simply, holding out her hands.

I stepped back, colliding with Zeke.

"Calm down, vampire," he said, adjusting the hem of his shirt. "It's only Darcy."

Only Darcy.

I felt the tips of my fangs with my tongue. "What do you want?" I said, inhaling the scent of Darcy's magic. *Cinnamon and allspice. Mulled wine. Sandalwood.* It was unique, almost comforting, and I shook my head, trying to shake off its pull. "Where's Haven? What have you done to her?"

"She's safe." Darcy cocked her head, her eyes assessing as she looked me up and down. From the outside she seemed ordinary, like any other late-30s woman in jeans and a sweater, but there was darkness in the threads that connected her to the world, a gunmetal undertone that contaminated everything.

"What's wrong with you?" I whispered, plucking one of the strands with a finger.

Darcy laughed, a surprised sort of cackle that lit up her face, and she moved forward slowly. "Haven was right. You *are* more powerful than you think. You proved it against my spiders—a test you aced, by the way—and you're proving it now. It's almost a shame to take it from you." She stopped right in front of me, tilting her chin. "Do you know what you are?"

"The *putere*," I said, my voice flat. "You know that."

"No." She shook her head. "What you were born as."

I paused for a moment, wondering why she cared.

"You're the same as me," she said. "Deep down, it's still in there. The magic. The power. The shared history." She grabbed my hands. "It's what links us together. And it's why I have to do the spell."

I pulled away, unnerved by the sorrow in her eyes.

"Don't even think about running," Zeke said, his voice close to my ear.

Darcy's eyes were bright. "It won't hurt, Emily. I promise." She waved an arm and Haven appeared, sitting in the middle of the field, surrounded by candles. The Impure Blade was beside her, along with all the other items needed to bind my powers. "It's time."

Haven lifted her head and screamed.

"Run, Em! Go!" Haven yelled, pushing up to stand. Her legs were shaking as she moved to the edge of the circle, and she reached out with her hands. A trail of sparks shot up her wrists as she moved too far beyond the confines of the candle-marked space, and she drew back, wincing. "I can't help you! I'm stuck in here."

I ran toward her, panic squeezing my throat. "It's okay. We'll figure something out." Turning quickly, I glared at Darcy. "Let her go."

"I can't," she said.

I stood as close to the edge of the circle as I could, breathing in magic and smoke. Earth and ash. "I won't help you if she's a prisoner."

"You have no choice, *putere*." A hand landed on my shoulder, fingers digging into my skin. "*Reserare.*"

Before I could move, before I could even think, Darcy pushed me forward, my body passing through the now unlocked circle. There were no sparks, no static electricity drawing at my bones, but the air inside was warm and brimming with power.

"You should've left," Haven said, steadying me as I lurched toward her. "You don't understand what she's planning."

"She wants to take my powers." I grabbed Haven's hand and pulled her toward the edge of the circle. "She's no different than Mr. Olaru."

Darcy sniffed. "*Claudere.*"

My arm hit the reinstated barrier and I swore as electric tingles spiked over my skin. "See?" I said to Haven. "She's just another asshole who thinks she deserves more power than she's got."

Darcy shook her head, her features twisting. "You're wrong. I knew Mr. Olaru. I worked for him—at least he thought I did. He never figured out that most of his flunkeys were working for me. But I never wanted what he did—power for the sake of power."

"What do you want then?" I said.

"Freedom." Darcy stared at me across the invisible barrier, our bodies so close we were almost touching. "Your parents made you think you were human, but you were always a witch. You still are, deep down inside." She whispered a spell under her breath and the grass around us lit up in a circle of flame, the fire stretching from candle to candle. "We have to hide our power. Our *magic*. But you barely got to experience yours at all."

I took half a step back. "And you thought you'd take

the rest of my powers so I don't get to experience them either?"

Darcy shook her head. "I'm doing it because I have to. Humans killed my ancestors—they killed yours too. Murdered them, because of what they were. Because they feared them." She stepped through the barrier, smiling as the golden sparks lit up her face. "Now it's time for *them* to live in fear."

"You're delusional," Haven said.

Darcy's jaw tightened. "I'm realistic. I know there are a lot of humans. And I know what's happened when supes have stopped concealing themselves in the past. You might think I'm stupid, but I've done my research."

"Clearly not enough," Haven muttered.

Darcy closed the gap between them. "I still have access to your mind, Haven. I can take control whenever I want."

Haven froze.

The circle burned with the scent of fear. With the scent of power and truth. Zeke laughed, still standing near the barn, but Darcy wasn't joking. She picked up the Impure Blade and turned it over in her hands, her thumb rubbing across the ruby embedded in the hilt.

My vision wavered.

My vampire surged.

The night around me turned scarlet, but I swallowed it down and turned to Darcy. "You don't need her," I said, lifting my hands in supplication. "Let Haven go and I'll do whatever you want."

"No! You can't." Haven swallowed audibly. "She's going

to destroy all of them. It's not about freedom—it's about revenge."

Darcy waved a disdainful hand. "Humans killed your ancestors too."

"You don't—" I started, but she lifted the Blade, the silver gleaming in the moonlight.

"I'm sorry," she said firmly. "But this has to be done. If we want supes to be free, we need a leader who's willing to do what it takes. And your abilities mean I'll be the most powerful supe in the world." She smiled, but her eyes were cold. "The humans will never be able to fight us."

Do something.

You have to do *something.*

I licked my lips. Vermilion wisps swarmed in my peripheral vision. Dragging in a breath, I let the scent of Haven's fear settle in my lungs. "You don't end up with my powers," I said to Darcy. "I've seen the prophecy. I know what happens."

Darcy picked up the vessel and set it in the center of the circle, then placed the orb behind the northern-most candle, the lamp behind the one facing east, and the half-used rosin cake behind the one on the west. She pulled a crystal from her pocket—a polished piece of moonstone— and positioned it behind the candle that marked south. Then she turned to me and smiled. "That wasn't real."

"But—" My arms clamped down to my sides, locking firmly in place. *Move.* I looked at Haven, whose eyes were wide, her body immobilized. *Breathe.* My gaze snapped back to Darcy's. "What did you just do?"

"Again, nothing more than I had to." She waved at Zeke, beckoning him toward us. "Take Haven and put her outside the circle," she told him. "I've waited long enough."

Haven screamed as Zeke lifted her through the now-unlocked circle. "Shut up, witch," he said, putting her down roughly in the grass.

"*Claudere*," Darcy whispered.

I breathed in slowly and let my vampire come to the surface.

"Not now," Darcy said, flicking her fingers and muttering a cascade of words in a language I didn't recognize.

My mouth closed.

My vampire receded.

Shit.

Darcy smiled. "Let's begin."

Lifting a hand, she pushed me—with magic—to the center of the circle. I grasped at my predator, trying to hold on to the hunger, the rage, but it was muted, like it had faded in my chest. *What have you done to me?*

"Don't fight it," Darcy said. "Think of your ancestors, the ones who were drowned, the ones who were burned. Know that you're doing this for them."

I screamed in my blood.

I screamed in my head.

"I know how much you care about other people," she said, pressing her fingertips against my forehead. "It's why I put so much pain into that fake prophecy. I knew if you felt it, you'd do anything you could to stop it from happening. *Get what you need for the spell,*" she said in a perfect imitation of Haven's voice. "Thank you for making it so easy."

The pain.

I thought ...

I thought I'd caused it. That I'd become so like Mr. Olaru, I'd ruined the world.

"Oh," Darcy said, her gray eyes softening. "You didn't understand. What I showed you—it was never about you becoming like him. You care too much about the world for that to happen. If anything, you feel too much. And that will only destroy *you*, not the other way around." She stepped back, her hands falling to her sides. "I can't hear you anymore, so think whatever you like. But I hope you understand, you'll be a hero for this."

She bent down and picked up the vessel, then positioned my arm above it, the Impure Blade held over my wrist.

No.

Tears streamed down my face and I screamed in my heart for my predator. For everything I'd done. For everything I'd lost.

Purple threads flickered to life around me. They were pale and weak, an imitation of my power, and as the Blade touched my flesh, the world turned gray, then red, then slowly faded at the edges.

I closed my eyes.

"That's it," Darcy said. "It won't be long now. I'm going to gather your blood, bind your powers, then I'll take them for myself. I'm going to make the world a better place. And you'll thank me. I promise." Her fingers touched my forehead again, her mind reaching for mine. "I won't let you down."

You've already let me down.

You've let your ancestors down.

Darcy slapped me across the face. "You don't know anything, bitch."

The purple threads burst back to life. Using nothing more than my thoughts, I pulled at the one that linked her with the Impure Blade. It was thick, a vibrant-hued purple underscored with gray, and it wavered dangerously.

I pulled it again.

"Stop it," Darcy said.

The thread snapped tight, and the Blade dropped to the ground. Darcy swore and bent to pick it up, but I twisted the thread that linked it to me, lifting it and holding it behind my back.

"If you ruin this, every member of the Order of the Silver Thorn will be out for your blood," Darcy hissed.

Her control slipped.

"I don't care," I said, finally able to talk.

She slapped me again.

She smelled like rotting leaves, the scent of her anger mixed with soot, with fear. Her gray eyes were hard, and when she opened her mouth, the words of a spell already on her lips, I drew in a breath and shoved the purple strands of magic down her throat.

Feeling rushed back into my limbs.

"You don't get to stop this. I planned this for *months*." Darcy covered her mouth and coughed, her face screwed up in anger. "Do you know how much time I spent watching you, sitting through Haven's classes, suffering through her daydreams, pushing and pushing until her defenses broke down?"

"I don't care."

She lifted her hands, twitching her fingers. "I made her weak—susceptible to infection. The day I finally broke through, the day I was able to talk through her mouth, I knew it would all be worth it." Her fingers moved faster, gray threads tracing the air around her hands. "I could finally get to you."

I sliced at the threads with the Impure Blade, watching in horror as I missed. They flew toward me, winding around each other, tethered to Darcy's wrist.

"You won't let me do the spell?" she said. "Fine. We'll be linked instead. Bound together by a magic that's darker than you could ever understand."

"No!" Haven yelled.

I swung the Blade again.

"To the left," Haven said. "Right there!"

She screamed, but I couldn't look. I split three strands, cleaving them down the middle and turning them to dust, but the fourth wound around my arm. It was cold, so unlike the violet threads I'd become used to, and I shrieked as it pierced my skin.

"Stop it!" I yelled.

"*Khohdash vehd indhagh.*"

I pulled my mental wards tight, slamming them against the power of her words, but the thread kept digging, squeezing around my arm. Sliding the silver blade flat against my skin, I gritted my teeth against the burning pain and sliced across, then up, creating a gash in the side of the thread.

"You can't win," Darcy said, twitching her fingers.

"Watch me." I gritted my teeth and drew on everything I had—every ounce of strength and fear and rage—and split the dark gray thread in two, watching as it twisted out from beneath my flesh and crumbled to dust, blowing away on the breeze.

My vampire surged.

It grabbed onto the anger, to the strength of emotion still sweeping through my blood.

"She's making another one!" Haven yelled.

Shit.

A scarlet veil curtained the world.

With a scream that echoed across the field, I launched myself at Darcy, throwing her to the ground. "I could end you," I whispered, dropping the Impure Blade beside me and grabbing her wrists. "I could steal your powers. Become the witch I was always meant to be."

"Do it," she said.

My fangs shot out as I lowered my head. "AB positive. My favorite."

Somewhere behind me, Haven screamed, and my fingers tightened around Darcy's wrists, pressing them into the dirt. The hunger ripped at my stomach, sending shockwaves through my veins.

Do it.

Take it.

Drink.

Drink.

"Get away from me, bitch," Zeke said from somewhere beyond the circle, and Haven screamed again.

Control it.

I dragged in breath. Then another. My hands were shaking, but I let go of Darcy and picked up the Impure Blade. "Everybody freeze!"

Darcy stood, laughing. "You can't stop this. I told you —you care too much. You won't—"

Thunk.

"—hurt us," she said, before she crumpled to the ground.

The lamp lay broken beside her. It had been so close. I hadn't even thought. I'd just picked it up and hit her.

"Em!" Haven yelled. "She's unconscious—the circle's broken."

I turned and ran, scooping up the orb—I couldn't leave my family heirloom—before I collided with Zeke. He pushed me into the grass, but I kicked up with my feet, my shoes connecting with his knee.

"Fuck," he said, his face turning gray as he dropped like a stone.

I pushed up to stand, sidestepping his attempts to grab

my ankles. "We have to go," I said to Haven. "Can you run?"

"I don't know, but … you have to leave me. Darcy's still in my head. Wherever we go, you'll be in danger. She'll—"

"Shhhhh." I grabbed her arm, tilting it so the silver mark faced up. *Where is it? Why can't I …? There.* I hadn't seen it when I'd looked at her before, and I hadn't seen it when I'd been fighting with Darcy, but it was there, plunging beneath her skin—a thin black thread, flexible and strong and almost invisible, even when I narrowed my eyes.

It took five tries to sever it.

Four breaths.

Three screams.

Two scars.

"It's done," I whispered.

Haven nodded, pressing a hand against the blood that ran from the two cuts in her arm. "Thank you." Gaze shifting, her eyes widened, the whites showing all around. "He's behind you."

I turned.

"You dislocated my knee, you bitch," Zeke said, storming toward me. "You won't—"

"Fuck off, Zeke." I let him get as close as he could, then kneed him in the groin. Smiling, I reached for Haven's hand. "Let's go."

Two hours later, I was sitting across from my parents at Coffee and Cake, my cello in its case beside me. I'd just come back from Ms. Maguire's office, where I'd spent an hour with her, Mr. Green, and Miss Lassila, explaining everything that had happened. They'd had the SCC dispatch a team of officers immediately, but Darcy and Zeke had already disappeared.

"Are you going to eat that?" my dad said, nodding at the untouched piece of chocolate cake in front of me.

I stabbed it with a fork and sighed. "I wish we could go back and start over."

"What do you mean?" my mom asked.

"It's just … I think we did everything wrong. You shouldn't have lied to me, but I shouldn't have frozen you out. I didn't even try and see things from your point of view."

We wanted to keep you safe.

We did it for your own good.

"Oh, Emily." My mom put her hand on my arm. "If we had any idea what you'd been going through …"

I broke off a piece of cake and shoved it in my mouth. Maybe Darcy was right. Maybe I *did* make stupid decisions based on my feelings—because I wasn't able to handle my own pain or anyone else's. Maybe that's why I didn't let myself recognize what was going on with my parents and my friends.

"I'm sorry," I said, reaching for the napkin.

"So what's going to happen?" my dad asked. He'd

always been more interested in moving forward than looking back. "Are you going to keep your powers?"

"I …" I set my fork down and sighed.

"You don't have to decide right now," my mom said, glancing sideways at my dad.

"No, it's …" It was hard to know what to say. Or how to say it. My parents and I had spent so long apart, and I'd spent so much time hating them. I'd spent so much time hating *myself*. "It's complicated, I guess … but I feel like these powers are mine now. They helped me save my best friend."

Mr. Olaru was gone. I couldn't feel him in my blood anymore; he hadn't been part of the decisions I'd made when I'd severed the connection between Haven and Darcy. Maybe he'd never really been there at all. *What I showed you—it was never about you becoming like him. You care too much about the world for that to happen.* How could Darcy have seen me more clearly than I'd ever seen myself?

I shivered, turning at the sound of the old-fashioned bell at the door.

Logan, Cayley, Thomas, and Haven walked in, a tall man with auburn hair and brown eyes right behind them. He made a beeline for the counter, and Logan paused, staring down at the floor. After a moment, he followed the others to my table.

"Hey," he said softly.

"Hey." I turned to my parents. "This is Logan. And Haven, Cayley, and Thomas."

"I'm Christopher," my dad said, extending a hand.

"And I'm—" my mom started.

The tall man cleared his throat as he walked across the room. "Jessica?" he said. "Is that you?"

"Silas!" My mother stood, her eyes widening. "You haven't changed a bit. It must be … what, over twenty years since we last saw each other?" She turned to look at my father. "This is Silas Ashworth, an old friend from college. He's a—"

"Dryad," my dad said, standing and shaking his hand. "I can tell."

"Your reputation precedes you, Christopher." Silas smiled broadly. "I heard all about your work as a beginning agent when I was interning at the SCC during graduate school. Everyone said you were on track to make Deputy Director within five years. But then you disappeared." His gaze shifted to meet my mom's. "Both of you."

"Secret business," my mom said smoothly. "We were undercover."

"I'm afraid we can't give you any details," Dad added.

They kept talking, reminiscing about things that had happened before I was born, and Logan touched my shoulder. "You wanna go?" he whispered.

I picked up my cello and stood.

"You're leaving?" Mom said. When I nodded, she got up and wrapped her arms around me. "We'll see you tomorrow, okay?"

I nodded again.

Cayley stopped at the counter for cupcakes and donuts

while the rest of us went outside. The door had barely closed behind us when Logan gathered me in his arms and kissed me. "I thought I'd lost you," he said, resting his forehead against mine. "When you didn't come back to the auditorium and no one seemed to know where you were, I … panicked. Left the brochures on the table and scoured the entire school."

Cayley walked toward us, shuddering. "At least you weren't turned into a rabbit."

Haven leaned against Thomas. She looked frail and tired, but her complexion was rosy, her eyes clear and bright. "At least you didn't have the leader of the Order stuck in your head for months on end," she said.

Thomas stiffened.

"I'm fine," she said. "Honestly, I think Emily's driving was worse. I used a spell to hotwire Zeke's car and …" She started laughing, gesturing wildly as she remembered. "She couldn't figure out which lever controlled the turn signal, so we were going ninety along the roads back to school, and she kept turning on the windshield wipers and swearing."

"It wasn't that funny," I said flatly.

Haven grinned. "It was exactly what I needed."

We walked a little farther down the path, the moon hanging low in the sky. Each footstep was a relief, a reminder that I was exactly where I was supposed to be. I didn't care that Mr. Davis was mad I'd skipped out on the refreshments. And I didn't care that my teachers were pissed I hadn't turned up to each interview. I'd started mending my relationship with my parents, and I was with my friends, who—despite our secrets and problems—would do anything for each other.

"I got double chocolate with sprinkles," Cayley said as we sat down on the lawn beside a flowering garden. She handed me a cupcake, then gave another one to Haven. "You guys deserve something nice after everything you've been through."

It was the most uncharacteristically nice thing I'd ever heard her say.

We sat and ate, the five of us talking about everything from Darcy and Zeke's escape, to the way Haven's parents had threatened to pull her out of school when we finally arrived back, to the way Ms. Maguire's eyes lit up when I handed her the Impure Blade in her office. Thomas apologized for his drinking. And Cayley told us she'd never confess to the things she'd done as a rabbit.

"This is nice," I said, lying back in the grass and reaching for a donut after a group of passing parents congratulated me on my performance.

Logan's hand brushed mine.

"It won't be nice for long," Cayley muttered under her breath.

The sweet scent of artificial perfume filled the air and I sat, lifting the still half-full box of cupcakes. "Hey," I said tentatively, holding them out as Vanessa walked past. "Do you want one?"

Vanesa's top lip curled. "Why would I want your leftovers, mosquito?"

Cayley started to stand, but I pulled her back down. "It's fine," I whispered as Vanessa stalked off. "I just … feel sorry for her now I've seen what her parents are like."

Cayley snorted. "It's possible to have horrible parents and not be a dick. Ask me how I know."

"How do you—"

"Not a literal question," she said, rolling her eyes as she got to her feet. "Anyway, it's been a long night. I'm outta here."

She brushed the crumbs off her shirt and walked away, catching up with Mia, who'd just turned onto the path ahead of her. A few minutes later, they were followed by Haven and Thomas, who left the rest of the food for us.

After finishing the last donut, Logan reached for my hand. "I guess we'd better go," he said as the warning bell rang.

We threw the takeout boxes in the trash, then walked down the path to our dorms. Almost everyone else had gone inside already and it felt like we were the only two people in the world. It should've been romantic, but something nagged at my conscience. Something I knew I should've said a long time ago.

"I'm sorry," I said.

Logan slowed. "What for?"

"For being self-absorbed. For not listening to you. For not thinking about anyone but myself."

"I don't …" Logan sighed, then kissed me softly on the head. "It's okay."

"It's not. You've been going through stuff and I haven't

been here for you. I haven't been here for anyone." I swallowed hard, my mouth uncomfortably dry. "But I want you to know that I'm trying. And I'm listening. To whatever you need to tell me."

"I'm fine. Really. But … I do have to tell you something important."

My stomach clenched. "Yeah?"

"I got my key back." He held up a familiar-looking, scratched, brass key. "Haven—or should I say Darcy—slipped it from Ms. Maguire's pocket in the infirmary, just after she confiscated it from me. It's how Zeke got into the school to find you."

"So you can …"

He nodded. "I can come up to your room again. And … I forgot to give you this. My dad delivered it to me just before I took off looking for you." He handed me a pretty pink envelope with my name on the front. "My sister's getting married over summer. And Dad said I could bring someone. So … would you like to be my date?"

I gazed up into his eyes, then went up on my toes and kissed him. "I'd love to."

NEWSLETTER

Thank you for reading *The Sapphire Eclipse*! If you have a few moments, I'd love it if you could leave a review on Amazon or Goodreads.

To be the first to know about new releases and updates—and receive a free copy of a prequel novella—sign up to my mailing list via my website!

www.amyhartbooks.com

ACKNOWLEDGMENTS

A big, enormous thank you goes out to Wynne, Mender, and Lani, for the chats, the memes, and the insightful comments on my drafts. Thank you again for putting up with the million messages about the blurb. You guys are awesome.

Thank you to Clare, who has read so many versions of this book! And Hamish, Zoe, and Alex, who are just generally really cool.

Thanks Mum and Dad for everything. I love you guys.

To Rianna, thank you for always being so supportive!

A huge thank you to Ian for always believing I could do this.

And to Connor and Ava, thank you for being the best kids ever! And for the motivational penguin. Love you lots and lots.

ABOUT THE AUTHOR

Amy Hart is the author of young adult paranormal novels about vampires, witches, and other magical beings. Her love of paranormal fiction began at an early age when she would routinely check out the maximum number of books allowed on her library card. After growing up and completing a Bachelor of Arts, a Bachelor of Music, and a Master of Arts (Hons) in Art History, she found her way back to fiction. Born and raised in Auckland, New Zealand, she adores cookies, singing, and collecting too many journals.

For more books and updates:
www.amyhartbooks.com